SPEAK !

Harvey Price

Publisher: Harvey L. Price Jr.
Hoquiam, Washington

ISBN: 978-0-9819220-1-0

Library of Congress Control Number: 2008906884

Manufactured, printed, and bound in the United States of America by Minuteman Press, Olympia, Washington; and by Phil's Bindery, Seattle, Washington.

FOR

DALLAS AND PATRICK

ACKNOWLEDGEMENT

Again, I must honor the infinite patience and insight of my wife, Jeannie, for her willingness to listen and critique each word of this book. Likewise, I want to again recognize the masterful skills of the Hicker's: Tom, for his uncanny ability to see my many mistakes and make the necessary corrections, even after I have reread the script countless times; and Liz, for her ability to create order and a finished product out of the chaos I present her due to my lack of computer skills. They are both masters of massaging the printed word.

And finally I must recognize the precious gift that my mother had and tried so hard to pass on to me, that of appreciating what is humorous and what should be seen as such. Her laughter filled any space she occupied at a given moment, as did that of the entire Swisher family. I owe them so much, each of whom must be laughing at this moment in an ever-joyful eternity.

Greg

Photo courtesy of The Daily World/Macleon Pappidas

FOREWORD

This story is a humorous fantasy, with an undercurrent of suspense blended into it, along with a dash of social commentary and an ongoing series of magical and mysterious events that continually unfold. It is told by Greg, a middle-aged Blue Healer, who hopes to have an adventure traveling cross-country, as he meets others and speaks publically about matters of concern. Beyond that, most everything else that happens is the story is a total surprise to him and to the majority of his fellow travelers.

Sometime before the story begins, its narrator mysteriously begins to speak. And in the preparation for his trip, he is able to enlist a bird, a cat and another dog, all of whom also talk. They are joined by two children, recently orphaned from brutal and menacing circumstances; an elderly couple and eventually a wizard and his companion. Transformations and otherworld revelations abound in this story that soon becomes a cosmic rescue mission. It is earth's last chance, and it all depends on these ten travelers enlisting the aid of birds, animals and trees everywhere.

INTRODUCTION

ONE: "I'VE GOTTA BE ME"

Ok, maybe it's in everyone's best interest if we lay down a few ground rules. For me, I'll try to be as accurate as my circumstances will allow. Actually, I don't think it's in my nature to be misleading. After all, you don't get the title of "man's best friend" by going around spreading gossip or making false statements to the press.

So, first off, I promise to set forth as accurate an account of what happened as I can. The only drawback to that promise is that I really don't have much of a memory. For me, each day is special but easy to forget. And if, as I've heard tell, I'm supposed to cram six or so years of my life into one of your calendar years, then the events, places and all the little things that we did can get jumbled at times. That's where help from my travel companions came in.

Then, there's rule number two. Aside from my nine other traveling companions, there is no way to accurately verify what actually happened to us.

You just have to trust me. I did try to keep a running record of each day's events, along with some stray (my apologies to some of my kind that I've associated with in the past, for the use of this term) thoughts of mine. Because, as I've said, having the long-term memory of a cucumber, if I didn't get it all recorded somehow that same day, whatever happened the next day would automatically deposit the previous day in my 'lost and never to be found again box', the same place where I guess my brain is supposed to be.

Speaking of which, many folks, like you, who I ran into or, around and around, were more likely to be preoccupied with the size, quality, functional level, alertness, creativity and remaining capacity of their brains. It made me feel fortunate that I had no concerns like those, because I am fairly certain that I don't even have one. That being the case, it makes it easier for me to handle each day, more or less, as it comes along. As I've said, I hardly remember what came before it anyway. But, just the same, Rule Number Two says we must trust each other.

Rule Number Three. This is not a story for the faint of heart. Prepare yourselves for some surprises, for there sure were a few for me. Myself, I always like an action-filled tale. You probably wouldn't have gotten as far in life as you have, if you didn't as well.

And now there are a couple of rules for you out there who might have stumbled onto this story, and are really desperate for something to do with your time. For you, and probably including assorted farm animals, things that have wings, pet owners, truck drivers, pretty women who say how cute I look and want to pick me up, captains of industry, city officials, people in uniforms, and those who wished today had never happened; please don't look for hidden meanings in anything I say. To project some kind of symbolism, long-lost truths or historic milestones into the telling of this story is missing the point entirely. For me, it was just enough that it happened. Our trip was a mighty fine adventure that also served as a rescue mission. In addition, a few messages were left along the way for our audiences to ponder. To put it simply, I had always wanted to travel. And when the opportunity to do so came along, I trudged along with it.

That leads me to Number Two for you. You must not be under any illusion about whom or what I am or what I can do. To start with, not surprisingly, I cannot remember when I first realized I was picking up, my then, 'owner's' lingo. As best I can recall, I was born about five years ago, along with three sisters and two other brothers. All of us were more or less born at the same time, or as you so precisely say, at a single, 'birthing event'. My knack of talking later became rather excited dinner table conversation, when the day before that my 'owner' asked me to, and I quote him here, "be good now, and hop into this tub for a nice bath". It was one that as far as I could tell was filled with mountain-spring, ICE WATER and an ENTIRE BOX of detergent. You couldn't see the edge of the tub for all the overflowing soap suds. Instead, I suggested, kind of under my breath, that "I'd rather

3

go outside and take a leak". To me, by that time, my participation in daily events was all about honest self-expression and setting your own priorities.

Soon thereafter, I realized that not only was my memory poor, but that I couldn't read or write. It was all about this same time that I had started to remind everyone that I was, when it was all said and done, just a dog. So you need to remember this. Unrealistic expectations of what follows will do neither of us any good; it will frustrate you, and it will cause me needless identity issues.

However, before I go further, I must tell you I had to correct a misstep I took in 'outing' my ability to talk. Plus, I must confess a bias. My first mistake was saying anything to an adult. I confess now I didn't know any better. There followed countless, public episodes of Howard, my then primary owner or handler, trying to get me to talk, after that initial compulsive outburst of mine. Awkward as it then was for him, I would respond with faux barking, howling, and occasionally blend in some yodeling to heighten the confusion. And following the episode by the bathtub, I rarely ever spoke in an adult's presence again until preparations for our trip began, unless, of course, it was for a valid reason or a good cause.

"Why?" you ask. Because in the time I lived at Howard's, I listened closely to many of his family and friends as they came and went. And for hours, on end, I lay around watching T.V., sometimes late at night when all the family had gone to bed and the volume was turned down. Invariably, at least it appeared to me, adults seemed caught up in how to make money out of a surprise and how to create misery out of happiness.

Kids, on the other hand, particularly those seven years old or younger, just enjoyed the surprise. And as I later found out, so did an endless assortment of other flora and fauna. With the passage of time, it appeared to me there was a small number of adults, and most of the rest of creation, who eventually just took my speaking in stride. But most adults I met in those days wanted to hire a business manager and book me on a tour when they found out.

One last housekeeping chore...before I forget. You probably should know a few physical characteristics about me, in case you pass me on the street. And, of course, I'd like you to know my name.

The name issue had loomed large for those first four years of my life. Howard called me "Bob", if you can believe it. Now, where he came up with that totally confounded me. I was never sure if it was because I reminded him of a family member or because he was using it as a verb, related to something I did with my head. Right off, after my decision was made about what I wanted to do with my life after that day at the bathtub, I began a process of selecting a new name.

First, I took major categories and broke those down into possible names I could adopt. For instance, there were the traditional dog names: Trixi, Mitzi, Spot, J.D., Mr. Mumbles, or Cuddles; names of food products: Kix, Chips, Pepper, Peaches, Gouda, Weiner, or Muffin; names of liquid refreshment: Suds, Bubbles, Earl Gray, Mocha, or

Chardonnay; legal terms: Tort, Bailiff, Habeas, Exculpatory, or Judge; anatomical names: Muscles, Dendrite, Sulcus, Mito, or Vagus; geological: Mesozoic, Tectonic, Berg, Palisade, Erosion or Lava; Astrological: Cosmos, Carbon, Continuity, X-246, or even Pluto, for heaven's sake. But nothing seemed right somehow.

In the end, I chose "Greg". It sounded more in charge, less servile or dependent. For instance, if Howard were to yell out to me, "Here, Bob, get the stick! Go fetch this stick!", as he heaved a piece of hickory firewood down a steep hillside. I could then reply, if I wanted to, "My name isn't Bob, you dweeb. It's Greg. And I don't fetch anything." I could even add, "Furthermore, who does, for that matter? Besides, if you want me to do something, you will ask politely, saying something like, 'Yo,! Greg, would you mind checking on the time? I believe the NFL Game of the Week is scheduled to start at 2 p.m. I'd sure appreciate it, if you would.'"

Of course, we never had this conversation, because I can't recall speaking to him again, after I took my new name. And it wasn't too long after this name change that I began to make plans for the future.

That leaves the one, final trivial bit about me, a brief description of my appearance. Overall, I think I resemble your basic dog; at least I have the usual attachments. My tail and nose are both tapered at each end. My ears are somewhat stubby, and my legs really could have been longer. I'm not necessarily complaining, but they seem, to me, too short for my body.

6

Which if I had any grounds or the opportunity to complain, it would be regarding my body. From what I've seen in magazines, on T.V. and in various movies, it looks to me as if my body resembles the world's largest sausage, one that grew hair in various shades of white, gray, black and blue.

It honestly looks like someone, as an afterthought, attached leftover dachshund or miniature poodle ones onto my boiler-shaped frame. Imagine if you will a five gallon bucket, painted in the mixture of colors I previously mentioned, shrunk into a ten inch diameter cylinder and then had four inch legs attached. Add a tail with absolutely no useful length or purpose on one end and ears that seem to wiggle constantly on the other. And I am so embarrassed to say that my tail and the rear half of my body also wiggles constantly. To complete this picture, my eyesight is rather poor, so I tend to stare. Altogether, it's like you have an immense Polish sausage, wiggling out of control at one end and fixed at the other end just staring at you, with a look of "haven't we met somewhere before." It unnerves me just to describe it.

One other thing. You need to know that this other-than-human ability I have to talk isn't limited just to me. That's one of the strange parts of this story. And, I guess, that's the final rule. Don't be shocked by what comes next. It seemed like each day offered a new adventure or surprise. But, for now, let's pick up the story a few months after my owner, or as I preferred to think of him, my landlord, realized his precious, "step and fetch it" blue healer had transformed himself into an equal opportunity, and soon-to-be temporary house guest. Because folks, it's like the crooner sings, "I've Gotta Be Me".

THE BEGINNING

TWO: ATLANTIC CITY

Now that we have all the introductory business behind us, it's story time.   And it begins in Atlantic City.   I lived, or co-existed might be the better word, with Howard and his family in a small, wood-framed house four blocks from the ocean. The most important thing about that house was that it was built up off the ground, with large basement windows facing the street.   That extra height above ground level meant the covered, front porch, which easily encompassed the largest area of the house, had a full view of whatever was happening in the neighborhood.   And lying on one of its old arm chairs, I could look in the front window and watch T.V. or keep tabs on anyone new prowling the neighborhood.   It was also here that I hatched out my plan.

Because I spent most of the day, and certainly all night, on that porch, it was easy for me to slip off, whenever no one was looking or too busy to notice, and head off to the Boardwalk.   I loved that place. In the summer I could practice herding groups of unattended children, who might be playing either on the beach or on the boardwalk. It kept my genetically-endowed skills honed. After all, you could never tell when an odd herd of sheep or cattle might appear in town. I always kept myself in peak condition for such an emergency. And in the late fall and winter, whenever there was a fierce storm, I had the place to myself. I could then practice my oratorical skills or to bark as long and as loud as I wanted to.

It was a good life, but I wanted something more. I had an itch, and it wasn't from one of my resident fleas either. I was beginning to feel driven to leave town, to be an apostle to the masses, if you will. But I didn't have any idea why or to whom exactly. And I was also beginning to have an urgent sense that it wasn't just sheep, goats, chickens, turkeys, cats and cows that needed their wayward behavior redirected; it was Howard and all his kind, as well.

So, step by step, between my life on the porch and on the boardwalk, the way forward became clearer. First off, I needed a crew. I couldn't do this alone.

Besides, by now, I was beginning to feel the need to lead. And yet leading, as we all knew in those days, had nothing to do with aptitude, skill, good sense, integrity, or honesty. You just had to look around you. Did any of those who proposed to be your leaders appear to have anything resembling good sense? Of course not. It would have been the greatest comedy show on earth, if they weren't so serious about what they were doing to us. So, in keeping with our evolving American tradition of rewarding dysfunctional leadership, which, wouldn't you know, was now rapidly becoming a world-wide phenomenon, despite being a dog, I chose to enter the leadership circus. I certainly couldn't do any worse. Mercy me, look at the White House! I bet you could gather a collection of farm animals and let them randomly choose courses of action, and it wouldn't be any worse than what we have now. They could govern by pawing their feet or pecking at assorted cubicles, filled with thousands of individual slips of paper, each one with a suggestion to do something, e.g. plant some squash next spring, change your underwear, wear different body cologne, clean out your garage, make one friend today, call Aunt Betty, convene a committee, bomb somebody, anybody, immediately, etc., etc., and it would be better than the obtuse excuse for governance and deliberation that went on then. Even I could do better.

By Valentine's Day of that year, I climbed down off the front porch and headed downtown to begin the process of selecting who was to be led.

I had a particular spot that I usually went to when people watching or "doing the boardwalk", as I liked to call it. But that day I decided it was time for a change. This time I headed out onto The Steel Pier. That would give me a view of both the main boardwalk and the shoreline. I needed to survey all possibilities. Finding a place to sit, between a couple of old wooden benches, I made myself comfortable. However, due to my lousy eyesight, I didn't notice that I had company and that I was apparently in the way.

"Top of the morning to you!" was the first outburst I heard. Looking around, I saw no one nearby. Next, the invisible voice called out, "Can you spare a dime or something for dinner?" Turning around to see if someone was yelling from the beach underneath me, the voice, lower this time, squawked and said, "Up here, meathead. Can't you see?"

Arching my head upward and behind me, there perched on the railing was a HUGE white bird, with a sash of bright yellow feathers hanging off the top of his or her head. "You can talk!" was all I managed to cry out.

"Surprise!! Surprise!! SO CAN YOU!" it replied. "Now, THAT is really impressive! Most dogs I know only bark or scratch for extracurricular activities. You're different. I could really make some money with you in my act. But first, you need to move over; you're sitting in front of my hat. It's for the donations."

"Do you always talk so much?" I asked. "It seems to me if you did, someone would grab you and keep you locked up or on display is a sideshow of some kind. Aren't your kind of birds only supposed to talk about crackers, toilets, various household objects and the time of day?"

"My kind of birds!" the massive bird yelled. "Listen to it!" it added. "Not only does it talk, but it has acquired a condescending and discriminatory attitude." This large feathered creature then trained its judicial gaze down upon me, the odd-looking dog that I am, sitting with my head turned sideways, looking rather bewildered. "Anyway, right now, you're definitely hearing the exception to my usual tourist hustle. Normally, I keep the conversation simple and direct. You know, what you indirectly referred to as the 'Polly wants a cracker' sort of natter.

"But what about you? Aren't dogs, these days, pretty much limited to various vocal ranges of barking and howling, with growling and panting thrown in on special occasions? I can't recall having a conversation with one before. Are you some kind of windup toy or computerized dogbot? Do you do housework? Special security jobs? Babysitting? Run on batteries? And avoid having to do any of the usual daily potty things?"

"Yep, Nope, Nope, Nope, Nope, Nope and Nope." I replied, with some smugness. At that point, I explained about my talking ability's onset and that I limited using it with only small children and, it appeared now, with strange birds.

"Do you do any tricks, tell jokes or do imitations?" the white and yellow-crested bird persisted, apparently not put off by my monosyllabic answers and a rather pedantic accounting of my vocal history.

"Nope again," I answered. But to show off my grace under fire, I stood up and walked around in a circle. Once in front of the perched bird, I stopped and peered, as usual, with my head jutting forward like a tortoise does, when examining something new in its neighborhood. It was clear the bird was unimpressed with that maneuver.

"You're kind of a short, stocky fellow, aren't you? And I notice you tend to stare. It's kind of unsettling. Is that due to a nervous habit or do you need glasses?"

She hit a raw nerve with that question. It was the first time anyone mentioned that about me. Before then, I always thought I struck a rather handsome pose. Funny, it's amazing how little we know about how others see us. A mirror is not necessarily the best reflection of how we are seen by others. "Well, probably it's because my eyesight isn't top notch. Do I squint as well?"

"Yep," she replied. "But if it's a handicap, I can deal with that. I just wanted to make sure you weren't trying to check me out. Anyway, do you have a name?"

"It's Greg," I replied with some pride. It was the first opportunity I had had to tell anyone. And in announcing it, I was probably a little too proud and loud, because a couple of tourists passing by, at some distance, turned their heads towards us. I immediately went into a squat-and-scratch maneuver, and the bird did a mock preen. These maneuvers decoyed my exuberance. And, luckily, the two continued to amble off, looking at each other and laughing, shaking their heads, like they had probably drank too much the night before. Following up, I asked, "What's yours? And what kind of bird are you?"

"Waddles," she surprisingly answered. "I walk funny, and drag my tail feathers when I do. So, you won't catch me too often just walking along. I prefer to fly or to perch. Walking always seems to prompt a variety of comments and snickers. It's humiliating…"

"Well, then," I answered, "we have something in common. I stare, and you waddle. We both have issues perceived by others as either odd or funny. If, like me, you don't like your name, then change it. I did. Mine used to be 'Bob'. Pick something you'd rather be called and that will settle the issue."

"Fair enough," Waddles agreed. "Then I want to be called 'Rita' from now on. I've always liked that name. It's a short name, but it has two syllables, so it rolls off your tongue."

"Whatever," I mumbled under my breath. Already, I realized that this creature had to be a female. But I didn't want to appear sexist, along with condescending, during my first encounter, so I just tried to smile and said louder, "that's a nice name." Secretly, I hoped that in the future, any decisions she made wouldn't be accompanied by too much explanation. Too much background information gives me a headache, and it REALLY confuses me. And, besides, as a leader, I truly want to be seen as inclusive, and having just a dash of good judgment and fair-mindedness. So, she's different. What am I? A pair of finely polished, dress shoes? You just have to look at me to see there isn't anyone else around with as many quirks and hairy warts. And she would give the troop some class and intelligence. Finally, I added, "In fact, it's a great name."

To that, Rita cocked her yellow-crested head and appeared to smile. "Good. I'm glad you like it. Now then, my next question is what are you doing sitting out here on a chilly February morning? Are you just out for a stroll, or are you one of those fellows who likes to look at the passing girls?"

"On the contrary," I responded. "I'm beginning to implement a mission of discovery and also one, possibly involving some rescue work."

"Going where and doing what?" She quickly countered.

"Well, my initial plan is to leave here"

"Hmm, that's a creative start for a trip," she replied.

"What I mean to say," I continued, ignoring the sarcasm, "is that from here, the trip will involve traveling all the way across the country to the Pacific Ocean. I hope to end up somewhere around Seattle. And along the way, I hope to meet all kinds of people, preferably, mostly small ones. As well, I hope to meet folks like you, anybody or anything that will share some time with me. There are issues that need to be discussed, ideas implemented, and projects started. And the trip is designed to help plant the seeds for this to happen."

"Now, THAT'S A TRIP!" she cried out. "Are you going alone?"

"No, I haven't firmed up that part of the trip, but I'm sure others will have to accompany me. I can't do it alone, and I would need other representatives along to share their experiences and insight…and maybe some money…"

"Ahh, so you need money as well," she pressed. "Isn't that the way with a guy? Manufacture some story about saving the planet, then put out your paw for a small donation towards your next escapade or sordid tryst."

"It's not like that at all," I countered. "This is, honest-to-goodness, what I am going to do, with or without anyone else or any money. It may take a little more time to get organized, if that's the case. But I'm determined to go and do what I say."

"Ok, ok, if you say it that way," she replied with less tension in her voice, "I'll reconsider your motivation. How, then, will you know who is right to be in this chosen group of fellow travelers? Do you have a list of their needed qualifications, job descriptions, or skills sets?"

"Well," I began, "that's not so easy to answer. Look at me... It's not as if I qualify for much of anything, except to make loud, dog-like noises; eat full bowls of freeze-dried kibbles and round up anybody or anything that is in a group of two or more."

"I get your point," she said with some resignation. "BUT, you can talk. That has to be something in your favor, even if you limit its application to inanimate objects or children who are just learning to form words themselves. Maybe to entice someone to tag along with you, you could add to your resume that you like to travel and that you would make a swell tour guide. At that point you might start attracting individuals who could be screened for selection."

"Great idea," I responded, gratefully. "And I do like to travel, even if has been limited to four city blocks. At least that's a start. So, what do you say? Would you like to join me in this quest? I think you meet all the qualifications, even if I don't."

"How long do you plan on being gone?" she asked, thoughtfully. "And what kind of resources do you need to get started? Do you have any idea who else needs to be recruited for this journey of yours? And are you open to suggestions?"

"Sure I am," I answered, feeling somewhat relieved, that maybe there was a chance this operation might actually get launched. "I'd say we'd be on the road for at least five months. And we need money to purchase two or three small wagons, the ones with wooden side rails all around. Then we need to buy some horse tack, enough to provide harnesses for a couple of us to pull the wagons. In addition, we need to buy extra supplies such as clothing, tarps, ropes to start the trip and to get some props for any performances we might need to give to raise money and awareness along the way. And finally, we need to be able to purchase food throughout the trip for each of us.

"As far as who else needs to be recruited, my list is small. Actually …I don't have one. On that subject I am wide open for suggestions and advice."

Sighing as she spoke, Rita then replied, "Honestly, I can't for the life of me understand why I am doing this, but I'll volunteer to be one of your fellow-travelers. I've about exhausted any potential rewards this city has to offer. Probably an extended change of scenery and making new acquaintances would do me some good. Besides, the money I make is coming in slower and less each week. But for what it's worth, I have saved up some, and that will be my stake in this venture."

"You're serious?!" I yelled.

"Yeah, but you've got to promise me one thing," she answered.

"Sure, what's that?" I eagerly replied.

"That you will not go around everywhere we stop to set up camp, layover, or bivouac and then proceed to lift your leg and mark off your territory. It will set a bad precedent for everyone else. And it will no doubt cause a chain reaction that could go on for hours on end. You, and everyone else in our party, will have to accept that the world at large is not your territory. You cannot carry on that crazy ritual of claiming someplace is yours just because you've stained an assortment of shrubs, telephone poles, car tires, tree stumps and fire hydrants."

"Ok, I see your point," I replied thoughtfully. "And it's a deal. That will have to be stipulated in the contractual agreement that everyone has to sign or mark. Now, can I ask something of you?"

"I guess so," she answered with some hesitation.

"Would you please take off and fly some around the pier and a little way out over the ocean to let me see what you're like in flight? All I've seen, so far, is you sitting on this railing, and I'm curious to see what you look like flying."

"So is my acceptance based on my ability to fly? What if I had a birth defect or a mid-life injury to prevent me from doing so? Would you then have to try to recruit a local pigeon?"

"No, no. Don't get me wrong. It's not a job interview requirement. I'm just fascinated by flying. And to know someone who could fly would almost be as good as doing it myself. Please…"

"Alright, if you put it that way. Here I go."

And after saying that, she unfolded her wings, sprung off the dingy, pier railing, flapped her three foot wing span two or three times, caught a gust of ocean-driven wind, and soared up into the dark gray sky. It was like something you could set to music, like a fine symphonic overture. Her brilliant white plumage, with the dash of yellow, was breath-taking against the blackening clouds. And, boy, could she fly. She did flips, barrel rolls, vertical dives, cartwheels, and then she skimmed along the shoreline like a bullet. Swooping up from underneath the pier, she arched over the boardwalk and landed effortlessly back on the railing. And she wasn't one bit winded.

"That was just amazing!" I stammered. "I'm always so proud of myself when I can just leap off our front porch; skip down its flight of stairs and not stumble, landing on my chin. Your flying is artistic; it's like a masterpiece. Thank you."

"Well, you're welcome," she replied, only slightly out of breath after that display. Preening a few feathers that got disheveled mid-flight, she added, "It's not good when anyone takes their abilities or talents so for granted that they become smug or suspicious when someone asks for a demonstration. It is nothing I did or deserve that blessed me with that ability. And it's certainly not mine to feel superior or selfish in sharing. Talents are gifts, and gifts are to be shared. And I thank you for making me aware of that.

"Speaking of which, I think I know someone

who has a few talents you might be able to use in your troop. She does acrobatics. And, if you don't come on too strong with your doggy mannerisms, she might even talk to you. If you have time now, we can go see if she is available for you to interview. But we'll have to go below the Boardwalk to find her. She, and I, both live down there."

"You bet," I said excitedly. "The sooner we get the team together, the sooner we can begin to arrange the materials and supplies for the trip. Do you want to fly or just walk with me to wherever your friend is staying?"

"You'll get lost for sure if I just give you directions and then fly over. Better that I stay with you," she cautioned. "And it will give me a chance to fill you in a little better on what you will be seeing."

Our walk to her home was unusual, to say the least. There I was, an overgrown kielbasa, wearing a Dick Tracy hat that Rita used for her patrons to toss money into. Inside it, she kept a string cinch-purse, which I had to wear around my neck. She actually carried the money she earned each day back and forth in that purse, gripped in her foot. The hat was her prop that she ferried back and forth in her beak. Cinching the purse was a clever combination of beak and foot movements, which she managed with effortless ease. She was so good at that maneuver I believe she could have changed a flat tire, if she could drive a car.

And of course beside me, was this waddling Cockatoo, dragging her tail feathers, as they swept side-to-side with each step she took. But Rita looked resplendent. As we walked, her head was only slightly lower that mine, but it still required that I both turn my head and look somewhat down towards her. This placed me in an awkward position, because then my vision, such as it is, was reduced further. I ran into people, benches, trash cans, baby strollers and other curious dogs as we engaged in our serious conversation. Our conversation was low, but anyone with any imagination could not help but have been puzzled, both at the spectacle and at our heads nodding.

We walked north once we left The Steel Pier, weaving our way along the Boardwalk for about a mile. It being a Sunday morning, the walkway was at least passable, and the hundreds of bicycle and skate board riders had not started zooming along yet. Plus, it was cold. Winter was not over, and it appeared to me something was brewing out over the ocean. The swells were huge, and the sky was an ever-darkening grayish black. I sensed snow was next.

Once we got to where Rita wanted to leave the Boardwalk, she motioned to a ramp that zigzagged down to the beach. After we got to the sandy area, she again motioned me to head south and back up into the rocks. They were piled as far as you could see in either direction, about one hundred feet from the shoreline. Once at their front edge, she had me crawl even further back into an opening, formed by these immense boulders, obviously placed there centuries ago to prevent erosion. And behind that was a tunnel, at least six feet high and wide that stretched back toward the city. It was then

I realized that unwitting saloon customers must have been shanghaied or press-ganged onto sailing ships through this passage. It had been forgotten and abandoned, but not before someone had rigged up some dim, overhead lighting. The tunnel was well above the high tide and storm surges, so it was dry and comfy. Add a few smelly, old blankets for a bed, and I'd call it home.

At the end of the tunnel there were some boxes, a homemade roost, an old metal storage cabinet with stacks of bagged cat and bird food, along with some aging fruit and vegetables and a few different colored, braided throw rugs. It was neat at first glance. But on top of one of the boxes was a large, calico cat, her back arched with every hair standing perfectly straight, like a porcupine. Moreover, she was making continuous, guttural, growling noises. It was very annoying, and already I was becoming peeved. It was so typical. No, "Oh, Rita, I see you have a new friend." Or, "Welcome, we don't get many visitors; it's nice to see you." Or, "Hi, my name is Fritz. Have we met before?" Instead, I'm met with instant hostility… cats!

"Greg," Rita began, "I want to introduce to you my roommate, Winky. Everyone calls her Winks, for short. And I'm sure she won't mind if you do as well."

"From what I am seeing and hearing," I couldn't help but reply, "I'd say she'd mind very much. And, most likely, she'd prefer I drag my sorry backside out of here."

"Don't be silly," Rita answered. "She's just

23

a little shy with strangers."

"Hmm," I muttered, but with increased impatience, "If this is a demonstration of her shy self, I can't wait to see what her reaction would be to someone she is really uncomfortable being around. And you said earlier that you wanted me to be warm and open to a relationship with her. Possibly you need to counsel your fetching friend here with that same message. And don't tell me this is her at her best. If so, then this interview is officially over…this just can't be happening to me."

"Winks! Now make nice," Rita counseled. "Greg, here, has come to interview you for a wonderful opportunity to travel and perform. He was so impressed with me that he hired me as well. I told him about you, and he was anxious to see your act. And as you have probably already noticed, he isn't like the usual dogs we come across. He actually TALKS. Say something to her, Greg. Speak up, so she can hear."

Clearing my throat and trying to control the countless generations of inbred desires, needs, drives, and quite frankly, the absolute JOYS of chasing uppity cats, I made myself speak slowly and measured. "It is nice to have a chance to meet you, Ms. Winky. My name is Greg. And if you would be so kind, could you give me a small demonstration of your gymnastic talent. I'll just stand back a ways and give you some room."

As I did so, it was obvious the two of them glanced and nodded at one another to confirm my sincerity. I let out a deep breath, fighting the tendency to sit down and scratch at a long-term resident flea, having its way with me. But I was afraid it might look like a displacement activity to both these individuals, indicating that I was nervous. When, on the contrary, while I was very upset about the rudeness of this cat, I, indeed, was experiencing a blue-ribbon itch in progress. I tried to smile as I backed up, but on me, when my mouth turns up like a smile, my tongue wants to hang out, and it looks more like I've just had the pleasure of passing some painful gas. So, instead, I just tried to cock my head slightly, looking up at their ceiling, as if I had until next summer to wait for her to perform.

And at this point maybe a little explanation of their living room setup might help set the stage for what happened next. As I mentioned before, there were only scattered boxes, a cabinet, and that perch that I recognized on first glance. What I didn't describe was the perch. It was not what you imagine. It was at least four feet across, with industrial strength bracing underneath. It stood about five feet off the ground. Attached at one end was a swing-like device slung underneath. In addition, on the other end, underneath, dangled a small mock ladder that nearly touched the floor. Its rungs were spaced wide apart for some reason. The other two items that I failed to mention before were a rather large and overstuffed mattress just in front of this perch, and dangling down from the ceiling was a rope with a small swing also attached to it.

Now in the time it took me to describe this to you, after these two made eyes at each other, the cat took two steps, then leaped five feet across the room and landed on the top of that perch. That, in itself, was pretty exciting. Given my bulk and low center of gravity, I'm always so proud when I can just trot a little each day. From that point on, the show began. That cat proceeded to walk along the perch, which was no wider than the end of my tail, and while doing so, she started doing summersaults, back flips, straddles, and head stands. It was as if she was trying to qualify for the next Olympics Balance Beam competition. But she was no sooner done with that when she slithered down the little ladder and did some hanging off the last rung, weaving in and out of the other rungs as she did. Then she sat on the swing hanging off the other end of the perch and waved at me. Finally, she climbed back on the perch and leaped across the room and landed on the hanging-rope swing. Once on that, she got it to swinging wildly; and when it was at its highest point, she jumped off and did a midair summersault, landing on all four feet on the mattress, facing me.

"How's that?" She asked me, with just a hint of breathlessness in her voice.

"Well, I never..." I replied. This was the first opportunity I had to really concentrate looking at her, without being mad or frustrated. Sure enough, she was a Tabby cat. But she was a large one. When she eventually sat looking at me, it was obvious she was at least two to two and half feet tall, just sitting. Her coat had deep white, gray and black swirls. The colors were rich, not faded or blending into one another. Her head was very large as well, matching the immense size of her body. It was clear she had not missed any meals since living in these quarters. But it was her eyes that stunned me.

They each were easily the size of a quarter. And they were a brilliant yellow. "That was a show-stopper," I announced. "If you would be interested, you are hired. Rita and I both can fill you in on the details later. Right now, I need to gather my wits. Your act was stunning. Where did you learn all that?"

"It just came naturally," she answered, her voice filling the hideout with its mellow tone. "Since I can remember, I have been swinging from tree limbs, clothes line poles, roadside mail box supports, and school and park playground equipment. Then when I was about two or three years old I began to talk. At that point the people, whose home I lived in, became overly interested in both my new-found abilities and in my acrobatics. They were going to sell me to the highest bidder. Within days of my becoming aware of this development, I clammed up and hit the road. It was about a year later I met Waddles, and we moved in here."

"Excuse me," the then, now self-named Rita, interrupted. "With Greg's recent urging, I have officially dropped that name and chosen to be called 'Rita' from now on." Doing a mock preen, she added, "It suits me better."

"Sorry," Winks apologized. "I didn't know. But I would agree that it is a much better name than 'Waddles'. It's like my name, which I got following an early injury to my right eye. It left me with a tic. My vision was not affected, but my eyelid fluttered uncontrollably. The household occupants that I stayed with at that time chose the names, 'Wickums', 'Winky' or 'Winks'. They thought it was catchy and cute. But like you, Rita, I always thought it demeaned my physical presentation. I wanted, in turn, to start calling them by their peculiar quirks: 'wimpy', 'whiny', 'wonky' and 'woozy'".

Then I suggested why she didn't change her name as well. If desired, she could have various names, e.g. a stage name, an official name, a secret name, even a pet name, which I immediately regretted, having said. It just slipped out, exposing my lingering distrust of cats and my still wanting to taunt them. I knew this deep seated urge was going to take some time to control. After all, it was such sport to goad a cat. And, don't forget, I am still just a dog.

"Alright, I will," she announced. "Let's see, what would I like to be called? It's a tossup between 'Jasmine' and 'Jennifer'."

"Do you want to answer to both?" I asked, realizing when I did that I was sliding into my not-so-subtle, taunting self again. But I did feel later, upon some self-examination, that she did leave herself open to it. Why couldn't she just choose a name? It's the dallying that drives me crazy. I was beginning to sense I might have to go on some medication in order to successfully enlist these talented individuals. I made a mental note: get a prescription for my possible mood swings, and do it soon.

"No, silly, I can't have two first names. I think I'll choose 'Jennifer'; it's got three syllables..."

It was at that point I knew I would now have to add to my list of upcoming trip essentials a case of Jack Daniels. But, as serenely as I could muster, I managed to say, "That's great. 'Jennifer' it is. What do you think Rita?"

"Oh, I think it really suits you, Winks. And from now on that's your name. Upon occasion, I may call you 'Jen' or 'Jenny', if that's ok."

"Sure, it is," the recently renamed Winky replied.

And so it was from then on. In the meantime, I now had a headache.

"Folks," I said, with some finality in my voice. "I must be on my way. From what I observed when Rita and I were walking over here, it wouldn't surprise me if we don't have one heck of a snow storm later today. I need to skedaddle home. What's say we plan on all of us meeting at the Pier, just like Rita and I did today, at 11 a.m. next Sunday? We can plan our next moves then. But if the weather turns sour, we'll just keep aiming for that same time and day of the week the next week. Is that ok with you two?"

Both nodded their heads in agreement. And it did appear to me that they seemed happier than when I first met either of them. That did give me a boost, despite the future potential for personnel problems, which seems to accompany any venture, involving two or more individuals. Diversity does have its positive aspects, but sometimes it sure seems like you're trying to herd an impossible collection of personalities, attitudes, and backgrounds. And let me say, one more time, if there is anything I know something about, it's herding.

After saying our 'good-byes' I trudged down the long tunnel and wiggled my way out of the boulders onto the now booming, incoming high surf. There were snow flurries and the waves were now crashing onto the lower rocky barrier. I had to do some careful maneuvering to get across the slippery rocks onto the ramp that led to the Boardwalk. Once on the Boardwalk, the flurries had changed to blowing snow. It was a blizzard. And by the time I got back to my front porch, I was frozen and exhausted. For once, I was relieved to be picked up and brought inside the house. I was sincerely grateful to the family that day. They, no doubt, saved my life. And I later dedicated this story to them, for what they did for me that day.

Beyond that, the storm, or series of storms that followed, prevented our threesome from reuniting for the next three weeks. And by that time I had a surprise for them.

THREE: FLO AND THE KIDS

I think it was at least three weeks before I saw Rita and Jennifer again. And it was just before seeing them that I had my next encounter with fate. The series of nor'easters, with the accompanying piles of snow, had finally moved away from the New Jersey shoreline and by sometime in the middle of March we had steady sunshine again. That was enough for me. It was porch time. Don't get me wrong. Like I mentioned earlier, my adoptive family thawed me out and gave me another chance at living a better life. And I will always be grateful to them. But I belong outside, running in the wild, with wind blowing through my flowing mane, exploring new frontiers, and herding something. I had to fulfill my destiny. Furthermore, I hoped Howard and company knew that my leaving was nothing personal. Honestly, it almost felt like a cosmic force was pushing me onward.

So, around 8:30 on that mid-March morning, I struck off, heading nowhere in particular. Spring was slowly peeking out from winter's final snow and ice storms. Buds were well formed on the maple, cherry and apple trees, scattered in the neighborhood, and I noticed a few Robins darting back and forth, as they called crisply to each other. I longed for the musical notes of the songbirds, the warblers, the larks, the orioles, and red-winged blackbirds but instead, more and more I only heard the harsh calls and squawks of the jays, starlings, crows and robins. The sounds coming from the trees, meadows and marshes were becoming more like the adults around me, scolding, loud, harsh and dull. It had to be different when we got started on our quest. I knew we would find the music again somewhere.

But just as I was strolling along, consumed by my thoughts and reverie, WHAM!, a buffalo-size dog struck me. For her, it was like she just stumbled over a soft cushion. For me, it was like I had been run over by a fully, loaded bus. She quickly recovered her loss of balance. I was sent tumbling over and over into the nearby gutter. Dazed and confused after I stopped rolling, when I was finally able to look up, I saw peering down at me the biggest dog I had ever seen in my life. Her face filled my field of vision.

Unable to focus completely or comprehend what had just happened, I managed to mumble, "Was it you who hit me? If it was, you should carry some kind of travelers insurance."

"You talk!" the huge form answered.

"Yeah, but do I need to now yell for help? Are you finished with me yet? Or is there more you have in mind? I don't carry any money on me."

"No, I am sorry to have nudged you off the

sidewalk..."

"Sorry?" I interrupted. "And 'nudge' is hardly the word I'd use to describe our encounter. You flattened me. Holy smokes! How big are you, anyway? And what are you? I've never seen a head so big in all my life."

"Again, let me apologize for stumbling over you. I was running away from my handler."

"You mean there is someone bigger who is chasing you?" I asked in fear and wonderment.

"Absolutely, and he will be coming soon. I need to hide somewhere and fast."

"Well, if you can help me get up out of here, I can hide you over on my porch. You can pretend you're our outdoor sofa."

By the time we both managed to get settled on the porch, me with my front paws hanging off the top steps, looking like something out of a Norman Rockwell painting, and Buffalo Dog well hidden behind the countless boxes and toys kept on the porch, along trotted a very large and menacing-looking man. He stopped in front of our house and looked both up and down the street and side to side, finally focusing on me. Given the serene pose I had struck, he just shrugged and jogged on, calling out, "King! Here King! Come to Papa!"

Hearing that made me want to stick my front paw down my throat and gag myself. Where do these guys come off sounding like they are our relatives? He sure didn't look like the daddy of this range animal I had hiding behind me. Maybe one day, when I am through with this pilgrimage across

33

the country, I'll try to organize our kind and get some respect and equal rights. After all, everyone else is. Between all the agendas: political, social, ethnocentric, economic, and personal that seem to dominate the airways, newspapers, magazines, and countless electronic devices, it only seems reasonable that us dogs, and possibly cats, should organize and demand our rights as well. I've seen some pretty sorry outcomes from these social trends, and the world certainly doesn't seem like a happier place to live in. Maybe if we four-legged individuals, feathered comrades, bark-covered species, water-dwelling creatures and other assorted flora and fauna came forward with our demands, a little composure and common sense would be infused into this mêlée. It just seems to me that this equal rights issue has been too one-sided for too long.

And as the burly sort passed on into the next block, I turned to the refugee behind the boxes and called out, "He's gone. I think you're safe now. You can come out of hiding."

"Thank you for protecting me," the huge dog said, as she crawled out from under the piles of long-forgotten toys. "That's it; I'm not going back to that house again. I'm making my break from being someone's 'pet' as of right now. And that only leaves one other decision for the moment. Where will I go?"

"Do you have any relatives close by?" I asked, still a little overwhelmed and hesitant, given the collision we had earlier and not feeling completely over its aftereffects.

"Are you kidding?" she replied. "I'm a purebred, Siberian Husky. And my closest relatives are at least 5,000 miles away! Just look at me. Do you think I belong here? Atlantic City is the land of poodles, schnauzers, Jack Russell's, and Pekinese's. It's definitely not Husky land. How I wish I could go back home, where I belong."

Now all this conversation had set my mind in high gear. This dog could pull a trainload of small red wagons across the country. And certainly, she could handle one or two of them with ease. Anyway, it was worth asking, but I thought I should approach the topic gingerly. Maybe I should get to know her a little better first...

So I started with, "The man chasing you, he called you 'King'. Is that your real name? It doesn't exactly fit you, does it?"

"Of course not," she exclaimed. "I'm a female, and I resent the term being used by those so-called, dog breeders. That bozo knew who and what I was, but he wanted a male dog instead of me, so he just gave me that name anyway. I wanted so many times to yell back at him, 'If you're going to call me anything, call me 'Queen'', but I didn't want to let on I could talk. That would have been the end of me for sure. He'd had me auctioned off on eBay the next day after that revelation. Can you imagine it, an advertisement asking for bids on 'one female Siberian Husky, that I call 'King', who has a vocabulary approaching 7,500 words? Speaks with a slight New York accent.'?"

"Yeah, I see your point," I answered. "So why don't you change your name now. It seems to

35

be something I've been seeing a lot of these past few weeks. Animals of all varieties have started talking in my presence, as well having identity crises regarding their old given names. Join the trend. Change your name."

"Great idea," she announced. "From now on I am Florence, which rhymes with Lawrence, my most favorite name. But you can call me 'Flo'".

With an undetectable shrug, I pronounced, "You got it," and secretly I sensed that maybe I was going to really like this individual. "Flo it is. Next, I need to ask you if you have anything special you like to do? Do you have any talents or hobbies? What gives you pleasure or happiness?" Already, I was beginning to sound like a Human Relations Department Supervisor. Leadership so often redirects your daily interactions with others around you in ways that you have little desire to adopt or natural ability to perform. Just look at me. I felt myself becoming Corporation Dog, Atlantic City's newest mogul.

"Well, I can't think of any off hand," Flo replied. "But I really love to sing, whenever I am alone and no one is looking or watching. As far as being happy, I'd say it will come with setting a new course far away from Ralph, my now, past owner."

Seeing this as my opportunity to probe further, I then asked, "Could you sing a verse or two for me from one of your favorite songs?"

Immediately, Flo launched into "Springtime in the Rockies" in a rich contralto voice. She followed that with "Show Me the Way to Go Home". Hearing her sing so beautifully, I knew she had talent. So, following the conclusion of her singing I asked, "Flo, would you like to join a group of us who are planning a trip across the country, eventually ending up in Seattle? It promises to be an adventure, if nothing else. But my other hope is that we may open the eyes of those we meet to begin the process of change. Would you be interested in coming along?"

"It would be an honor for me to accompany your group. Can you describe who all will be coming along and how you plan on managing day-to-day?"

"Sure," I answered. "Let's take a walk, but in the opposite direction from where Ralph was headed. We can walk and talk; and I'll give you all the details up to the present moment. And actually, it will probably be a good idea that all of us begin graduated, walking training to prepare for the trip ahead. I know I'm really out of shape from being shut in most of the winter. I've gained at least five pounds. I can tell because it makes my skin so tight my hair is beginning to stand straight out. I'm beginning to look like I stuck my paw in a light socket."

Nodding her head in agreement, Flo and I struck out, heading south from my porch. It's in the direction of the less affluent neighborhoods, but ones with the most elegant, old homes. It's my favorite part of the city. The magnificent old chestnut, hickory and oak trees form canopies over the streets. Years ago, I have heard, it was the American Elms that provided the most shade, but most of them are gone now due to the blight. Wrought iron fences

37

and poorly maintained honeysuckle and holly shrubs line the sidewalks, which are buckled and broken from uplifting, aged tree roots. The area looks tired and unkempt, but it speaks of an age when the city's citizens took more care: of their surroundings, of their bodies, of their families and animals, of attaining maturity and a proper sense of their place in the world around them. The neglect and abuse of the area now reflects the decline of the individuals who live there, and even more sadly, of the society that is supposed to care about them.

We walked and talked, undisturbed, for at least an hour after leaving the porch. But it was as we rounded a very large corner house, with its sidewalk bordered by a wooden picket fence that had had its' last coat of whitewash paint years ago and now was mostly hidden by a bramble of ivy and weeds, that we heard whimpering. They were the sounds of hearts' breaking. And they were cries you could not pass or ignore.

Immediately, Flo and I went into high, investigative gear, with our noses close to the ground, sniffing the area both outside the fence and, eventually after finding an opening in some splintered slats, inside the fence. Eventually, and simultaneously, we discovered, burrowed in the deepest area of the undergrowth, two small, very terrified children. They both looked to be seven years old or younger, so that made the next decision easy for me.

"It's ok," I began. "Neither Flo, here, nor I, will hurt you. And we won't let anyone else do so either. We'll protect you from whatever harm you have experienced. But can you tell us what is wrong?"

Lifting their heads up to see who was talking to them, their eyes widened in wonder. "You can talk!" the oldest-looking of the two exclaimed.

"Yes," Flo and I said simultaneously. Following up immediately, I continued, "And we need to know why you are hiding here. Not only that, but we need to know what has made you so unhappy. Your cries are so forlorn sounding. Are you hurt? Do you need to see a doctor?"

"No, no, please don't take us to anyone. They will only separate us, and we'll never see each other again. We've seen it so many times with our playmates. And we are not cut or anything like that. We are just sad."

"Why," I kept pressing.

"Because everybody is gone."

"When are they coming back?" I asked, feeling that maybe this wasn't such a crisis after all.

"Never. They are dead," came the awful response. "Somebody came into our house early this morning and began shooting everyone. My little brother and I were the only ones able to escape out our bedroom window and hide here, or I am sure they would have hurt us too."

And again my only response was "do you have any idea why this happened or who it was that did this?"

"No, but my brother and I have seen one of the men a few times coming to our house occasionally with some packages. He would just leave them and go away, but not this time. And there was more than one person today, but I don't know how many." After explaining that, they broke down, sobbing mournfully.

I looked at Flo and her at me, both of us unsure what to do next. Fate, it seemed, had deposited a Special Delivery Package to us, but there were no instructions accompanying it as to how to handle it or where it should go from here.

Finally, I spoke up. "Flo, why don't you stay here with the children? You can snuggle up to them and get their body heat up. They must be nearly frozen. No telling how long they've been huddled out here. You'll be a great comfort to them. In the meantime, I will try to get inside the house and see what I can find. We need to at least attempt to confirm the little girl's story. And then, if we do confirm it, we have got to figure out what to do next."

That decided, I did a crouching, slow walk to the back of the house. The rear door was broken open, hanging on one hinge. Someone had obviously entered the house from here. There was glass scattered over the entryway. Maneuvering around the glass and scattered kitchen utensils and furniture, I entered the hallway. It was there I saw my first body. Not wanting to track through that area, I went back into the kitchen and entered what had to be the dining room. This entire room and the living room were in shambles, and lying on the floor next to the old fireplace was another body. It appeared to be a man, and the one in the hallway was a woman. Making my way upstairs, I found two more bodies, of older children. All were dead. It

40

was the most gruesome sight I ever saw. What happened here on this day was nothing short of savage. I thought to myself, 'what kind of species does this to itself? What pathological drive leads to this kind of behavior, one that includes slaughtering its young?' Realizing that I had seen everything to confirm the child's story, I made a hasty retreat back to Flo and the children.

"It's true, Flo," I said as I leaned down to where she had spread herself around the children. "There was a terrible crime committed in that house. I found four people dead, two were older children. I'm sure if the killers had found these two, they would have murdered them as well. We need to get them out of here."

"But where to?" Flo interrupted. "You sure can't take them to your residence or mine. And the authorities will separate them for sure if they go to a Foster Home or some shelter."

At that, I sat down and had a scratch. It's something I do when I need to think seriously about an issue. A few minutes passed as the children appeared to fall off to sleep and Flo laid her head down beside them.

"I think I have a plan and a place to shelter them, but we have to move quickly, before someone else comes here and finds this carnage and these children. We need to head, as quickly as possible, to the beach. There should be an access pathway at the end of this street that leads directly to ocean. Once there, we won't look so suspicious to everyone, just two dogs and two children walking along the shoreline. But it will be a long hike for these two.

We will have to walk under The Steel Pier and about a mile north of it to the place where our other troop members live. It would be safe for them there. After getting there, we can figure out what to do next."

It took some effort and coaxing to get the children up and moving. I guess you can't blame them; it was a wonder they were able to function at all. And they were brave little tikes. Up until the time we starting actually walking away from that awful tragedy at the house, the little boy had said nothing. It was clear he was in deep shock from what he had witnessed. Hoping to break down the barrier somewhat, I asked them what were their names, by first introducing Flo and myself. The little girl told us her name was Bernice, but that we could call her "Bernie". Her younger brother was quiet for a while longer, and then said his name was Wallace, but that we should call him "Wally". After that Flo asked them how old they were. Bernie said she was seven and Wally was six. We, in turn, told them I was five and Flo was six. This really impressed them, our talking so much, yet being so young. I started to explain about dog years compared to human ones, but quickly felt it was too much information for now and ended up just saying "thank you" for the complement.

By the time we reached the beach, it was clear that the school kids were now making their way to class. The streets were filling with commuters, school buses, kids on bicycles and people of every description walking. I had warned the children not to look up or around, but to just go straight to the beach. Flo, being the largest, walked on the street side of them, while I trotted along on the other side and slightly to their rear. Flo and I kept a tight perimeter around them. Of course, it was quite natural for me to assume this role. I do take some pride in my ability to form up a group and move them along. But this time it was a much more serious journey.

Reaching the beach was nerve-racking, but the children were real soldiers about it all. They didn't cry, fuss or look particularly out of place. No one paid us any attention. It was an immense relief to finally be on the sandy shoreline, and particularly to find that it was at low tide. If it had been storming, along with a high tide, we'd had even more problems. There was no way we could have walked undetected through the main part of town.

It wasn't long, however, before Wally became weary and said quietly to Flo, who was walking next to him, that he had to sit down. "I'm really tired Mr. Big Dog," he said.

Flo looked over at me, and equally as quiet said, "I'm going to stop a minute and lay down. You and Bernie try to get Wally to climb on my back. Then tell him to hold on tight while I stand up."

We all did as instructed, and amazingly, Wally wiggled himself up on the broad back of that Husky. Holding on to his leather collar, he managed to stay on as Flo slowly stood up. Once up, his feet were a good foot from the ground, he being small for his age and Flo being just plain big and tall for hers. Bernie, without being told, walked close to them, making sure her brother was stable. And at the pace we were walking, there was little likelihood he'd topple off. Flo didn't walk with an unsteady stagger, but rather with a lope. There was a natural gracefulness about her, as if she was pretending to pull a sled over the frozen tundra in Alaska or Siberia, but at a slow and careful pace. The horror these children witnessed just a few hours earlier was eased somewhat, as the two of them looked at each other and smiled. To me it meant, at that moment at least, they felt secure.

We arrived at the opening to the underground den where Rita and Jennifer lived approximately two hours after leaving Wally and Bernie's hiding place. To finally arrive there was a great relief to all of us. However, I wasn't sure who might be in the living quarters at this time of day. And certainly I didn't want to shock Rita and that cat by bringing my three companions inside without their foreknowledge and permission.

"Why don't the three of you sit or lie down outside here, while I go in and see if anyone is home. It will be safe for all of you here, but I want to make sure someone is inside. It is their private home, and I don't want to just barge in. There's been enough of that kind of behavior, and much, much worse, today. It will only take a few minutes to see who's there. I'll be right back out."

This was greeted with nodding heads and some relief. All three of the newcomers to this ever-growing troop collapsed on the beach, now being warmed by some rare, March sunshine.

Making my way through the maze of

boulders into the tunnel entrance was a little awkward, it only being the second time I had done so, and the first time Rita had led the way. Probably because of the bright sunshine outside, it took me a while to get accustomed to the dim light coming from the other end of the tunnel. Feeling like I should announce myself, I began saying, in my more official voice, "Rita, Jennifer, it is Greg. Are you home? I'm coming in. Please don't be alarmed. I am alone at the moment. Do you hear me? Rita? Jennifer? It's Greg."

As I got closer, still repeating myself over and over, there finally came the reply, "Greg who?"

Now this already had been a somewhat stressful day for me. And by now, you've guessed that patience was one personality trait I seemed to have lost or maybe it slipped someone's mind to ever issue some to me. In addition, this had not been my best day. A truck-sized dog had run over me. I had discovered a terrible crime scene. I had adopted two very small children and one hippopotamus, dressed like a dog. And all three of them were now very hungry, thirsty, tired and already probably on missing persons and dog posters scattered around town.

So it was with some testiness in my voice, when I replied, "Greg C. Schmidt from the Animal Control Department of Atlantic City, that's who." This was followed by a brief flurry of activity and throat clearing at the other end of the tunnel. Waiting, for what must have been for them a rather disturbing pause, I then added, "Not really. It's just Greg, your soon-to-be, cross-country, travel guide…how many other Greg's do you know anyway?"

"Not funny," came the echo-like reply. "You should know we have to be so careful about whom or what enters this area. Besides, someone may have overheard a conversation we had in the past and just used your name to gain access to our shelter. Anyway, enough said, what brings you down here? I thought our agreement was to meet on The Pier."

Knowing Rita's voice, I advanced more relaxed into their lighted room and briefly explained my situation. Jennifer was also there but appeared to be asleep. However, I knew she was pretending. I could tell by the way she swished her tail, every now and then, during my monologue. Whether it was a way of agreeing or not with what I was saying, I had no idea. Who's to fathom the emotions and reactions of cats? Certainly, not me.

After about ten minutes updating them, I suggested that I go ahead and get Flo and the children for them to meet. At this point Jennifer opened her eyes, sighed, and whispered, "Knock yourself out…" I turned quickly before I said something I might regret, shaking my head as I left the full light of their den.

Upon arriving back at the beach front, I found my three other companions sound asleep. Flo was the most difficult to arouse. She must not have slept for days, given the depth of her unconsciousness and the effort I had in waking her. Finally, I had to crouch down by her exposed ear and bark as loud as I could. It's not a real commanding bark. Rather, it has a high pitched, hysterical quality about it. It's been described as a cross between someone getting a car door slammed on his thumb, while being told he has just won $185 million in the Power Ball Lottery. But it had its desired effect.

Flo jumped up, twisting her head side to side as she did, mumbling "Quick, someone must have their thumb caught in a car door." As he did, I turned my head towards the two fully awake children and gave them my toothy smile. "Works every time," I proudly announced.

At that point I suggested that the three of them follow me into the tunnel. It was hardest for Flo to maneuver through and around some of the smaller spaces in the jumble of boulders. Eventually, all of us cleared them and we were able to walk upright in the poorly illuminated tunnel. Wally and Bernie walked behind me, with Flo behind them. Both Flo and I continued to be very concerned about their emotional status. They needed to feel safe and protected as much, and as soon, as possible.

Entering Rita and Jennifer's living area, I announced, "Well, here are my new friends, Bernie, Wally and Flo." Rita, by this time, was standing regally on her perch, and Jennifer was behind one of the piles of boxes, with just her head peering around the corner of the box. The rest of her body was hidden from view. It is very hard for Rita to show much emotion with her face or mouth. A bird's beak has an unfortunate resistance to expressing emotion; it basically just moves up and down. As far as I could tell, Rita's only way to gesture physically what she was feeling or thinking was to shift her yellow, head crest one way or the other. At this moment it was standing straight up, like a Mohawk haircut. I had no idea what that meant, but I later thought maybe she was displaying her parliamentary pose. As for the cat, she had this 'Welcome to my lair,' exaggerated smile, which displayed a full row of upper and lower teeth. It covered a full three quarters of her face. It suggested whoever she was smiling at was most likely to be on the menu for her next meal. For just once, I wanted to…

Having already briefed these two on the circumstances of finding the children, I didn't feel the need to go into that any further. I simply motioned for Rita and Jennifer to show some hospitality. It was Rita who spoke first.

"Good morning," she began. "My name is Rita. And I am glad to meet you. Welcome to our home. That said; let me also introduce you to my roommate, Jennifer or Jen, for short. She's the cat grinning at you from around the corner there," pointing to the other side of the room.

And surprisingly, Jennifer spoke up immediately, as she minced around the box and came into full view. "How do you do? I, too, am pleased to meet both of you. Which one of you is Bernie?"

"It's me," Bernie said shyly and sinking fast into a further state of shock. This time it was not from the horror she witnessed earlier this morning, but from seeing and hearing a bird and a cat now talking to her. "How did you learn to talk?" she asked, ducking her head as she did, for fear it was an improper question to ask at this time.

"Basically, we just listened to those around us, watched T.V., listened to the radio, and practiced day and night. But, like might have been explained to you by Greg, here, we don't talk freely to everyone," Rita interjected. "There is a very limited audience we speak that way to; it's isolated to a few non-human types and to children 7 years old or under."

"Well," Bernie pressed, "I'll be eight in another month. Does that mean you'll no longer talk to me then?"

"No, but it's only because we were introduced to you when you were seven."

"I see," she said. "What kind of bird are you? I've never seen one like you before."

"I'm a Greater Sulphur-Crested Cockatoo," Rita answered with great pride. "And unlike the others in this room you have recently met, I can live up to 50 years, provided I look out for my health and avoid unnecessary stress and anxiety."

"Like what?" Bernie asked.

"Like my not having any conversations with adults, would be one example. They are an absolutely crazy lot, for the most part. The first two of them who kept me, treated me like I was a stuffed animal, like I had no sense at all. They kept saying the same words to me, over and over. Things like, 'Pretty boy', when in fact I wasn't; 'Good morning, daddy', which obviously he wasn't; 'I want a cracker,' which definitely I did not; and 'Good night, Polly,' when I planned on staying up most of the night practicing my vocabulary. It wasn't until I sought a different living environment that stress was no longer an issue. And, you're right, there are not too many birds like me around these parts; we primarily live in the south Pacific area. But don't ask me how I ended up here, because I don't know."

"Is it the same for Jennifer? Is she also from far away?" Bernie continued.

"No," Jennifer answered. "Like you, I am from around these parts. I was a house pet for a couple of years. During that time I acquired my speaking ability. After that, I decided to hit the streets and leave the domestic life behind. But, on the other hand, the feral life held no charm for me. I met Rita a few weeks after I was on the road, so to speak. She had already started her panhandling gig on The Steel Pier. After watching it for a day or so, I asked her if I could join her act. She auditioned me and afterwards agreed to let me work with her two days a week. The other five days a week she works independently. It was on one of those five-days, solo performances that Greg first met her. But, the long and the short of it is that I've never seen anything beyond a three square mile boundary of this room; I'm definitely a local gal, so to speak."

Looking around, Wally finally got up his nerve to ask, "What's going to happen to us? I want to go home! I want to see my mommy and daddy!" And then he broke into sobs, as did Bernie.

It was Flo who stepped up at that point and gently coaxed the children to lie down. Tearfully, they crawled under some blankets in the corner of the room. Flo then lay down beside them to comfort and warm them, which she did until they were able to drift off to sleep. In the meantime, everyone else in the room would have to think what they could do to make life better for them. While that was happening, Jennifer and I scurried around the living area looking into boxes and the cabinet for extra bedding. It was obvious there was no food or drinkable water for the children, so that was the next problem we had to face and try to solve. But everyone quickly agreed that getting them into some recovery sleep was tops on our list now.

About thirty minutes passed before Bernie and Wally were sound asleep. Flo and I worked to cover them with the extra blankets. How or why they were stored there we didn't bother to ask. There wasn't time to probe or conjecture. With a sigh of relief we backed away, holding our breath that they would stay asleep once we finished. And they did.

Then Flo turned to the three of us and said, "Things have gotten a little more complicated, due to our rescuing these children. Adding further to both their problems, and ours, are that their future in this city is grim. They are probably being sought after by those killers right now. And no doubt the police want to question them about they saw and heard during the commission of this crime. On top of that, the State Child Welfare Department is also probably looking for them for immediate placement in Foster Care. It's almost as if we've become accomplices in this tragedy.

"Right here and now, we have to do some serious thinking and planning. We've become involved in an incident, not of our making and in a rescue, not of our choosing. We acted out of urgency and fear for the safety of these two children. It was not a rational choice. But from this moment, and for the immediate future, what happens to them is our responsibility.

"While I was with them on the beach, I did ask them if they had any relatives living in the area. They said there were none. It seems their mother came out East sometime before they were both born, looking for work in New York City as a dancer. She eventually ended up here in Atlantic City where she dances in one of the larger, casino's stage productions. They were both born here. But Bernie thought they do have a grandmother living in Washington State, somewhere near Tacoma. She has never seen them, and as far as they know, she is their only living relative."

It was at this point that I spoke up. "Are you thinking what I think you are?"

"Possibly," Flo answered. "If we plan on going cross country..."

"Hold on a minute," Rita exclaimed. "We? Did someone invite you?"

"Yes," I said. "I did. And the reason I did is that Flo has a singing voice of professional quality. Go on, Flo, sing a song for them. It won't awaken the children. In fact, it might calm them even further."

"Alright," Flo replied. "But it will be muted. I definitely don't want to wake them."

Clearing her throat and briefly humming a key, she then sang a lively version of "California,

Here I Come."

Repeatedly, Rita and Jennifer both turned their heads back and forth from Flo to me throughout her singing. It was obvious they were impressed.

"I see your point," Rita said. "Flo has a real fine voice. And we could use her in the show."

"I agree," Jennifer added. "With me doing gymnastics, Flo singing and you doing mid-air cartwheels, we will have a good act. Greg can be the M.C. And maybe the kids can sing along or dance to the music."

Rita spun around to face Jennifer, exclaiming, "you're suggesting that we take them with us on the road?!!"

"Yes," Jennifer answered.

"And I agree," Flo added. "The thought occurred to me when I was talking to the children on the beach. What do you think, Greg?"

"They're traveling with us will complicate the trip's logistics, but I guess getting food and other supplies was going to be complicated anyway. And it's possible that having them along will ease that problem somewhat. But it still doesn't solve our problem of what to do now with their care."

"Well, if you all have decided to do this, I suppose I'll go along with it," Rita added, "but let my reservation be on record."

"Ok, Rita," I said. "We sure wouldn't want it left unrecorded that you had concerns. However, it will be in everyone's best interest if ALL of us gather our thoughts and come up with solutions as to how we can make it safe and nurturing for these children, now and on the road."

FOUR: THE CHILDREN MUST DECIDE

It probably goes without saying that the next few hours in Rita and Jennifer's living area, under the Boardwalk, were filled with arguments, compromises, short-term and long-term goals and objectives, major and minor decisions and pouts. If you think having mature, enlightened, rational discussions and agreements, without self-serving hidden agendas, has become impossible in the centers of our national government, you should see what happens when you get a parrot, cat and two stray dogs together trying to formulate a plan. And through it all, those kids slept soundly. It was as if they subconsciously knew that we had their best interests and welfare always in mind. Moreover, somehow we finally agreed on how to proceed. And, afterward, it sure made me reconsider my doubts about there not being a benevolent Guiding Hand, helping to conduct the business of living, especially when love is your primary motivation.

Of course, as mentioned previously, acquiring food and liquid for the children was our primary concern. We ultimately had only one avenue to explore in accomplishing this. It was to have Rita fly over to DiAngilo's Market and see if they would help. And you will need some background on how this came to be. It was all news to me as well.

It seems that Rita had not been doing her pay-for-view, Steel Pier monologue and show-stopping, mid-flight maneuvers too long before Frank DiAngilo wandered by. He sat down on a nearby bench and watched Rita perform her act countless times. And he saw the passers-by's put money in the hat she had placed in front of her pier-railing perch. It fascinated him, because if someone took the time to really study Rita's act, they would have noticed that both her monologue and flights were different each time. He knew this bird was something special.

Eventually, as evening approached, and the crowds faded, he got up and walked over to Rita, who was just about to jump down and collect her day's wages and fly home.

"Excuse me, may I speak with you a moment," Frank began. "I have been watching you for some time now, and I've noticed a few things."

Aware of his presence, Rita immediately became leery and prepared to fly off, reluctantly leaving her day's earnings to this stranger. "What do you want?" she nervously asked.

"Don't be alarmed. I mean you no harm, and I don't intend to take your well-earned money. I just wanted to speak with you."

"What about?" Rita pressed.

"Well, for instance," he began. "Where do

55

you live? Is it with a nearby family? And if not with a family or someone, where could you live that's safe? And if you are on your own, how do you manage to get food and water? It's no secret; you parrots require a special diet to stay fit and healthy."

"Why are you asking me these things?" Rita asked in return.

"Because, if you'd let me, I'd like to help you.   That's all.   I know by watching you all afternoon that you are very special, and I suspect that you are not living with anyone. They wouldn't let you out of their sight. Not with what you can do. I wouldn't either."

Rita recoiled somewhat at that remark. "What are you suggesting?   And why should I divulge anything to you?" she answered.

"Three reasons, I'd guess," he replied. "One is that I admire your act and would like to stop by regularly to see it and not arouse suspicion on your part and not have to pay each time I do. Another is that I and my family own and operate a grocery store not too far from here. I would like to work out an arrangement where you could get the supplies you need from me and one of my children will even deliver them to your residence. And finally, like I said, neither I nor my family would have any intention of harming you. We would just like to help you. That's all I am offering. Some help."

"How will I know you are serious and can be trusted," she asked, letting her guard down somewhat.

"Why don't you gather up your money and

the hat and follow me home. My family and I live in an apartment above our store. It's just a few blocks west of the Boardwalk, on the north end of town. I'll walk back and you can follow me, flying overhead. I'll set a perch outside the store, where we often set out the Special for the Day, and you can land there. Any time during the day you can come and order what you'd like. But, there is a catch. You have to pay for what you order. I'm a businessman, and I expect you are a business bird."

The rest of the story about Frank DiAngilo and his family is the stuff of legend. They did and do exactly as he promised, as long as Rita paid them. Every Sunday she went over to the store to place her weekly order for her and Jennifer; and every Monday, when the crowds were less at the beach, one of the five family members brought the groceries and other miscellaneous supplies over and set them outside their opening in the boulders at a designated time. They would stand there while Rita ferried the supplies inside the tunnel. On some days, when Frank brought the supplies and had the time, Rita and he would sit down and have lunch together and talk about anything and everything.

But today was Friday, and Rita was unsure how to proceed with our plan for getting the children food and drinks. The decision was finally made for Rita to fly over to DiAngilo's Market and sit on the perch until someone in the family came out. If it wasn't Frank, Rita was to say she needed to speak with him, that it was an emergency. Further, it was decided that she had to confide in him what had happened to the children's family, how we came to have them and what we were planning on doing. The one small detail she purposefully left out was that we all spoke the local dialect. We fully realized that he may not agree to any of it and refuse to have anything more to do with Rita. But it was a chance we had to take. We really had no other alternatives.

And, God Bless him, he decided to help, at least to provide the children some food for the short term. Unbeknownst to us, Frank and his family had little faith in the welfare system, or in most all government entities for that matter, and letting the menagerie of a bird and various animals have a go at caring for the children, seemed no worse than letting the wave of attorneys, bureaucrats, and social workers mess with these children's lives.

With that arranged, by later that same afternoon, Frank himself delivered the food and a few other supplies. Probably, it's safe to say, he was never the same after Flo, Jennifer and I explained to him how grateful we were for his help.

Immediately following that experience of his having a very brief, two-way conversation with a cat and two dogs, Frank did recover enough to stammer, "Tell Rita we've got to talk, and now that I've met you three, it must include all of you and the children as well. Also, tell her I will come over tonight at 8 p.m., and take all of you back to my house to meet with my wife and I. Tell her this meeting is important. All of you must come! Meet us at the top of your ramp on the Boardwalk. But for heaven's sake, DO NOT TALK to me or to yourselves once you're up there! An animated conversation amongst a collection of animals and two missing children will attract a crowd, even here in Atlantic City."

"Sure," I replied. But it was an answer which only appeared to make him more nervous. Saying 'Hi' could have been a trick anybody could have learned. Replying with 'Sure' was probably not on his customary word list for four-legged talkers. I could tell right away, after this brief exchange, that this had not been a particularly good day for him. Shaking his head, in utter disbelief as he staggered off, it must have seemed that his life was swirling into an Alice, or Frank, in Wonderland vortex, and he was its captive.

Following his halting, but clearly stated, directive that we meet him later that evening, we turned and looked at each other with rising fear and anxiety. We began to feel that our mercy mission was about to turn into a disastrous mistake. What for us, caring for one another, even someone of a different species, was hardly questioned. For these humans, being kind and generous can so often be judged as meddling, unnatural, perverted or immoral. And tragically, what species on this planet, or maybe anywhere else in the cosmos, kills and tortures multitudes of its own with such precision and determination. Given these thoughts, I straightened up my sagging midsection, stuck out my scruffy chest, lifted up my raggedy ears, and said, "We have a job to do, despite what anyone may think or feel. Let's get this food and other items inside."

Nodding their heads in agreement, Flo and Jennifer each said in unison, "Yeah, that's right," and "You bet. Let's do it."

59

There was now an unspoken determination to follow through with our rescue of these children. And for now, our primary job was to get some nourishment into them. Frank had brought some cartons of fruit juice and milk, along with those small boxes of breakfast cereal and some ready-made sandwiches. Also included, but unknown to us at the time, were blankets and clothes that Sophie, his wife, had insisted Frank bring as well.

Upon reentering the underground living area, we were encouraged to see both Wally and Bernie awake and sitting looking up at Rita, putting on a show for them. But for an additional calming effect, she was talking constantly throughout her routine. She was spinning round and round on one end of the perch, then jumping up and down off it, higher and higher each time, then jumping off onto their bedding and rolling over and over, again talking constantly as she did. Finally, she gently crawled up each of their arms and sat on their small shoulders. They were hypnotized by her performance. And for the first time both were giggling at Rita's silliness. She was a master performer, to be sure.

Being able to look closely at the children for the first time, I saw that both Bernie and Wally had red hair. Bernie's was in long curly locks, like something I had seen in those older movies I used to watch late at night when everyone was asleep. They reached down past her shoulders. And even in this dull light it was a rich, almost burgundy red. Someone loved her very much to groom and style her hair so beautifully. Her face was still rounded, not yet becoming sculptured with cheek, jaw and chin bones. And even in the reduced light, I could see her green eyes as she turned back and forth watching Rita's act. Aside from her facial features, she appeared too thin for her age. She was maybe four feet tall. Her clothes belied the frantic moments before she and Wally escaped from the horror in their home early this morning. She had on faded blue jeans and a blue checkered, flannel shirt that appeared too big for her. Her well worn shoes were like those popular running shoes that could be purchased for around ten dollars. In short, she was as beautiful as a china doll, but dressed hurriedly for flight. She laughed easily. And when she spoke, it was not always clear. She hurried her speech, and rounded off some words ending in r's and slurred some s's, as she did. She seemed like a delightful child. 'Who would want to hurt her in any way?' I thought. Adults…

Wally's head was covered in tight-knit, red curls. It was wavy like some of the prissy poodles I see swaggering up and down the Boardwalk. And did he have freckles! His face was covered with them. He had a happy face, with an easy smile, even after all that had happened to them today. After their nap that afternoon, he was giggling constantly at the antics of Rita. For someone his age, he did appear quite small. And thin. I think both children had had a hard life up to and, obviously, including today. Both looked like they had missed more than a few meals, and that many others they had were too meager. His eyes, also, were green. But his face, unlike Bernie's, was drawn. He definitely was more fragile than Bernie. I could tell that right away. And I knew, if and when we ever started our journey cross-country, and if they were with us, it would be Wally that I'd have to watch carefully to see that he didn't get overly exhausted. My hope then was that the trip would make him stronger and erase some of the terrible memories of this day.

Like Bernie, his clothes were threadbare. And he only had a light jacket on, which was pulled over a hooded, light blue jersey. His trousers had holes in them, with both knee caps fully exposed. One shoe had no laces; the other one did, but the shoe was mismatched.

As the youngsters were talking and playing with Rita, Flo and I began to sort the clothes and food. Sorting, as you can imagine, is not a refined or delicate matter when it comes to dogs. And of course that upset Jennifer, who prefers that things be done with tidiness and daintiness. Tossing her head in muted disgust, she proceeded to gently carry over the smaller food items we had brought in and set them by Wally and Bernie. Meanwhile, with a flourish of nose shuffling and paw scratching, Flo and I had the girl's and boy's clothing arranged in two piles. Not stacks, mind you, which is what Jennifer insisted we do. Making stacks of things is something humans, ape-like animals and cats do. Dogs make piles. It's just our nature, and we're kind of proud that it sets us apart from the obsessive-compulsive species. Making piles indicate a more liberal and relaxed individual. Whereas, making stacks represents a tweedy, uptight or more controlling one. Show me someone who does piles, and I'll show you a happier sort. For instance have you ever seen a dog cry? Or, take for example, kids under the age of seven. Who's happier? Someone like me? A child under that age? Or those 8-94 years old and cats?

So, it wasn't long before Flo and I had the clothes separated and had to interrupt Rita's act. We told the kids to pick out some warm clothes and change into them. We also had each one wrap them self in a blanket. This area had gotten colder and damper since I first came here. All I could think of was that it must have been due to the recent weeks of snow and ice storms we just had. Anyway, Flo and I were very concerned they would chill and become sick. We hoped our efforts were in time to prevent that from happening.

Immediately after finishing dressing, they spotted the food and drinks that Jennifer had neatly arranged in front of Rita's perch. Eagerly, and without saying a word, they each ate and drank most of what Frank had brought them. Finally, as they were about to finish, Wally looked up and saw the four of us staring intensely at them eat. "What?" he asked. He appeared a little frightened, like he was now going to be our supper.

"Oh, nothing," I replied. "We're just happy you like the food and are eating so much, so fast. It reminds me of when I sometimes attack a bowl full of dog chow, after cruising all day in town and forgot to eat.

"Which also reminds me, I have been gone all day and my family is going to be concerned.

Maybe I can get Frank to telephone them; and tell them he found me, that I had strayed far away, but that I am ok. And he could add that he'll drop me off there later on this evening after we finish our meeting."

"What meeting?" Rita challenged. "I don't know of any meeting this evening with Frank."

"I don't reckon you do," I replied, "because we haven't had time to tell you."

"What then are you talking about?" she pressed.

"It seems Frank and Sophie wanted all of us to come over to their house at 6 p.m. tonight for some kind of meeting. He said it was urgent that we do so. And he left no room for any excuses not to come. We're supposed to meet him at the top of your Boardwalk-access ramp. And we're to bring the children with us as well."

"What's it about?" Rita interrupted.

"We don't know," Flo joined in. "It didn't seem appropriate to ask him. He seemed a little unhinged with all of us talking to him. I think he thought it was just you, Rita, that had that ability. But, like Greg said, he was insistent we all come and meet with them."

"But what time is it now?" Jennifer whined, not wanting to be left out of this discussion. "We could already be late and not know it."

"It is 5:45 p.m.," Bernie proudly announced, still chewing on a ham sandwich and holding up her left arm to reveal a colorful, large dial, wrist-watch.

"Thank you, Bernie," I gratefully acknowledged. "Maybe you and Wally can take the rest of your sandwiches and the milk cartons with you, because it looks like we ought to head off to that meeting point right away. I don't think it would be a good idea to keep Frank waiting or wondering if we are even coming."

Within five minutes we had collected ourselves, and proceeded in single-file out the tunnel. We carefully weaved our way through the entrance-hiding boulders in the murky, evening twilight and then over the fog-shrouded, sandy shoreline until we finally reached the ramp onto the Boardwalk. As we finished climbing up and looked to see if there might be someone watching us, Bernie came over to me and leaned down to show me her watch again. She noted that it said 6 p.m. We just made it.

Upon our reached the Boardwalk, Frank walked up to us. "Good, I'm relieved everyone made it on time. I didn't want you to spend too much time up here waiting for me, nor did I want to appear conspicuous just waiting for you," he told us. "Quickly, let's all go over to the side street that is straight ahead of us. My truck is parked over there."

We bunched up, like we did coming from the children's home to Rita and Jennifer's place earlier that day. Rita asked Frank what the truck looked like; and after he told her, she leaped into the air and flew over to it. She knew there would be a greater risk of attracting attention if she was to tag along with us.

Frank then led us over to a brownish red pickup truck. It was a late 1950's or early 60's

Apache, Fleetside Chevrolet. It looked tired but large enough to easily hold all of us. Frank unlocked the passenger side and asked the two children to ride in front with him. He then signaled to the other four of us to climb or fly into the open bed.

Now, I have to admit, for the first time publicly, that I had never ridden in a pickup truck, or more precisely, in the bed of a pickup before. But I had always dreamed of doing so. It always looked like so much fun. Honestly, I had never even ridden in a car before. You can just imagine my excitement at this moment. And wouldn't you know, once we all got in and Frank started the engine, I started barking... It was just too much for me. I danced back and forth, going from side to side, barking the whole time he drove the truck. I barked at cars, trucks, buses, girls walking on the sidewalk, at trees, parking meters, fire hydrants, at anything that moved or couldn't move, at cats in particular, and at tall buildings. It was pure glee, and I had to share it. But once we came to a full stop behind Frank's grocery store, I was met with four sullen and vexed individuals.

"Nice, Greg," Rita chided me.

"Really cool," Flo added.

"Do you feel better now?" Jennifer asked, and then offered, "That was so humiliating and so like a dog."

But, at least, Bernie and Wally sided with me. Wally, opened their side of the door and excitedly shouted, "Boy, wasn't that fun, Greg! You sure had a good time! I'd never ridden in a truck before.   It was ggrreattt!   And can you BARK!"

Bernie, ever the polite one, smiled at me and nodded her head.   I knew right away she approved. Her sadness couldn't allow her to express herself with such exuberance at this time, but she was happy for Wally and me.   It was at this point I decided I really liked these kids, and I hoped we could be life-long friends.

Frank, on the other hand, didn't show embarrassment or particular annoyance at my antics, but he sure didn't congratulate me on my performance.   He just mumbled, as he closed his front door and looked at me, "If you ever..."   And then he instructed those of us getting out of the truck bed to tend to any personal business that might be pressing before we went into his home.   This, I thought at the time, was very prescient of him, because with all that had been happening over the last twelve hours, I had not had a chance to relieve myself.   And as it turned out, such was also the case for Flo.   Jennifer, as I later learned, had a little female problem with her bladder and had to use the facility quite frequently.   Rita, wouldn't you know, just lets her 'wind blow free', so to speak, as she flew.   That kind of made me shutter.   What if everyone had the ability to fly?   The world then would be an even more difficult place to cope with, I thought.

"Meet me back here, at our front door, in five minutes," Frank instructed, as he opened, what I thought was his back door, and let Bernie and Wally in.

Actually, it really wasn't the front door, that was pretty clear, but I didn't feel then was a good time to correct Frank. I had drawn pretty heavily on my reserve of having-just-met-him good will. But for accuracy's sake, I must tell you that it was the back door. We were parked in what must have been an alley.

Frank's front door is the grocery store's front door. We were coming in the back way. His store was in the middle of an older block of blackened red-brick, late nineteen century row houses, all fronted with different stores or shops facing the street. But his particular store took up a good four or five of those spaces. It was big, as was their apartment. Still, we were to make our entrance from the rear of that block-long building.

Be that as it may, as instructed, we each scatted to find a most private spot, and I watched Rita fly off in the darkening sky to 'do her business' aloft. I thought, as she flew off, if I had that ability, I'd certainly be barking night and day. There would be, as there are now, song birds, squawking birds, chirping birds, birds who cried the sounds of haunting vespers, but then there would be me, a barking bird or, more specifically, a birddog.

We each arrived back at the BACK door as Frank opened it and smiled. "Come in," he invited us, "and welcome to our home. Let me introduce you to my wife, Sophie. Our children are away tonight, so it will only be the two of us here."

Sophie came forward and greeted each one of us individually, calling us by our recently acquired names. She had a naturalness about her that instilled trust. She looked straight on at you. There was no shifting her gaze or turning her head, as if this was a mechanical gesture she was performing and was anxious to move on to more respectable and important guests. I liked her right away. In fact, I sat down, when it came my turn to meet her, and held out my right paw to shake paws/hands. And in my most sincere manner I said, "I am very pleased to meet you, Sophie."

She took my paw and shook it warmly, smiling and giving me a wink, saying, "I hear you enjoyed your trip over...", and then she moved on to meet Flo and the others. I was captivated. I'd play fetch with her all day, if she wanted to. That's how taken I was with her.

Frank was another matter. I had yet to hear him laugh or even see him smile. His dark hair and tan complexion, along with a Roman nose and brown eyes provided him a handsome, but serious, face. He had a medium, almost athletic build. Both he and Sophia were trim, no doubt as a result of all their years running the grocery store business. If I had to compare, I'd say he was the veneer, and she was the foundation of that couple. But, understand, those were just my first impressions. Dogs can be too quick to judge; like others you may know.

Without any fanfare, as soon as Sophie had been introduced to each of us and had the chance to hug and cuddle the two children, she gently took each by the hand and escorted them into their den. Following behind her, Frank then asked us to come with him. Once in there, we could see that they had prepared some food and drinks for each of us. Mind you, it wasn't like a meal you set out for guests from your office or church study group. There were bowls on the floor for us four-legged guests, a make shift perch lashed together for Rita with a couple of tin cups of food and water attached to it, and a folding card table with metal chairs set up for the children. Beside Sophie and Frank's individual, easy chairs, they each had a T.V. tray with a serving of small sandwiches and hot tea.

"Please sit down and let's have something to eat while I introduce the reason we asked you to come over here tonight," Frank began. "And while you are making yourselves comfortable, I will begin. During the course of this conversation, Sophie may interject her ideas and concerns as well. In fact, it was her idea that we get you over here right away. She and I are both extremely concerned about the situation that you have gotten yourselves into. None of it was done maliciously or haphazardly, of that we are certain, and we salute all of you for your bravery and compassion.

"First off, we need to tell you that there is no way you can manage to care for Bernie and Wally in your living area or with your limitations of acquiring needed supplies. With their permission, we would like to have them live here for the short term, until your trip details are finalized. We understand that their only known living relative, a grandmother, lives somewhere in the Puget Sound area in Washington State. And we know that Bernie and Wally's last name is Appleton. Your hope, as is it ours, is that when you arrive in that region, you will be able to find her and reunite them. We couldn't agree more with that plan. Staying here in Atlantic City only heightens the likelihood that they will be separated and be placed in some kind of temporary shelter, eventually becoming lost and forgotten in the state and county bureaucratic shuffle.

"But, like you, we have no legal authority to keep and hold them here. In the eyes of the authorities, we will be breaking the law. From Sophie and my perspectives, however, we will let these two say what they would like to do. Enough has happened to them, at such a young age, and they deserve the right to make some decisions themselves as to their future course. And if they say they would prefer to stay here in New Jersey, and not live with either your band or with us, we think that is only fair and appropriate. We would then help you to relinquish them to the proper agency.

"On the other hand, if they decide to stay within our group, it's our firm belief that they should be here until time to leave on the trip, if that is also what they would like to do.

"We would have to home-school them. And if they are only here for a short time, we will have to keep them pretty much isolated from the public, particularly in this neighborhood, where everyone knows our family so well. If two unfamiliar children suddenly show up, questions will be asked and their wishes and welfare will be threatened.

"Moreover, if they do decide to stay with all of us, we must get some kind of identification made up. Traveling cross country will require that certain ones of you must carry I.D.'s. Otherwise, you are certain to be detained for questioning. So, let me ask Bernie first, "Do you go to school?"

"No," she replied quietly.

"Have you or your brother ever gone to kindergarten or elementary school?"

Again, Bernie replied "No, sir."

"Have you ever seen your birth certificates?" Sophie interjected.

"I don't think so," Bernie answered. "We hardly ever left any apartment or house we happened to live in. Mom always said she was afraid someone might get suspicious about what she was doing, or who was taking care of us."

"You poor tykes," Sophie sighed. "They have been faceless and nameless. But by your mother's efforts to protect you and herself, she possibly provided you an avenue of escape from a hopeless and tragic situation."

Frank, having heard this, then spoke up. "If that's the case, then this leaves open the possibility of establishing identification for both Bernie and Wally. I've got family connections in New York City, who themselves have connections, and between all of us, we can develop a temporary I.D. At a later time, maybe we can get copies of their birth certificates from the local country courthouse, once they are safely settled with their grandmother. Then their real identification can be established. I would suggest they be temporarily identified as our grandchildren and, as such, have our last name. I'm sure I can arrange this with our relatives in the City.

"What do you say, Bernie and Wally? What is it you want to do? Would you like to stay here in Atlantic City and let the people here take care of you and put you in another home? Or would you want to stay with us, and then in a few weeks maybe leave on a trip to find your grandmother who lives out West? It's your decision. None of us will mind whatever you decide. We want you to stay where you want to and be with who you want to. And everyone here knows deciding this now, or anytime, isn't easy or fair. You've been dealt a terribly loss, in the most horrific kind of circumstance, and we just want to help you what little we can. If you'd like, the two of you can go back into one of our bedrooms and talk it over. Take your time. And whatever you decide will be fine with us. Ok?"

"Alright, Mr. DiAngilo," Bernie quietly answered. "Come on Wally, you and I need to talk."

"Let me show you the way," Sophie said, taking the children by their hands again. "Would you like me to bring you some milk and a cookie while you talk?"

"Yes ma'am," Wally said eagerly.

And for the next fifteen minutes the group of us sat or perched quietly while the kids were in one of the back rooms. Then, without warning, the sound of running footsteps were heard pounding down the hallway and Wally was the first one to appear, shouting, in a sing-song voice, "We've decided, we've decided. We're going to stay with you and then go on a very long trip." And following him, soon thereafter, was Bernie, smiling weakly, wiping some stray tears off her face. "That's right," she added. "We want to be with you, and then we want to have you help us go find our grandma."

A collective sigh was heard throughout the room. The adventure was on.

FIVE: GETTING READY

Obviously, Rita, Flo, Jennifer and I would have loved to have the kids stay with us in the underground room, but what little collective good sense we had told us that Frank and Sophie's request was the best choice. Bernie and Wally would stay in their home and be home-schooled by the DiAngilo family until we were ready to leave on the trip.

The next decisions to be made that same evening were which of us were going, how to travel, what to take, and what roadways to use. The discussions and arguments went far into the night, with the children falling fast asleep early in the evening. Frankly, it spared them seeing me at my most hysterical.

The one, more civil, discussion we had during this meeting involved the wishes of Sophie and Frank to accompany us on our upcoming, cross-country trip. They said that their 38 years in the grocery business was long enough and that their older children wanted to take it over anyway. It was time for them to change the direction of their lives, and this trip would open the doors for exploring that direction. They even admitted that neither of them had been any further from Atlantic City than New York City. Of course, I could trump that narrow radius, with mine being from my handler's house to the Boardwalk. But that moment wasn't the time for one-upmanship or one-updogship, as this case clearly was.

They made the case, and quite convincingly I thought, that to have the two children along, with only talking animals to support and care for them, was a clear invitation for constant harassment and probably some serious dog-pound time or much worse. Having adults present would lend a family atmosphere to the journey, and it would provide adequate support and safety for the children. Another plus was that it would also give cover to the children's false identities, until they could resume their real ones, once they were united with their grandmother.

But our agreeing to that plan only led to the arguments that followed, which ended up having me race madly around the house, shouting, "This isn't a recreational vehicle, road trip!"

That's because they insisted on renting a large RV and driving us all the way to the West Coast. Luckily, that didn't fit into the overall plan Flo and Rita had either. Flo began to howl, in a mournful arctic, barren-wasteland, contralto voice. Rita became unhinged by all my yelling and Flo's howling and began to squawk like she was lost deep in some jungle rainforest. Jennifer, of course, pandered to the DiAngilo's, now becoming the most likely source for her next meal. She just paraded around their feet and legs, purring, as if to say, "Listen to them! Aren't they a bunch of ingrates? You can count on me. I'll happily ride with you in your R.V. "Unmoved by her shameless treachery, I even threatened to begin my insane barking again, if other options were not considered.

Finally, in a desperate attempt not to have the entire population of Atlantic City's southwest corridor at their doorstep, Frank called out, "Ok, ok, it was just a suggestion, for Pete's sake! What is yours? Or do you even have a plan?"

Coming to a complete mid-air stop, and simultaneously doing one of my less-witnessed, 180 degree about-faces, I came to rest about two feet in front of Frank and gave him one of my straight-on, head half-cocked stares. It is usually disarming, if for no other reason than the recipient hasn't any earthly idea what I'm going to do next. Ninety-nine percent of the time I just stare, but on this occasion I spoke.

"Yes we do," I calmly replied. "Using a big, lumbering, overpriced, glorified bedroom-on-wheels is not our idea of travel, particularly for what we need to do. Ours is to be a different kind of journey. Maybe it's not like the Burke and Wills trek across the Australian Outback, or Lewis and Clark's Corps of Discovery, or Marco Polo's travels across multiple continents, or Columbus' sailing the mid-Atlantic or even Livingston crossing the equatorial jungles of Africa, but still it is a journey of exploration and discovery. We want to find out what makes life so special. What enhances it? What detracts from it? Who lives it the best, or the worst?   And if it is not being lived, as it was originally conceived or designed to be, what needs to be added, subtracted, or altered to do so.

"And to accomplish this we need to have 'boots on the ground', as they say.   We must walk this land from shoreline to shoreline.   And we must listen, watch, learn, interact with whoever we encounter, even going so far as all of us communicating with them."

"Fair enough," Frank said pensively.   "But how do you plan to travel?   If you are taking the children, they certainly can't walk all that distance. And if you, for the sake of argument, agree Sophie and my going along will give your troop added protection and legitimacy, how are we to travel? Believe me, neither of us can walk that distance either."

"Well," I began, "up to a few minutes ago, our travel arrangements had been pretty well thought out.   However, if you should accompany us, that's something new to consider.   But first things first.

"For the original six of us, I envisioned Flo and I would pull three wagons.   I'd pull one, and she would handle the other two.   I've seen the wagons down at Archie's Toy and Bicycle Shop on the Boardwalk.   They sell and rent their equipment.

"They are the classic red ones with wooden side rails, the ones with the thick, ten inch high inflatable tires.   They are heavy duty.   We would have to have them modified by removing their single, metal handles that are usually used to pull them, and substitute a set of leather harnesses.   They would be attached where the metal handle used to be, by drilling holes in the swivel axel. The tack would be similar to what is used on dog sleds.

"As I said, I would pull Wally, because he's the lightest, and Flo would pull Bernie in one wagon and supplies in the other. Flo's second wagon's handle would also be removed and it would be permanently attached to the first one. It would be pulled in tandem. In addition, there would be a perch, four feet in height, welded on the rear end of that second wagon. Rita could ride there when she wasn't out investigating the road and facilities ahead of us.

"The trickiest part of this caravan is having someone build a squirrel cage-like apparatus that would be attached to the back of my wagon. It would have a single axle through its center, with twenty inch wheels attached. The cage would be about twelve inches wide, enough to allow Jennifer to fit comfortably inside. It would be made of aluminum mesh, and opened at each end. The cage would turn whenever the wagon was moving, but when Jennifer was walking inside it; she would generate additional power, especially for going up hills. When she wasn't helping in that way, she would have to walk along side us. We will have small saddle bags made for her to carry when she walks outside the squirrel cage."

"Alright," Frank acknowledged, looking at Sophie as he spoke. "But now, what about us? As I said, we cannot walk. I suppose we could drive a car or van."

"No," Rita exclaimed, jumping into the conversation. "A vehicle like that would be too big, too fast. It just wouldn't work."

"What do you propose then?" Sophie asked, turning her head toward Rita.

"Well, I'd suggest a bicycle of some kind," Rita answered.

"A bicycle," Sophie exclaimed. "I couldn't possibly ride a bicycle across country, up and down mountains. It would just be too hard on me."

"But what about a tricycle?" I asked. "I've seen those nice ones at Archie's. Some are called 'Bents'. The rider sort of reclines in a very comfortable looking padded arm-chair seat with a backrest. It has a basket behind it to carry packages and supplies."

"Again," Sophie argued, "how would I manage getting that up and down steep hills or those tall mountains we'll be crossing, further out West?"

"Some, I've seen," Frank interjected, "even have electric motors on them. I think their called motorized tricycles. And you could get some kind of small utility trailer to attach behind each of them. We could each get one and be able to carry extra supplies. What do you think? Sophie?"

"Well, maybe," she replied. "Do you think we could go down to Archie's and rent a couple of them to try out and see how we manage?"

"You bet," Frank answered. "Now what do you think, Greg and Rita?"

Looking at Rita, Flo and Jennifer, I could see they were nodding their heads that this was a real possibility. And I thought having one trike in front of our caravan and one in the rear just might work. "Ok," I said. "Go over as soon as you can and try them out. If they work, you have some time to order them and begin some training to get into shape. The same applies to us. Flo, Jennifer and I will need to start running in the sand to build up our strength and stamina.

"And while you're at it, and now that we've touched on the subject, I think we should review what other specific supplies we will need. The sooner this list is known by all of us, the sooner each of us can begin searching for the items, some of which may require special effort and expense to get. And some may require the services of a seamstress or purchases from an old-style, country store."

"What, in particular, are you considering?" Sophie and Frank both asked in unison.

"Yeah," Rita and Jennifer, both chimed in. "I don't think you have even shared that with us," Rita added.

"Probably not," I responded. "Flo and I talked about it on our way over to the Boardwalk earlier this morning, just before we found Bernie and Wally. I guess a lot has happened between then and now, and it was a low priority.

"So to begin with, we need to get tack for those of us pulling the two sets of wagons. Also needed, both for the wagons and the tricycles, are some of those bright orange warning triangles, red reflectors, and headlights. For safety and protection, maybe someone could locate a couple of those old- style airmen, pullover, leather caps for Flo and I to wear. We could then attach small headlamps to the top of each of them. They would be turned on in heavy traffic, when it's foggy or in the twilight, if we are still on the road.

"Additionally, we need to have leather booties made for Flo, Jennifer and my feet. Otherwise, we run the risk of wearing our paws off with all the walking that is ahead. I know we will look silly, but, as it is, the pullover caps aren't going to give us the look of crisply dressed, New York, Wall Street brokers."

"I like it," Jennifer interrupted. "Just call me 'Puss 'n Boots', from now on."

I smiled wanly at her, but secretly, I did appreciate that she was not objecting or complaining, for once. And then I continued with the list, explaining we needed props for our various acts. And to questions about that I explained that we were to perform for audiences, in order to make money and to encourage participation in question and answer sessions or in lectures we might want to give. Our performing, in other words, served two functions. It would give us revenue, and it would provide an avenue for broadcasting our messages.

And next, I mentioned the supplies we needed for shelters: a tent for Sophie and Frank, a large fly for us to meet and eat under, small tarps to drape over the sides of the wagons at night, and a larger fly for our act to be performed under. Finally, we needed a camp cook stove, pots/pans, extra clothing and food. All consumables would have to be bought along the way. Having listed all that, we then had to decide who would look for what and where the items would be stored, until it was time to assemble it all and set off.

But, then, I sat bolt upright, stopping

mid-sentence and exclaimed, "We haven't decided yet, and for all time to come, who's going, where we are going and what roads we're taking to get there. I say it's time for a vote, before we go any further in this discussion."

Looking around the room, and particularly at Sophie and Frank, there were the usual looks of surprise at my rashness and sudden outburst, usually pretty much unrelated to anything previously being discussed. And yet, there followed a chorus of "you bet, yep, why not, time's a' wasting', what took you so long to ask, and let's do it."

I suggested we vote on three separate issues. The first was whether Sophie and Frank accompanied us and that their mode of travel would be by bicycle or tricycle. The second was whether our final destination, after leaving Atlantic City, was to be the Seattle-Tacoma area. And finally, we needed to decide whether we were to travel on side roads or on main highways. In addition, because we needed to start immediately being open about how we felt and thought, I also suggested our voting should be by a show of hands, paws and wings. All that was agreed upon and the votes were cast. Surprisingly, and to my relief, all the items passed. Secretly, I had begun to feel much attached to Sophie and, even somewhat towards, gruff Frank. Their going with us was important. It would give Wally and Bernie a better chance of success with their new start in life.

Rita then brought up the issue of paying for all this. She offered to donate all her earnings toward the trip, but had no idea how much it amounted to, because like me, she couldn't count. Sophie asked Frank to bring her earnings back tonight, after delivering us to our respective homes, and she'd count it. We all knew that the DiAngilo's were going to have to bankroll the major portion of the trip for now, but it was everyone's desire that our performances would generate a self-sustaining income once we were on the road. And later we hoped to repay them as well.

All that was decided, and other minor issues had been settled, both kids awoke and realized what had taken place. They, too, were relieved it worked out as it did. We all began to dance or hop around the living room, some on two feet, others on four feet. Sophie turned on a recording of some Italian music, and that did it. We sang, danced, had something to drink and munch on, congratulated each other on our new horizons ahead, and felt truly thankful for Wally and Bernie. Their grieving was far from over, but at least they were to be safely sheltered and protected.

The one last bit of business that had to be sorted out, which was done in the days that followed, was to determine the cross-country routes we would be taking. Unanimously, we all opted for going on the less traveled county roads whenever possible. They would take us through the heartland of America. Our intention was to avoid any of the bigger cities along the way. The side roads and staying clear of the metropolitan areas offered all of us safer passage in the long run. We needed, wherever possible, for the roadways to have paved shoulders. We hoped to travel mostly on those surfaces. For everyone's safety, travel would only be during daylight hours. We realized, at the same time, we'd be doing a lot of camping along these roads, often on private property. To avoid any conflicts, we always hoped to get permission to do so. And besides on private land, we also envisioned camping in city, county, state parks, and school yards and on church properties. Basically, we anticipated we probably would be staying overnight just about anywhere someone would let us.

The party broke up about midnight. Frank said he'd drop me off at my residence and then take Jennifer and Rita back to the Boardwalk. Flo was invited to stay with Sophie and Frank, which given the amount of food she ate, was a relief to Rita. Likewise, I wasn't sure how to manage that issue at my house, if she stayed with me. Hiding and feeding a 90 pound animal was beyond my ability to do subtly. Frank insisted the three of us ride up front this time, as he drove us to our residences. He wanted no more outbursts from me. Still, even riding in the cab of the truck was so exciting. I just had to close my eyes and hold my breath most of the way, otherwise, I knew I'd start jumping around and barking. It's what dog's do when their happy. So?

Arriving home, I crawled up on our front porch and laid down on my bunched-up blankets, after resorting them a bit. It was cold, but snuggling up inside them, I got comfortable and warm. It had been an eventful day, and the future looked bright. It was good to be alive, I thought, as I dropped off into a deep sleep.

THE EAST COAST

SIX: UNDERWAY

The next four weeks were a blur to me, as I guess were my last four and half years of life. Give me day-to-day existence every time. Trying to recall all these past events and conversations has given me a terrible case of the mange. In fact, I itch so badly that everyone now makes fun of me, whenever they see me scratching. You see my mangy parts are solely on the top of my back. You try scratching that with your hind leg sometime. So to do so, what I have to resort to is lying down on my back, on an old, bumpy, gravel-strewn drive-way, with all my legs positioned up in the air. (Where did you think they'd be, lying on the ground?) You see, I'm still a little testy about all this. Next, I start pedaling my back legs, slowly at first, and then as I get a little body momentum going, I pedal them faster and faster until my entire lower body is moving across the gravel, side-to-side. And, wa-la! I'm now enjoying an exquisite scratch. I'll even rest a little bit, because it is tiring doing this. But I just pick up the momentum again after I'm rested, still lying on my back of course, and the ecstasy continues. I can continue doing this for almost an hour or at least until a crowd assembles…

So, anyway, you get my point. Remembering is a struggle for me, and I'd appreciate it, if we ever do meet somewhere that you don't mention this scratching business. After all, I don't know anything about your quirky or embarrassing antics. I only mention this in an effort to provide as complete a picture of our preparations and recording of this adventure as possible. And I ask you; wouldn't you do the same for me?

As I said before, the weeks after that first evening at the DiAngilo's were filled with constant meetings and trial runs, in which we had to determine what harnesses would work best for pulling the wagons, how to get the squirrel cage apparatus to operate properly for Jennifer, and what modification of Flo's wagons was necessary for connecting them. Sophie, as it turned out, was an accomplished seamstress and was able to make four pairs of boots for the three of us pulling or pushing the wagons. She even incorporated miniature steel toes and cleats in all of the boots. And they had lace-up tops. To me, they looked all-the-world like the boots used by the loggers in the Northwest. I was so proud of them that I began to wear them on the beach when Flo, Jennifer and I worked out.

Due to Sophie's ability to anticipate and prepare for the unexpected, she added two rather luxurious additions to our original lists of supplies and equipment. After rearing five children, what else would you expect? Her ability to forecast and problem solve never ceased to amaze me. In this case, she insisted that we construct canopies to be raised over the seats on the tricycles and over the wagons. The children, Frank and herself needed extra protection from the more severe and persistent rainstorms that we were bound to encounter in route. Everyone, except Flo, Rita, Jennifer and I, had full rain gear, with hoods, as well. When the canopies were raised on the tricycles, they looked like something I'd seen on T.V. in the streets of Manila.

And the other accessory she insisted on was a two-way radio set for herself, Frank, the kids, me, and Flo. Flo and I had them incorporated into our leather helmets. Any messages that had to be relayed to Jennifer, if she was working in the squirrel cage, were the responsibility of Flo. And messages for Rita had to be relayed by Frank, provided she was sitting on the perch and not soaring over the countryside.

All our equipment was kept in a storage warehouse that Frank had built years ago on their property in Northfield, on the city's outskirts. It was too far away for all of us to walk to. This meant we only went there if he drove us. But sadly, when he did, Frank always made me ride in the cab of the truck

. It was a big enough building that once the wagons were modified and we had all our strapping, we could practice pulling the wagons inside. And this is where Frank and Sophie also assembled and kept their motorized recumbent tricycles, with their attached utility trailers. In the countryside, surrounding the warehouse, they practiced riding and pulling their cycles and trailers.

There was one last very important issue that I have nearly forgotten to mention, and that is the status of Wally and Bernie. Events, both on that day we found them in the bushes and I made those gruesome discoveries in their home and in the following weeks after our meeting that evening with Frank and Sophie, need to be described to you.

First off, soon after Flo and I made our discoveries, someone, and most likely the murderers themselves, decided there was too much evidence left at the crime scene, so they returned and apparently doused the interior of the house with gasoline. It burned down with such savage ferocity, we later found out, that it destroyed all evidence that Wally or Bernie even existed. Like I mentioned before, they did not go to school, and there was little evidence outside their home that they were even inside. They had no identity outside the walls of that now, burned-out house. Even their grandmother in Tacoma, as we later found out, was unsure of their existence.

Next, there was the issue of Frank getting their identification papers. True to his word, he was able to travel to New York City, contact his sources that arranged for that kind of work, supply them with recent passport-size photos for each child, and later secure New Jersey I.D. cards for them. And they were given the temporary names of Wallace and Bernice DiAngilo. There was apparently a nominal fee charged for this service, because even his contact people in New York had heard of the murders in

Atlantic City on that March day.

Having accomplished that, it was our troop's hope that the children were relatively safe now. At least the murderers were the only ones looking for them and not half the government authorities on the Eastern Seaboard. And by their leaving the area permanently, we hoped that would eliminate the threat of the killers ever locating them.

And on the evening of April 15, we finally had assembled all our clothing, camping equipment, tents, tarps, food, water, vehicles and some extra money to hold us until our performances starting paying our way. It was decided we'd have a party for the people who had helped us get ready and who had supported us, but we had to have them swear secrecy as to what we were up to and, most importantly, what some of us could do. That meant, of course, that Howard and his family were invited, as was Sophie and Frank's extended family, Archie's bicycle shop staff and Jacob's family, the fellow who owned the country store in Steelmanville, where we were able to locate our tack and leather goods for our boots.

And to thank everyone, we decided to do their first, full-dress rehearsal for them. It was complete with Flo singing, Jennifer doing acrobatics, Rita soaring and doing loop-the-loops, all the while telling off-colored jokes, Frank playing his accordion and Sophie her fiddle, while Wally and Bernie danced, and with me doing my Master of Ceremony's shtick. There had been no preliminary warning as to what any of us could do, say or sing. Even I had none for how well Frank and Sophie could play their musical instruments. As well, Sophie or Frank had never seen our entire act, so everyone was pretty amazed at it all. Or maybe stunned would be a better word. I know Howard kept shaking his head in disbelief. Here, all along, he and the family thought I had a classic case of hyperactive, attention deficit disorder, and that I could only whine and bark. Life is full of surprises they were to learn that night, as we hoped others would experience in the course of our upcoming journey.

Everyone slept over in the large warehouse. No one was in any shape to drive that night after the partying was done. But come sunrise that next morning, we all lined up outside the warehouse, with Sophie in the lead, followed by my and Flo's wagons, and Frank in the rear. With everyone sworn to secrecy about what they witnessed the night before, we all waved, barked, shouted, squawked and headed off on the road leading northwest to Clarksville. Our adventure had begun.

SEVEN: NEW JERSEY - PART 1

Maybe to keep you from getting too confused and disoriented, and to keep me focused on the task of writing this account, I will first give you our travel route in each state that we were to cross. That way you could follow our journey, as the story unfolds. This will be followed with the actual events as they occurred, more or less, depending on how well I recall them. I have had Flo, Rita, Jennifer, Frank and Sophie reread and correct my work, but even at that, we all got caught up in making this journey. None of us were that good at remembering the details. But, believe me, I'm trying. And now for the journey itself.

The route through New Jersey went from Steelmanville→Clarkstown→MaysLanding→Wey mouth→Pinelands National Reserve and Newtonville→Hwy 538→Franklinville, under I-55→Farrell→under the New Jersey Turnpike→Swedesboro→Hwy 551 → Repaupo Exit on I-295 → across the Delaware River through Chester, Pennsylvania, to Long Wood Gardens near Red Lion, Pennsylvania. It was here we began walking again.

There was little fanfare as we left Steelmanville. Sophie and Frank's family, along with scattered remnants of party goers, waved us off. In addition, there were about twenty local folks who gathered to see what in heaven's name was going on. My bet was that they all thought we'd be lucky to make it to Clarkstown, just up the road. And, honestly, at that point I agreed with them. I was as nervous as..., well as..., Jennifer. I hadn't eaten much the last two days, I was so excited.

We had tested our two-way radio headphones repeatedly in the days leading up to our final departure, and at the moment we started off, Sophie announced, "Jersey Wagoners, mount up! Let's be on our way, you lads and lassies...Westward ho!"

It kind of made me proud to be addressed as a "lad". I've never felt any particular need or desire to be a direct descendent of humankind, but 'lad' had a nice ring to it. Being addressed as "dog" or "doggy" sometimes had a pejorative connotation. "Lad", on the other hand, made my chest swell with pride, as I strained on the reins of my wagon load, and moved forward. Taking my first step was a milestone. And as I thought about it, at approximately six inches per step that meant I only had 31,680,000 more to take before we arrived in Tacoma-Seattle, some 3000 miles from here. That thought, alone, almost led to panic, but I managed to stifle it by following up on Sophie's command, and shouted , "Gee haw".

Then over the ear phone I heard Flo's voice urge us on with, "Wagons ho."

And Frank yelled, "We're off to see the wizard," which as future events would soon reveal, this remark seemed remarkably uncanny.

And the children, almost in unison, cried out, "Whoopee."

And Jennifer sighed.

Within two blocks we were outside the town's city limits and Sophie was peddling onto the paved shoulder, leading us into history. The terrain was level, for the most part, with only gently rolling inclines our first day on the road. On days not scheduled for performances or public gatherings of some kind, we hoped to travel eight hours. There would be rest breaks every two hours and lunch, with an accompanying hour's rest, after the first four hours of walking and pedaling. Our plan was to be settled for the night by 6 p.m., at the latest.

After we had been walking for about 30 minutes this first day, Wally tapped my on my rump and asked, "Mr. Greg, are we nearly there?"

My heart sank. I didn't have it in me to say, "Oh…, about 31,680,950 more steps". So, I was quiet, for a minute, as I thought of how best to answer that question. After all, it deserved an honest, but gentle, reply.

"Wally," I began finally, "we have a long way to go, and we will be on the road for many, many days. Honestly, I am not sure how much further we have to go or how long it will take us. But I will be here with you all the way. And I plan on making it as fun a trip for you as I can. You and I are going to become best friends along the way, and to start with I need to ask you a favor."

"What's that, Mr. Greg?" he replied.

"Well," I began, "sometimes I get a really bad itch that needs to be scratched, and by having all this gear on me to pull the wagon, I can't scratch it. I'll need you to help me, when I ask you to. I'll tell you where to scratch it and for how long. Can you do that?"

(As I looked back on this time, I realized this was the beginning of my lifelong journey with this confounded mange, which finally came into full bloom, as I mentioned before, as I was preparing this story for you. I've decided that some folks and critters get awards, banquets and keys to the city, along with ribbons and medals for their acts of bravery and civic involvement. Me? I got a first class case of the mange.)

"Sure, I can, Mr. Greg. Do you need a scratch now?" he asked.

"No, I'm doing just fine. And one other thing, when we have our rest stops, you'll need to help get me out of my harness so I can stretch and go potty, like you do. As you can see, we'll be a team. I'll need you to help me, and I am going to do the same for you."

"Ok," he said, sounding rather thoughtful. "Then, let's play a game!"

"So soon?" I thought to myself. I'd never had an opportunity to play anything, except that stupid, "go fetch the stick", or pretend I was herding a group of animals or people. To satisfy the eagerness and loneliness of little Wally, I needed to think of something that would be challenging and fun.

And you have to realize that my world view is somewhat limited at this point. Bound up in the harness, pulling the wagon kept me pretty restricted as to what I could see or do. In fact, about the only vistas I had were of gravel, pavement, fog lines along the highway, beer cans, other roadside flotsam, and uncut grass and bushes. My travel horizon consisted of anything within a two to three foot half circle around me. It was possible that I might not even know what I was pulling. Frank could put anything inside my wagon, and I'd be unaware of what it was, aside from knowing that I was pulling more weight. So, with this as background for our games, I began to formulate a plan.

"Well, then, my Captain, and that is what I am going to call you, I have a game for you to play, or better still, both a game to play and an important duty to perform."

"Goody," Wally replied. "What?"

"I want you to tell me everything that we pass by, for as far as you can see. I want to know descriptions, colors, shapes, and kinds of trees, cars, trucks, bushes, grasses, crops, orchards, hillsides, mountains, streams, rivers, lakes, anything and everything. And then I want you to make lists of what you see and we'll have a point system attached to each thing, depending on its uniqueness and beauty. But, for anything thrown out along the way that you call out, like beer bottles, old tires, pop cans, points will be subtracted. And at the end of each day we'll tally up what you saw, add and subtract the points and see how much you come up with. And at the beginning of each day, you and I will guess what total points you have for that day. The one closest to that total at the end of the day wins. And we'll do that every day for the whole trip until we determine the overall winner. Then one of us will get a Grand Prize."

"What's the surprise?" he eagerly asked.

Feeling fairly proud of myself that I had gone this far, I was caught off-guard by this question. I was quiet for some distance after that. Being what I was, there were few options open to me. I didn't have a bank account, drive a fine car, own a fancy wristwatch, have a closet full of high fashion clothes or know anyone who did. All I had was me.

"You get me," I answered. "If you win, by the time we get to your grandmother's house, then I'll gladly become your partner and friend forever. How's that?"

"Do you mean it?" Wally asked.

"Yes. That's a promise. But we have to be dedicated how we play the game. No cheating. No missing days. But, by the way, can you count?" I asked.

He replied, "I can count to 100. Do you want to hear me?"

"You bet," I said. "And while you're doing that, I'll begin making up the list and the score for each item on it. You and your sister will have to write them down, as I list them off. Both of you do have a pencil and some paper, don't you?"

"I don't, but I know Bernie does. I'll ask her to help, and then I'll begin counting. But what about me? What can I give you as a prize, if you win?"

That led to an equally long pause in our conversation, as I considered his having the same dilemma as I did. Finally, I said, "Two things. One will be your friendship and the other will be a promise."

"What's the promise?" he eagerly asked.

"That you will always take care of your sister, even though she is a little older than you and make sure both of you finish your schooling."

"Well," he replied hesitantly, "I've never even been to school before, but if I ever do go to one, I'll promise to finish it and also to help my sister do the same. And I think being your friend will be easy. So I agree. But, I'm going to win anyway..."

"We'll see about that," I concluded, turning my head around to see him. Fortunately, he was all smiles by now and then started counting, "1,2,3,4,5,6,..."

And as he did that, I began my list. And over the next three days of travel and arguing amongst all of us in The Jersey Wagoners, the following list took shape. I will share it with you now, because it did play a role in some of the events that followed throughout the rest of our journey.

Wally's Roadside Game List
ADDITIONS

points	points
First small river +10	First Holly bush +25
All small rivers afterward +5	First Rhododendron bush +25

First large river +15

All large rivers afterward +10

All really large rivers +50

First small pond +10

All small ponds afterward +5

First small lake   +15

All small lakes afterward +10

First large lake   +20

All large lakes afterward +15

All really large lakes   +50

First large hill +10

All large hills afterward +5

First mountain +50

All mountains afterward +25

First large mountain   +75

All large mountains
    afterward   +30

All large mountains with
  snow   +100

All mountain ranges +100

First Pine tree +10

First Oak tree +10

First Hickory tree   +25

First Chestnut tree   +15

First Azalea bush
    +25

First Hollyhock bush
    +25

First Honeysuckle
    bush +25

First Lilac bush
    +25

First tulip   +25

First Daffodil +25

First Crocus   +25

First Iris   +25

First Violet   +25

First Hyacinth +25

First Rose   +25

First Camellia +25

First Wisteria +25

First field corn +20

First field sweet corn
    +35

First field with alfalfa
        +20

First field with
Timothy grass +30

First field peas +40

First field tomatoes
    +35

First field soy beans
    +25

First field pumpkins
    +35

First field sugar beets
    +30

First Spruce tree   +20

First Aspen tree   +25

First Fir tree   +25

First Redwood tree   +50

First Yew tree   +75

First Madrone tree   +35

First Pecan tree   +35

First English walnut tree +30

First waterfall +75

All waterfalls afterward +50

First deep canyon   +30

All deep canyons afterward +25

All cumulous cloud formations +15

Any funnel cloud formations +75

All dust devils   +20

All meteor showers   +50

All rainbows   +35

First apple tree
   orchard +35

First pear tree orchard
   +40

First peach tree
   orchard +45

First orange tree
   orchard +45

First grape vineyard
   +50

First grapefruit tree
   orchard +45

First lemon tree
   orchard +50

First blueberry bushes
   +40

First blackberry
   bushes +25

First   passenger   bus
   +15

All buses afterward
   +5

All passenger trains
   +20

All school buses
   +15

Any blue cars
   +30

Any 3 wheel
   motorcycles +35

All tandem bicycles
   +50

All long freight trains

+15

All deer/ other wild life +25   All cars made before
1950   +35

SUBTRACTIONS

points		points	
All beer cans	-10	All mattresses	-75
All beer bottles	-15	All tires	-40
All soda cans	-10	All hub caps	-30
All plastic bottles	-10	All building materials	-20
All large plastic bags	-20	All food packages	-25
All metal/wooden chairs	-40	All newspaper	-20
All overstuffed chairs	-50	All large cans	-15
All sofas	-75	All small cans	-10
All hot water heaters	-75	All sacks of garbage	-35
All stoves	-75	All refrigerators	-100
All washers	-75	All dryers	-75
All lamps	-35	All desks, cabinets, shelves	-45

The list grew in size and, at times, caused lengthy discussions about the point system. To settle any argument, I would fall back on the fundamental fact that it was my idea in the first place, so initially I made all the final decisions. Being a dog, in this case, had nothing to do with behaving like a mature and sensible person. And as I thought about it, my experience was pretty limited in the number of mature, courteous and thoughtful adults I'd known up until that time. I wondered if maybe they should be added to the Roadside Game List. But, I knew, without much further thought, that it was impractical, because anyone with these traits would be priceless.

Already in my short life, and again in preparation for this trip, I was learning that quality human beings, like Frank and Sophie, were national treasures. Maybe, I later thought, we'll devise another game based solely on the kinds of people we meet. First impressions are not the best gauge for judging people, but you're usually not too far off the mark, even after you've spent considerable time with them. But, on second thought, I let the idea slide. These children had already experienced the worst of humankind through their family's deaths. Nothing needs to remind them anymore, beyond what their nightmares must already do, of that. Besides, I guess each of us, even dogs, keep a watch list of personality types and behavioral traits that we try to shield ourselves from or at least shift into heightened awareness to avoid them harming us or those we care about.

All that aside, by the fourth day on the road, Wally and I began the game. And it wasn't long before everyone was involved, making side bets or calling out missed objects. But out of respect for the children, everyone always let them have the first chance to claim any new object on our list. Over time, as the game became more involved and the list grew and grew, I relinquished my grip, and decisions were made by a majority vote. See, even dogs can acquire some maturity.

However, this game did not substitute for the school curriculum material that Wally and Bernie had to learn. Before we left Atlantic City, Sophie contacted the New Jersey Education Department and got their grade level Home School materials. That work was interspersed with this game, the performances we did for the public, and just sight-seeing. By the time we had been traveling for a couple of weeks, both children appeared settled and content. They knew that they were cared about and that they were on their way to be with family. There were few moans or sighs of boredom during the entire trip. In fact, they were wonderful Wagoners.

EIGHT: NEW JERSEY - PART 2

Now, I don't know about you, the reader of this tale, but for me, the narrator of it, it's been my experience that the first of anything usually leaves the biggest impression. And certainly that was the case for our first day on the road, as we headed from Steelmanville, through Clarkstown, and on to Weymouth for the night. Roadway Alt. 559, as it was called, took us right along the shoreline of one of the Clover Leaf Lakes.

We weren't planning on scheduling any performances in New Jersey. It seemed too risky for the children, by possibly bringing unwanted attention and news coverage to us and to them. We weren't unaware of the ongoing threat they were under, being the only witnesses to their family's deaths. So, we decided prior to our departure that we had enough money to make it to Pennsylvania, before we needed to start our paid-on-admission performances. Mind you, we also planned on giving free performances as well, particularly for any children we met, but even that would not occur until after we crossed the Delaware River into

Pennsylvania.

But back to our first day on the road… The rain began about 3:30 p.m., as we passed along the lake front. And we still had another two hours to go before reaching Weymouth, where Frank knew someone who'd let us camp in their pasture. The campsite was just east of the township. Despite knowing that, we still had to get through the rainstorm to get there. And yet, as inconvenient as the rain was, it wasn't until the gusts of wind began, that this day became particularly memorable. It seemed the lake, which was now along our right flank at this point, provided a fertile playground for the wind to gain more confidence and strengthen. It became a gale.

Picture, if you will, Sophie and Frank with their canopies now hoisted up over their tricycle seats. Their canopies had plastic windshields that zipped up in the front and across their laps. Wearing those bright yellow rain pants and jackets, they were dry and comfy as they peddled. The children also stayed dry and warm inside their own yellow rain hats and coats and by being partially covered with the tarps that Sophie had embroidered with an elastic band around their edges. Those bands kept the tarps firmly in place around the perimeter of the wagons' sides and allowed the rainwater to run off easily onto the ground. They, thankfully, stayed in place through the storm

Rita sheds rainwater like a goose. It was no matter to her. The only indication of her being somewhat amiss was when I later saw that her yellow crest was pasted down over one side of her head. I was completely unaware of why she was so unruffled and clean until later, when she showed me what she and Frank had designed and built without my knowledge.

Jennifer was wearing her modified rain suit, as she jogged in her squirrel cage. It only partially covered her, so as you might expect, she complained enough for everyone. But at least, being somewhat shielded at the back of Wally's wagon, she was spared the splashing of oncoming or passing cars.

Then there was Flo and I, with only our leather, pull-down, flight helmets to protect us from the elements. Both of us faced the endless waves of water head on. But it wasn't just water. It was also dirt, gravel, cigarette butts (which, I soon enough realized should have been added to Wally's roadside list of undesirables) and bits of plastic shopping bags and newspaper that clung on, wherever they struck you. I honestly wasn't sure if I needed a snorkel or a football helmet with a full face mask before another storm hit us. My boots were so heavily laden with water that I began to slog along, like their soles were covered with sticky, industrial-grade glue. And all the while, due to my miserable eyesight, I was trying desperately not to run into Sophie's tricycle, as she weaved along into the head wind.

This first travel day came to an end with Sophie announcing excitedly that we had arrived at our destination. Everyone was so relieved to be stopping that they hurriedly took off their rain gear and dismounted the tricycles, wagons and squirrel cage without saying a word. Just at that moment they turned and saw me, motionless and dripping whatever it was that had splashed on me. I had been transformed into a roadside, garbage magnet.

"We made it!" Sophie shouted as she looked around to see the tree-covered camping area that would provide our first night's lodging.

And just then Wally, with worried innocence yelled to me, "Mr. Greg, there are lots of things on your roadside game stuck on you. Do you want me to count them?"

Spitting something on the ground, that tasted like road-surface soup, brewed from 75 years of tread-bare rubber tires, leaking crankcase oil, countless cigarettes and cigar butts, assorted candy wrappers and soda containers, I managed to sputter out, "Don't you dare!"

And at that moment I glanced back to see Flo. She was hardly recognizable. Her brilliantly thick, white coat, always so perfectly coifed and fluffed was matted and streaked. She looked like an oil drum, like one you might find behind one of those old, abandoned filling stations we occasionally passed on our journey, propped on wobbly, wooden legs, ready to collapse at any moment. The only thing I recognized about her was our leather, pull-down, flight helmet. But even that was streaked. The goggles were so filthy; I wondered how she saw anything ahead of her.

"Oh, Flo," I moaned. "I'm so sorry to have gotten you into this mess. I've made a terrible mistake. We can't go on like this. We'll be lucky if we don't catch the flu or something worse, after this deluge. Who knows what diseases have been tossed up into our faces today? Please, forgive me."

Immediately after my saying this, and Frank had just finished unhitching her wagon harness, everyone for a twenty foot radius experienced a little of what Flo and I had just gone through. She began to shake herself from the tip of her head to the tip of her tail. Her flight helmet flew off into the tree line, along with whatever unmentionables were lodged in her fur. Next, she launched about a gallon of roadside water, which showered over everyone and everything nearby. This went on for the next minute, sometimes less vigorous, but still non-stop. And when she was done, presto, there was Flo again, her white coat back in its full rich color and in proper order. She looked at me, smiled and quipped, "There, that will give everyone something to consider the next time they decide to mush through a monsoon-like rainstorm. Share and share-alike, I always say."

The shock of her suddenly doing this caught everyone off-guard. And before they could jump aside, they, too, were being doused with ode-d'-roadside-shoulder cologne, like Flo and I were. And then we all laughed, pointing at one another. It was our trip's baptism and journey lesson No. 1: when it rains hard enough to cause vehicle road spray, STOP AND GET OFF THE ROAD!

The spot Sophie and Frank picked did have a creek nearby, so Flo and I were able to completely wash off and then dry ourselves by Frank's camp fire. While we were bathing, tents for the kids and adults were erected. Ground cloths were placed under the wagons and tarps were draped over them to protect Flo, Jennifer and I, who would be lying underneath them for the night. Rita alternated sleeping either under one of the wagons or on her perch; it all depending on the weather or her mood.

Speaking of Rita, you may ask what happened to her during that first day's deluge. To answer that, I must propose a theory. My present thinking is that the longer you can spend time off the surface of this mixed up world, the wiser you become. And if you can't fly, get yourself up into a higher elevation. Look at the spiritual leaders who originated from the Himalayas. And look at the people, scattered around the world, who have the longest life expectancy: hand's down, they usually come from some mountainous area. My bet is that their longevity is due to their eating, drinking, sleeping and behaving more wisely. So, if someone can fly, they must have an even higher IQ.

That leads me back to Rita. She had an idea, one that hadn't occurred to us mere landforms, and spoke privately to Frank about it. The two of them arranged to have a fully covered roost built, opening only to the road behind Frank, and attached to the back of his tricycle canopy. When the canopy is pulled forward and secured in place for Frank, Rita's covered shelter is likewise fully deployed. She was dry and looking dashing, as always, even after Flo doused everyone else. She had anticipated his actions. Seeing this and learning about her shelter, I made it a personal goal to try to speak with some of those winged creatures who soar so high above us all. They must all be Olympic class geniuses, if

Rita is any indication.

It took us an hour to set up and also to break down our camp site for that first night. But as the trip progressed, we got quicker at doing both. For me, my first night's sleep under my wagon was perfect.

NINE: NEW JERSEY - PART 3

.   The next leg of our journey, through The Pinelands National Reserve, was where we experienced a dramatic change of fortune. I've tried to learn to take things in stride, but what happened to us the second day of our trip is still confounding to me. And I suspect it will be to you as well.

Rita, as it became her custom, left our company soon after we ate breakfast and flew off. She would do a reconnaissance patrol of the road and countryside ahead of us for the day. In doing this, she could report any road hazards, steep hill climbs or traffic problems that we might encounter. It became an immense help for our safety and comfort. On this particular day, however, there was a very different outcome.

As Rita tells it, she had been flying for a few miles into the heart of the Pineland Reserve, but rather than be directly over our roadway, she had veered off to the north about two miles. As she said later, she was just curious if the monotony of the oak and scrub pine trees went on and on forever. She also noted some time after this that she understood why this region used to be called the Pine Barrens. It was desolate country, at least in her estimation.

Frankly, I found it quite nice. After our journey was done, I found myself quite partial to the conifer tree species. Give me pines, firs, cedars, spruce, hemlock, redwoods and yew every time. Fall is the only time I particularly fancy the deciduous variety. But I digress.

What Rita saw during this over-flight changed everything for us. As she soared a good 1000 feet overhead, she happened to look straight down, and in a clearing, not much larger than two or three of our city lots, sat a small cottage. It appeared to have a two-foot thick, native grass or straw-covered roof, with a high, rock chimney, poking out from the middle of the roof. It definitely looked out of place, particularly when there were no other structures within that part of the Reserve. And, there was no road leading up to it. It stood alone in this clearing.

And in the clearing, in bright orange and magenta colors, were large three foot letters, spelling out, "RITA! DROP IN TO SEE ME. SIGNED, W. J. WIZARD".

Within minutes of swooping down to check this out, wondering all the while as she flew down, whether she was dreaming or simply having high-altitude sickness hallucinations, she confirmed the message was real. Stunned and bewildered, she immediately flew back to us, as we pedaled and walked our way westward.

"EVERYBODY!!! STOP!! I HAVE TO

TELL YOU SOMETHING! STOP IMMEDIATELY!" she cried out as she swooped down and landed in the middle of the roadway, beside Wally's and my wagon. "There is someone ahead, who wants to meet you. He lives in the woods, just off this road, a little way from here. WE HAVE TO GO SEE HIM! IT'S REALLY IMPORTANT AND AMAZING AND SCARY AND IMPOSSIBLE AND EVERYTHING!..."

Ok, so imagine yourself in this circumstance. Here was someone I had come to trust as highly intelligent and level-headed. Now I learn she is anything but that. Instead, I was convinced we had a bipolar, greater sulphur-crested cockatoo, who desperately needed to be on medication and who, sadly, would be creating imaginary people, places and things for the next 2,974 miles.

Politely, I remarked, "You've got to be kidding, Rita. There is no one living in this wasteland for two thousand square miles. It's a nature reserve, for Pete's sake!"

"NO! You're wrong, Greg," she snapped back. "You wait and see. Just up ahead there will be a turnoff to his home."

At that point everyone, including Jennifer, looked at each other and shrugged their shoulders. For the last six miles there had been no side roads or paths leading off this roadway. This area was devoid of permanent habitation, by anyone, and we all knew it. So, we politely smiled and resumed walking and pedaling on down the road, ignoring her pleading with us.

Rita, sensing our condescending attitudes,

simply stood in the middle of the road, cocked her head slightly upwards, and called out, "You wait, pilgrims. You've got one show-stopping surprise ahead of you in about two minutes."

Undeterred, we marched on, but with maybe a little more awareness of the unbroken, roadside vegetation. It was obvious to everyone that there were no side roads behind or ahead of us, and we could see far into the distance.

BUT, and this was a category 9.8, on the Richter scale, BUT, we were soon proved wrong. As we ambled along, each of us looking northward into the dense, scrub pine tree line, suddenly there was a parting of the trees and a paved roadway appeared, heading in a northerly direction. Shock would be a mild description of our reactions.

We all just stopped and stared at the opening, not 100 feet ahead of us. Finally, Sophie said that she would pedal up to the entrance of the road that suddenly appeared and read the sign that was posted just before its entrance. We all agreed that would be a great idea, particularly because it wasn't us doing it. Why be brave, I always say, when someone else is better at it. And Sophie, without a doubt was then, and always would be thereafter, my hero.

Moving cautiously ahead, she pedaled close enough to the sign to read what it said. Calling out loud enough so all of us could hear, she read:

"WALTER J. WIZARD
(Personal Affairs Advisor and Manager)
Our guarantee: No requests are too complex and no questions are too basic that we cannot help

you in your time of need or confusion. We help
with any of the following, but they are just examples:

-income tax garnishments.
-weight loss issues.
-home foreclosures.
-vacation suggestions.
-speaking to your boss about a pay
   raise.
-marriage counseling.
-helping settle the multiple universes
   versus a single universe
   debate.
-helping you understand what your
   house pet is saying.
-personal travel through the
   space-time continuum.
-how to prepare perfect short-bread
   cookies.
-what causes belly button lint and
   what you should do with it.

Just follow this road straight ahead until you see my
office.   The door is always open for fellow travelers,
like yourselves."

   After Sophie read this, I was the first one to
speak.   "This guy thinks he is a wizard of some
kind.   Can you beat that?"
   "But, Mr. Greg," Wally interrupted, "what
about that road just suddenly appearing. It wasn't
there before. I know, I was practicing looking for
roadside things to use in our game."
   Turning around to face us, Sophie anxiously
cried out, "Frank, I don't know what to do! I'm

afraid! This is so wrong. It just can't be happening to us! What are we going to do?"

At that point, Frank left his usual position at the rear of the line and pedaled up to the front. As he pedaled past me, I saw a look of fear on his face, and it scared me. Things, without any logical explanation, were happening and the sense of panic was beginning to take its toll on all of us, except Rita. Even Jennifer was losing her detached demeanor and acting nervous. How do I know this? For example, she wasn't sighing, rolling her eyes or shaking her head in disgust, and she appeared to be whipping her tail side-to-side more vigorously than usual. Flo hadn't uttered a word since Rita returned from her flight of discovery. That also worried me. I really needed to know what Flo was thinking. If both Sophie and Flo were upset and confused, then it was time for me to begin some type of displacement behavior, like herding, which would not be easy considering I would be dragging a wagon and Wally around, as I did. I needed to get some control of the situation.

By this time Rita had swooped in over us, from her middle of-the-road-sulk earlier. With some penance in my voice, I called out to her, "Rita, can you give us a better understanding of what's happening? What did you see that is up this road? Are we in some kind of danger?"

"Certainly not," she snapped back at me. "If you clowns had just given me another minute, I could have explained enough to prevent this immanent stampede. And it wasn't so much what I saw as what I felt and heard."

"Oh, that's encouraging," I interjected. "You had a good feeling about all this; now I feel a lot more reassured. I'm having a feeling, too, about now. It's divided into two parts: to begin barking and howling, and to herd your sorry behind out of here."

"There you go, again, acting just like a dog," she retorted. "The feelings came after I saw the large sign asking me to come down to investigate the cottage and after I heard a voice from inside it call out to me saying, 'tell Greg, Flo, Jennifer, Sophie, Frank, Wally and Bernie to join you and come have a cup of tea with me. I have something important and urgent to discuss with them.' Now, a voice, any voice from out of nowhere, that knows all our names, offers to help us in some way, and provides a paved road to his home, when there wasn't one before, is someone I'd really like to meet. And it seems you are all invited as well."

"It sure would have helped if you had seen this voice's face," Flo added, with some hesitancy in her voice. "This could be a trap of some kind. Although I have to admit, it is somewhat far-fetched, and possibly even a little extravagant, to provide a roadway that usually isn't there, for us to travel on. Maybe, if we go ahead and see who is behind this voice, we ought to unhook ourselves and leave all our gear aside. I want to be able to have the best shot at protecting myself and you folks. Besides, it'd sure be nice if we had a sign of goodwill about now."

And, amazingly, as she said this, a very large and sturdy-looking, kind-of horse, which I later learned was actually a mule, suddenly was standing on the just-appeared-out-of-nowhere roadway. It was a strange way of confirming our invitation, but it was effective, if not shocking to all of us standing on that highway. And then this strange looking horse spoke to us.

"Please come. Meet Mr. Wizard. This is not a trick. He would have come here himself, but he's preparing a surprise for you, and he asked me to appear before you to a lead you to our cottage."

"Are we the surprise?" I blurted out.

"No," the big fellow said. "It's something that will help you on your journey."

"He knows about that as well?" Frank exclaimed.

"Yes. There isn't much Mr. Wizard isn't aware of in this neighborhood. He's lived here a long time, it seems, and he knows about everything that goes on here and about," the mule answered.

At that moment Sophie turned to us and asked, "Do we want to vote on this, to see if we go down this new road or if we simply stay with the one we're on?"

"I say we vote on it," I replied quickly.

"Me, too," added Flo

"Ok, Frank," chimed in. "So let's hear from all of us who say let's take a chance that this invitation is legitimate and go see Mr. Wizard. All in favor say 'aye'."

And to my surprise, there was a chorus of "ayes", even from me.

Frank then asked, "Are there any 'nays'?"

There were none.

"That's exactly what Mr. Wizard told me would happen," the mule said. His name, I later learned, was Podesta, or Po as I came to call him. "He told me you were an intrepid bunch, and that he was anxious to meet you."

With that decided, we lined up again, in our usual formation, with Sophie in the lead, and Po just slightly behind and beside her. As Frank passed the intersection of the highway onto our newly discovered roadway, Rita, sitting on her perch looking backward, noticed that the foliage wove back into place, covering the entrance to the road we were now on, and this continued to be the case as we walked further into the forest. It was closing in behind us, as we walked in.

The only thing special about the road into Mr. Wizard's cottage was that there were flowers lining it on both sides. Behind them were the usual pine woods, mixed with some small oak trees and brambles. It was comforting to have the extra touch of color, but you knew it wasn't natural and that something mighty weird was afoot. I began to imagine that between then and sunset, I might end up being transformed into a frog or a toad, but one that still liked to herd two and four-legged animals. Somehow, I didn't think sheep-frogs would give you much clout with a bunch of strong-willed sheep. Maybe it would, if I could still bark, I thought…

It took us about thirty minutes to travel the mile or so from the highway to the wizard's residence. Admittedly, we were doddering somewhat. Our hesitation and awareness of the absolute strangeness of it all gave us pause and a sense of unease. We reluctantly entered the clearing that Rita had seen earlier and saw the cottage.

And sure enough, it looked like one of those dwellings you see in old-time paintings of thatched-roof cottages in the countryside of seventeenth century England. The same flowers that accompanied us on our walk into this place, bordered the front of the white-washed, native-stone cottage. They were tall, multi-colored lupines. Surrounding the house was a three-foot high, white picket fence. Inside the fence was a vegetable garden on one side of a curved black, slate pathway and on the other was an herb garden. Over the entrance into the fenced area was a grape arbor, with a sign hanging from its curved top. It simply announced:

"Walter J. Wizard, Esq."

Walking up to the gate, we then stopped and cautiously dismounted our respective conveyances and unhooked our various harnesses. All the while, unbeknownst to us, Po had quietly departed our company and disappeared behind the cottage. For all I knew, he had just fallen off the face of the earth. For by now, I expected just about anything to happen next, and it did.

As we stood in a semicircle around the gate entrance, the front door opened and out walked an old man. I say old, because I don't have much to base a judgment of age on. After all, with me being five years old and just about middle age, in human terms, he being ten years old would make him a senior citizen in my cosmos. I guess it was the rather long, white beard that prompted my assumption of his agedness. He had bushy, eyebrows that seemed to reach halfway up his forehead and cover over the tops of his eyes. He had to peer through the unruly strands to see you. His face was lined with deep creases, and yet his eyes, the parts I could see, were bright blue and moved quickly from each one of us to the next.

He was dressed in a pair of those striped bib overalls, with one strap unhinged, leaving the top of the left bib to hang over his protruding stomach. He had a hat on that looked like what I've heard described as a 'Big Apple' hat. It was a patchwork of multiple fabrics, made into a floppy cap, with a narrow brim that swooped over the entire front of the cap. Under the one secured strap of the overalls, he was wearing a long-sleeved, well worn, faded, pinkish-red, hooded jersey. Honestly, he looked all the world like he'd just finished chopping a cord of wood or just plowed a field of last year's corn stubble.

But most notable of all, he wore a magnificent and glowing smile that seemed to say all that was necessary to reassure us. And then he spoke.

"Welcome to our home. It is such an honor to have each of you come here. We were so afraid you might be skeptical about what Rita told you or too afraid of the manner you were escorted here and not come. My name is Walter J. Wizard, but you are to call me Walt. Please. Come forward, and I'll show you into our home. I've prepared some tea and a few mid-morning snacks for you. Come."

Without saying anything to each other, we filed down the garden path single file, just as we traveled in our convoy, with Sophie leading the way. As he turned to usher us through doorway, he held out his one hand in a welcoming gesture, as he held the front door open with the other. I noticed as I passed through that his hand was very large and calloused and that he was a big man. I stared up into his face as I began to pass through. There was nothing wizened about this wizard, I thought. If he was frail sometime before today, since that time he'd been eating his three squares every day or had been on steroids for a while. Because when it came to his turn to reenter his cottage, he filled the doorway with his huge frame.

He shook everyone's hand, paw or wing tip. And with each individual, he personally introduced himself. When it came my turn, before I even had a chance to give him my name, he said, "Indeed, at last, I get to meet Greg, the mastermind behind this all-important journey. I cannot thank you enough for what you've accomplished in bringing this band together and to our cottage. You are a persistent, merciful and most-brave lad."

There was that title, "lad", again. My, how my head swelled when I heard myself called that. Now, I was a "persistent, merciful and most-brave lad". It was just too much. I had to show my appreciation with just the shortest bark.

"Ruff," I said, thinking later that must have sounded truly intelligent to a wizard, but then I recovered enough to add, "thank you, sir, but it seems a little too early to tell if we are going to actually accomplish our goals."

And then, most surprising of all, he countered with, "Oh, yes you will. That is the primary reason you have been invited here. Your journey has immense importance, as you will find out later."

Once everyone had been admitted into the cottage, our third major surprise for the day occurred. The first two were discovering Rita's announcement of the cottage's existence was true and the second was the sudden appearance of the road leading here. Although, in all fairness, I should probably qualify that statement. Me being such a sheltered and provincial dog, there were many more than two surprises for me. For the most part, just about everything we had seen on this trip so far, including all of yesterday and today, came as a surprise to me.

Our next surprise was the room we entered into, upon stepping into Walt's cottage. It was huge, much bigger than the small exterior of the cottage should conceivably have. Whether it was a trick, such as an optical illusion, or something that I ate earlier this morning to cause me to hallucinate, it was clear right then, the appearance and disappearance of the roadway into here was just the beginning of Walt's surprises.

The room easily accommodated one very large table, with four wooden arm chairs on each side for all of us, and a larger arm chair at the far end, which I presumed was for Walt himself. The walls were paneled in oak, as best I could tell. At one end of the room was an immense fireplace, which still had an active, popping blaze. I couldn't tell how much room was on the other side of the fireplace, but it seemed like it was an equally large area as well. On the surrounding walls and floor were various richly colored rugs, shields, swords, banners, flags, cross-bows, helmets, and armored battle suits worn by knights hundreds of years ago. Hanging from the vaulted ceiling, held up, it seemed, by timbers bigger in diameter than Flo was, were more ribbons and banners, along with large circular, black wrought-iron chandeliers, suspended by large chains. There were at least twenty candles on each chandelier. The room didn't smell musty or moldy, like I'd expect, given its old appearance. It was warm, filled with rich colors, against the background of the soft tan color of the oak wall and ceiling planking. Actually, if my sense of smell was still as good as it used to be, the fragrance I noticed was that of freshly baked bread or scones.

"Please, take a seat or a perch, and while you have something to eat and drink," our host said invitingly, "I need to talk to you. Simply reach for whatever you want or need; you'll find it somewhere on the table, I assure you."

And he was right. There was enough food for twice the number of us, along with condiments galore. There were all the varieties of jams and jellies, you could imagine, as well as honey for our bread and scones. There were even savory dishes as well, if we didn't fancy sweets this time of day. There was a mixture of fresh fruits, which particularly caught Rita's eye. And there were jugs of hot tea and water for us to have endless refills into our pewter tankards. And, yes, there was beer as well, if that was what you wanted instead. Frank and Flo were the only ones to drink that.

"And as you make yourselves comfortable, let me begin," Walt smiled and continued. "You have been asked to come here for a very important reason. Podesta and I need to accompany you on your journey. Now bear with me, because I realize this is a shock to you. But let me continue before you object," which he said looking directly at me.

Quite frankly, given the sumptuous 'snack' we were being served, and the richly furnished surroundings, who could? But there was a sliver of doubt as to the wisdom on their coming with us that eddied around my extremely small brain. Why would someone with all this want to leave it and walk across the continent. This kind of living would hypnotize me. And yet, maybe that was the seed of my mounting doubts. There was too much abundance here; something was amiss. I needed to hear more from this guy or wizard or whoever he was. I found myself quickly losing my appetite.

"It's true, as my full name implies, I am a wizard. And from where I came from your surname was your occupation or title. As a further example of this Podesta, the talking mule, who guided you into our quarters, is actually a 'protector'. That being his occupation, his name is Podesta C. Protector."

This admission was met with giggles from Wally and Bernie. And Wally spoke up, asking,

"Can Po really protect us? Flo said he was a mule, and he seems pretty big and kind of slow moving to me."

"Thank you for asking me that, Wally, because that question brings me to my next comment and a small demonstration. Wizards, like me, have two ways of communicating. One way is as I am doing now, through normal speaking. The other is more indirect, but much more visual. And I do so," as he reached down and picked something up off the flood beside his chair, "with my wand.

"When it has its scabbard on, it has no effect. But, in my hands, with the sheath removed, there are distinct and immediate changes, which occur with certain, specific movements of my hand. Let me demonstrate for you, and to do so I have asked that Podesta come in through the back door and stand beside me."

And sure enough, in ambled this big mule and stopped beside Walt. What happened next is another example of how first experiences are indelibly etched in your memory. Walt quickly removed the cover around this brightly painted stick, or as I was later to discover, a metal object of unknown composition which when exposed to daylight shown with a brilliance that hurt your eyes to look directly at it. He then, from what I later learned was the neutral position of the wand, pointing directly forward, moved it quickly downward and then back to the neutral position. But he did that while pointing it at Po. There then followed a bright light, some misty haze or smoke, I couldn't tell which, and when it cleared, there stood a fellow, as big, if not bigger than Walt, dressed like a Roman centurion.

I never knew what experiencing an epiphany meant until that moment. But, without any further discussion, I knew this experience, and possibly my entire life henceforth, was NEVER EVER going to be the same again. Talking birds, dogs and cats is one thing, and is certainly noteworthy. But transformations of beings or species into other beings or species, that's got to be at the top of the cosmic list of things you do when you want to alter one's entire view of reality. My mouth fell open and my tongue hung out at the sight of this happening. And when I turned to look at Flo, she, too, was wide-eyed, breathing rapidly and squirming in her chair like she was going to bolt out of there before she was turned into a camel or something. But she was nice enough to say to me quietly, "Greg, your tongue is hanging out..."

"Everyone," Walt continued, "let me reintroduce you to Podesta, whom you obviously met before, but in a different embodiment. And you can now see, Wally, Podesta can protect us. He is a warrior, when he's not a mule. By waving this wand downward I can transform objects, animals, and people back to their prior or original status. And if I point the wand at Podesta and wave it once upward, he will be transformed back into a mule, which is what I will do for my mode of travel with you. The wand, in my hands, gives me the ability to transform animals and people back and forth to a different species. But for any one person or animal it can only be to that same one, particular species that

I first transformed them into. That's a choice I can only make once."

"Could you transform me into a wealthy and powerful government official, so I could begin making some needed changes and maybe have a truck of my own I could drive around in all day," I blurted out.

"No, I cannot," Walt replied. I cannot transform you into a particular person. And any transforming that I do is never done lightly or for amusement. It has to have a serious purpose."

"Well, it was worth a try," I sighed.

"Beyond that, I need to tell you what additional abilities I have with this wand," he resumed, basically ignoring my outburst. "If I point the wand at an object, and only an object; it will not happen for animals or people, and make a clockwise circle, like this."

And he did so, pointing the wand at a bowl of gruel, or something of that sort, sitting in front of him, and made a circular motion with that wand. Then the same puff of mist and smoke occurred, and when it cleared, the bowl was gone.

"Now if I just reverse the motion with the wand, pointing to the same area where the bowl was before, it will reappear."

And doing so, it did reappear.

"But you can't do that with us?" Sophie asked, with her voice obviously showing the strain of all this morning's revelations.

"No, Sophie," Walt answered. "I can only transform humans and animals and only into one particular change.

"Does it hurt when you do that to them?" she further probed.

"No, it doesn't," Po answered. "It is a harmless transformation. I am usually a little dizzy after each transformation, but that is all."

"How do you decide what form you are going to transform something or someone in to?" she continued the questioning.

"It's always a serious matter, requiring the most thoughtful and reverential consideration. I don't pretend to be God. In fact my becoming a wizard was based on years of examination and testing to insure that I would never delude myself or abuse this power and the trust it implies in having it. To become a wizard requires eons of your time for screening, testing and training. Only God is God, in whatever cosmic Verse you are in. But for the time being, the discussion of Verses is another revelation for much later on in your journey.

"Moving on, because I am well aware that your need to be further away from Atlantic City is very urgent, let me conclude this demonstration by showing you what happens when I point the wand at a empty space and move it horizontally to the left."

As he did so, where there was nothing but bare, dark, mahogany tabletop, there was now sitting a vase of flowers. "Again, this is limited to objects, not animals or people. It is somewhat like what you describe as magic. It's the most basic of the wand's capabilities. On the other hand, the most sophisticated capability is when I wave it, horizontally, to the right. But I will reserve doing that, or explaining its ramifications, until later as well. It does not serve our immediate purpose for me to demonstrate or discuss it now.

"Finally, I need to say that it is imperative that you, along with Podesta and me, resume your trip immediately. You are in grave danger the longer you stay in this region. I understand the reasons you chose your mode of travel. I have no intention of trying to convince you to make other, speedier arrangements. Your mission is a bold and daring one, and doing it as you have decided is courageous and, for the most part, appropriate. But Podesta and I will accompany you to insure you are safe along the way. But don't misunderstand me, I am still a wizard, and this is not an act of simple charity. Whatever I do, it is done for a greater good, far beyond what you can imagine at this time. You, too, are involved in that, even though you have no idea how or why at this time. That, as well, will be made clear to you as time goes on. For now, please finish your food and tea, while Podesta and I gather together the last of our provisions. We will meet you outside the front gate in fifteen minutes."

And with that, the two figures in front of us turned and walked behind the large fireplace, disappearing from view. And it was clear that we needed the next fifteen minutes to discuss what we'd just heard and to make sure the purpose for our journey had not been hijacked. Maybe we didn't have cosmic powers, or whatever Walt called them, or even much beyond growling and barking at any approaching threat or danger, but we did have our own reasons for this mission. We restated these to each other, with Frank and Sophie leading the discussion. And certainly we acknowledged the stunning, unbelievable impact of what we had just witnessed on our lives now and probably forever. And yet, with dogged (and the use of that word, in this context, makes me proud...) determination, we proclaimed to each other our fidelity and assurance that we would not let these beings, whatever they were and wherever they were from, alter our plans. Even Jennifer, to my amazement, arched her back, with hairs bristling down her spine, and vowed with everything in her power, to keep our plans intact. We left that repast with a renewed sense of purpose, and secretly, for each of us, with an unspoken sense of dread. Nothing like this would be happening to us unless there was something almost unspeakably possible or about to happen. But, united as we had become, we filed out of the cottage and up the front path to meet Walt and Po at the gate.

Walt was still wearing the same clothes he had on inside. But I did notice he was wearing mid-calf, high rubber boots, with his overall pant legs tucked into the top of them. He carried a large walking stick, which looked to have been carved out of some twisted, tree limb. He had on a small backpack, and I surmised inside it was probably his magical wand. Po, on the other hand, had now been transformed back into his mule persona. Boy, did I envy him... And he had a pack saddle on, which had a canvas cover over whatever supplies they were bringing. As I walked past Po, he appeared to smile, kind of like I do with my tongue hanging out, which created a kind of kinship between us that continued to mature over time. He then whispered under his breath to me, "let's go change some hearts and minds."

To which, I also smiled and replied back, "What other choice do we have: us beasts of burden."

And it was at that moment that Walt uttered the last words he spoke for the next two to three days, as I recall, or at least until we were safely on our way out of New Jersey.

"Thank you all for your patience and kindness in letting us accompany you. I know it is an imposition and a source of worry. We will not be a hindrance; that I promise. And, for your information, I will be walking, not riding. I've needed to stretch my legs for longer than I can remember, and now is my chance to do so. We will follow at the rear of your procession. Lead on Sophie." And that was it.

The roadway back to the highway opened up again before us and closed silently behind as we passed.

TEN: NEW JERSEY - PART 4

I've certainly never written a daily diary nor have I ever read one. Remember, I can't read. So maybe that influenced my decision not to recall this journey like one. It'd just be too tedious for everyone involved, specifically you, the potential reader, and me, the shaggy scribe. And it'd probably be pretty boring. So let me simply outline the sequence of days that followed and recount some noteworthy events that occurred along the way, at least ones which I, and the others, vividly remember. That way, you will get the gist of what kind of pace we maintained after leaving Walt and Po's cottage until we had our first, true rest stop, almost two weeks later at the Codorus State Park, near Hanover, Pennsylvania.

The next three nights we spent outside Newtonville, Franklinville and Swedesboro respectively. We opted not to camp in these communities, but pulled off the main road and camped in secluded areas. We wanted to avoid unwanted attention, which given our growing menagerie of people, animals, bird and wizard was getting harder to do. Sometimes I'd let my mind wander back to those earlier days of dreaming about this venture, about how simple and uncluttered it would be to travel, unfettered on the open road. Look at us now. I swear I thought the next addition we'd probably run into were a couple of hysterical giraffes, who needed our care and would join this circus act. There's that side of me that wants and needs to be nice, but mixed in is the more rangy side that wants to cut the traces and head cross-country, solo.

Anyway, it was a little before we passed under the New Jersey Turnpike that we began to run into your typical, metropolitan congestion and all the frantic traffic that brings. And with that, on our 6th day out from Atlantic City, near the Repaupo Exit, southeast of Interstate 295, we first experienced Walt's jaw-dropping, head-spinning, creative handiwork. Like was recorded earlier, our resident wizard had not spoken a word since we left his cottage. I was beginning to think he had mixed a bad batch or overdosed on some concoction he had probably brewed. More likely, I was beginning to think that he was one, moody wizard; not that I was any judge of such things. But that impression changed mid-morning on this day, when he called out from the rear of our caravan, "We need to pull off the road and head into that grove of trees to our right. Behind them should be a large clearing. No one, who is in the immediate vicinity, should be able to see us there."

Once we got ourselves parked and somewhat rested from the rush to get off the busy highway and into the grove of trees, Walt again spoke to us.

"Folks," he said, reaching back into his backpack and bringing out the wand, "I need to explain to you why I am doing what you'll witness next. We are about to cross the Delaware River over a toll bridge, and then enter into the busy industrial areas of south Philadelphia. It's no place for our band to be on foot, particularly if we are trying to maintain some anonymity. I have a plan, and I will ask that you bear with me while I initiate it. I apologize that it isn't something that is being put up for discussion and a vote. We haven't time to dally. We need to get out of New Jersey right away and to do so in the most cloistered way possible."

After saying that, he held the wand out in front of himself, walked over to where the clearing was spread out and there was easy access to the side road we just entered from. He then pointed his wand down toward the ground and swept it crisply to the left and let it remain motionless there for a moment. He may even have muttered some incantation, for all I knew, because by the time he was doing this, I had to ask Wally to give me a good scratch, and I was busy enjoying that. Forgive me, but I can't be everywhere at one time or record everything that is happening, and everyone else was so spell-bound they didn't notice either. So there.

Anyway, then we saw the same smoky haze and bright light as we witnessed in the cottage after Walt's first demonstrations with his wand. And as the smoke cleared, there standing before us, all bright and shiny, was an enclosed semi-trailer truck. Walking around to the back end of the trailer, Walt then reached up and opened the set of large doors and swung them open. Next, he pulled out a ramp, which was hidden underneath the bed of the trailer. I know some of us should have helped him, but we were all so shocked by all this, we just stood there and stared in stark silence. For me, I wasn't sure what was going to come running out of that trailer when he opened the doors. I fully expected anything from a platoon of Marines to a flock of fire-belching dragons. Luckily, it was empty.

"Now then", he continued, "we need to load our tricycles, wagons, carts and each of you inside. Podesta will also ride in the trailer. Frank will drive, and I will ride up front with him, in case we run into any problems along the way."

"But I've never driven anything like this in my life," Frank exclaimed. "And for me to navigate the busy Freeway and streets of Philadelphia in this thing would be suicidal."

"Don't worry," Walt reassured him. "I will empower you with that ability, once we get into the cab of the truck.

Now, don't get me wrong. I'm not trying to become the center of attraction in this adventure, but no one, I MEAN NO ONE, would want to drive a truck this BIG, any more than I would. And to ride up front in that huge cab! It was all I could do not to stand up on my hind legs and beg Walt and say, "Please choose me for that job. You can make me a truck driver, or better still, a truck. But I didn't. Somehow, I didn't think Walt would appreciate it, but I did notice Frank glanced at me and winked. He knew. He'd had his experience with me and trucks before.

"For the rest of you," Walt, continued, "I'll need you to load the wagons, tricycles and carriers on first, and then each of you needs to find a place, along the sides of the trailer and make a bed with your bedrolls or some tarps. We'll be riding in the truck for a while, particularly if we get into some heavy traffic. There should be some extra rope in our gear to secure the equipment in the front and to rope yourselves loosely to the loop straps on the side of the trailer. I don't want anybody to get hurt during this ride. We'll have the overhead lamps on throughout the trip, so it will be light enough to read, write or just nap. We'd better get rolling as soon as we can, Frank. Just let me help each of you staying in the trailer get everything on board."

After everything and everyone was secured in the trailer, Walt then looked at me as I climbed onto the ramp to crawl into my nook. "Hold on, Greg, you're riding up front with Frank and I. From what I understand you fancy yourself a good judge of truck rides. I'll need your opinion after this one."

I looked at Frank to see if he was smiling, like he had snitched on me about my first truck ride to his house. But he just looked at me and shrugged, indicating he had no idea where Walt was getting his information.

"Like I said before," Walt added, "you've been under observation by me for some time."

"How long," I blurted somewhat indignantly.

"Oh, for about four years, I'd guess," he replied.

"Four years! Why that's back to the time

when I first started to talk!"

"Exactly," Walt said with a broad smile.

I didn't know what to say. I had been manipulated and probably it was still happening to this day. I was being controlled by a cosmic magician. I was just a hairy puppet, who liked trucks. Sadly, I replied, "That makes me pretty sad. All this time I thought I was charting my own course in life. Instead, I find out I'm more a rudderless fleabag, simply doing whatever you decide or becoming whatever your wand creates."

"No, that's not entirely true," my now senior master answered. "While I did do a little maneuvering to help you, hopefully, speak, I had no hand in its actual development and progress. And, more importantly, I did not and could not have any control or give direction to your other abilities. By that I mean your insights, compassion and drive to change what you think is not right. That is all your own doing. Mostly, I simply maintained you on my radar, and many things you did and said both shocked, humbled and pleased me immensely. There is, however, one more surprise in store for you, as there will be for others in our troop, but that is something you'll discover much later on in our journey."

"For example, what did I do that shocked and pleased you?" I interrupted.

"As an example, there is yours and Flo's rescue of Wally and Bernie; that horrible tragedy was totally unexpected, as well as your participation in their rescue. The truth is you've made me very proud. You are definitely your own dog. So get up here in the cab, between Frank and I, and enjoy the ride."

The trailer doors were securely locked, the lights were turned on and two-way communication was maintained with our helmet radios. Frank then squared himself into the driver's seat and looked at Walt, asking, "What's next? I haven't a clue what I'm supposed to do now."

"Close your eyes," Walt answered. "And now I want you to put your hands on the steering wheel." As he did, the truck engine started immediately. "Now I want you to open your eyes and press on the two floor pedals. One is for braking and the other is for accelerating. There are no gears to shift. The engine will respond to your foot movement only. And as you turn the truck on curves or on streets, it will automatically self-correct to avoid traffic or other obstacles."

Frank did what Walt instructed, and then looked at me, smiling and shifting to get a little more comfortable in his seat. "Fasten your seat belts passengers and crew," he announced to all of us. "We are on the move again. This time it is to Pennsylvania."

THE EAST

ELEVEN: PENNSYLVANIA - OUR FIRST PERFORMANCE

Our route through Pennsylvania was divided into two sections, separated by our having to travel into Maryland and West Virginia in order to keep on less traveled roads. The first section took us through Chester→ Long-Wood Gardens near Red Lion, where we began walking and pedaling again→ Hwy 926→ Russellville→ Hwy 896→ Georgetown→ Hwy 372→ Sunnyburn, where we crossed the Susquehanna River→ Hwy 74→ Airville→ Hwy 116→ Hwy 425→ New Park→ Hwy 851→ Stiltz→ Hwy 216→ Hanover→ Hwy 116→ Gettysburg→ Iron Sprs.→ Hwy 16→ crossing the Appalachian Trail to Waynesboro→ Hwy 316→ Hwy 60 into Maryland.

You have to remember, thus far, my pulling Wally has only allowed me minimal appreciation of the passing surroundings and landscape. I relied entirely on Wally to tell me what he saw. And, meaning no offense, you have to grant me this one early observation.   Southern New Jersey, for all the care and concern that it had provided me, did not have the most diverse ecosystem.   For the most part, the trees were stubby and limited in variety.   The soil was sandy, and the outcrops of rocky cliffs, snow-covered mountains, pristine rivers and lakes were very few and far between, at least in that part of New Jersey.

That being the case, once I got settled between Frank and Walt in that mammoth truck cab, but only after Walt had to hoist me up into position, it was like I was in a U.S. Forest Service Fire Lookout Tower.   I literally could see for miles ahead and to each side, and it spooked me. Probably the only sounds I made in those initial moments were ones of quiet, shallow breathing, with some occasional whimpering.

The traffic congestion and the speed everyone was traveling, likewise scared me.   Soon enough, like when you ride in a smaller craft on rough seas, I began to maintain my focus on the horizon.   At that point my anxiety lessened, and I began to notice the remarkable sights around me.

The first revelation was my seeing the lofty toll bridge ahead of us, as we were about to cross the Delaware River into Chester, Pennsylvania. I couldn't help it, seeing the awesome, steel superstructure of the bridge and the huge, congested river below, filled with ships and barges, along with the countless train engines and freight cars on each side of the river, I had to bark.   It was just once and crisp.   Then I quickly followed up that exclamation with, "My, oh my, Frank!   What wonders do I see, both natural and manmade! Please excuse my outburst."

Looking northward, as we crossed the bridge, I could see the skyline of downtown Philadelphia. It seemed to stretch on forever. It sure didn't look anything like Atlantic City! But that sight didn't hold the fascination for me that the bridge and river did. There's something about dogs and big cities that doesn't suit my personality. It seems like any dog I ever saw on T.V. or in a magazine in a big city had a leash on and was being led or pulled along. To me, that isn't living.

And it was soon after paying the bridge toll and maneuvering the truck through Chester that I began to see, what eventually was to become a major obsession for me: my love for tall and magnificent trees. Everywhere I looked there were oaks, maples, hickories, elms, chestnut and walnut trees. Later, I began to imagine that I must be part druid, given my attraction to them. I longed to stop and have a conversation with one of those stunning life forms. And unbeknownst to me, Walt sensed this about me as well. The combination of my eventual love for them, and his awareness of this, led to some heart-pounding encounters for me further on in our journey.

Because of the heavy traffic, our drive into Bridgeport was stop and go, but Frank did great. It was just like Walt said. The truck seemed to maneuver on its own, provided Frank just nudged it along with the slightest movement of the steering wheel. The ride to the community of Red Lion was smooth and everyone in the trailer settled down quickly and peacefully for the duration of that trip. Me? I was as close to dog heaven as it gets. I just wished everyone in the back could have ridden up front with me, especially Wally and Bernie.

We arrived in Red Lion around 1 p.m. that afternoon, and, as before, Walt directed Frank to drive into a secluded clearing, which was surrounded by dense trees. All of us happily got out of the truck cab and trailer and reattached ourselves to the wagons and tricycles for our next leg of the journey. As we linked up and climbed out onto the roadway, Walt again positioned himself at the rear of our column. Pointing his wand at the truck, he circled it in a clockwise manner one time and the clearing was filled with smoke or haze. Within seconds, after it cleared, the truck was gone. He noticed me turning to watch this final act, but he only nodded at me. He again had returned to his silent state. "Wizards," I thought, "they really must have a lot on their minds..."

We arrived in Willowdale around 4:30 p.m. that same day. And along the way we discussed at length, using our headphones, whether we should begin our performances that evening. Because our funds were getting low, and we didn't want to depend on the creative powers of Walt to feed and clothe us, we agreed to stage it twice in this community. His help had been invaluable, to say the least, but we still felt the need to retain our identity and independence; it was part of our original plan.

However, it wasn't like we were some fully-outfitted traveling carnival or circus. We had no banner to advertise our show, nor did we have a shelter big enough to protect an audience of any size from foul weather. But wouldn't you know, Walt knew this as well. Where we relied on inspiration and good will, he apparently relied on infinite insight and magic, which is not a shabby combination, if you have an opportunity or option to choose them. What I'm leading up to is that as we were approaching the outskirts of Willowdale, he called out to us from the rear of our troop.

"Wally and Bernie, I have some handouts here I need you to take around to the various shops we pass by. Ask the store owners to please post one, if they will, so their customers can see them. And one of us will put them on a few of the scattered signposts hereabout, as we pass through the main part of town."

The handouts, as Bernie later read to me, said:

"Come one, Come all.
Why?   To see theNew Jersey Waggoners.
When? Today, April 23rd at 7 p.m.
        Tomorrow at 7 a.m.
Where? To the Big Top at the edge of town.
What for? To see and hear singing, soaring,
        slinking and slithering, serenading,
        sashaying, and slight of hand
        If you are really lucky, there might be
        some sermonizing, Greg style.
Who's welcome?   Everyone.
What's it cost?   Admission is free for
        everyone under age 8.   Donations
        gladly accepted for all others."

Wally and Bernie eagerly jumped out of their wagons, grabbed a hand full of these announcements from Walt, completely oblivious as to how they came into being, and began running from store or business to store or business.

The town's main commercial district was only two blocks long. And as I was to see countless times during our trip, there were numerous shuttered stores and offices through these two blocks. Those vacant spaces were, as I was later to learn, where individuals or families used to make a decent living year-to-year.

Now, many of these places were shells, filled with second-hand or recycled goods. You could measure poverty's infectious rate in a community or region by the downtown stores vacancy rate and by the number of secondhand or recycling outlets and stores. Reselling goods, be they packets of cigarettes, personal care items, furniture, or countless household items, signifies that an economic disease process is active and probably contagious. It was like a shadow creeping across the nation's landscape, a national transformation and with it an emerging economic darkness of third world poverty, was stalking the land.

And it wasn't just as a result of the population's migration to bigger cities, looking for better jobs. Frank and Sophie would later talk about the desperation that the vast majority of individuals and families felt in the New York City region. There was a desperation bomb ticking within the land, and our first chance to hear its ominous tick

was in Willowdale. But what do I know? Right?
I am, after all just a ...

"We've all got champagne tastes," Frank
would often observe, "with more and more of us only
having flat-beer, and loose change in our wallets and
purses."

Our parade pedaled and walked through the
main shopping district until we came to a large series
of vacant lots. They were where the business
district ended and homes began to sprout up on the
town's western and northern borders. Across the
street from the vacant lots was the town's only
elementary school and day care center. Scattered
over the lots were bottles, cans, and garbage strewn
amongst tall weeds and thistles. Even seeing this,
we all knew instantly that this was the ideal location
for our first performance.

Again, it was Walt who directed us on how to
proceed. "Everyone, please move to the far rear of
this large clearing. We'll set up our campsite there.
And before we attract too much attention, I want all
of us to move to the center of this area, but only after
you've stored our vehicles and equipment in the back
area. When you are done, come to where I am and
form a large circle, 50 feet in diameter. I'll help you
to stand in the exact spot where I need you to be."

Dutifully, but totally bewildered as to what
was going to happen next, we did as he instructed.
Within ten minutes we were standing in a circular
pattern, marking its perimeter.

"Now, please close your eyes," Walt
requested. "There is no danger, but I want to lessen
any shock or surprise you might experience next."

But, of course, I had to peak. Curiosity may do some kind of harm to Jennifer or whoever, as I've heard say, but staying alert and aware of what was happening around me was my stock and trade. I let the consequences of that approach to life take their own course. And what I saw next was another of those "Walter moments", as I came to call them. He held his ever-trusty wand in one hand and pointed it at the middle of the circle, and then he gracefully moved it horizontally to the left. In the middle of that circle an ever-larger, dusty cloud arose. What followed was a shocker. There before us was a genuine, life-size, circus tent that was fully deployed. And facing the street, behind me, stretched between two fourteen foot high, large wooden posts, was a gently, flapping banner, eight feet off the ground with six foot high lettering, announcing, "THE NEW JERSEY WAGONERS".

Given what had been happening with Walt previous to this, at least there wasn't a collective scream from all of us in the touring company. But we were, individually, still stunned. As everyone was gradually overcoming their shock at the tent's presence, we worked our way around to its front entrance. I was already there, standing transfixed and speechless. The doorway flaps were already pegged back, revealing a lighted interior with a stage directly facing the street entrance. There was a middle aisle, separating neatly arranged rows of white, wooden, Adirondack chairs. Multi-colored bunting lined the edge of the stage and the perimeter of the tent. Colored pennants cordoned off the entranceway from the overhead banner to the tent's entrance.

"What do you say?" Walt, beaming with self-satisfaction, asked us as we stood spellbound in the tent's doorway. "Do you think this will work?"

Well, I can tell you now, it sure did. And it was far beyond anything we could have dared to imagine. Come 6:30 p.m. we had set up camp, eaten, dressed into our respective performance attire, arranged props on the stage and around the tent, placed programs on all the chairs and set two slotted, donation kettles on small tables at the entrance. Having done all that, the ten of us, Po included, took our seats at the back of the stage and waited to see if anyone would show up. And I do believe, glancing over at Walt, even he seemed a little tense and anxious about whether anyone would. But, to everyone's credit, we were all determined to put on the show, whether it was to a full house or to an empty one.

It wasn't until about 6:45 p.m. when a few people started trickling into the tent. No one, apparently, had noticed its miraculously sudden appearance on the vacant lots. At first they arrived individually or as couples. Then groups of families started coming in. Finally, there was a steady stream of townsfolk who filled the aisle and entranceway. We knew then we were going to have a packed house. Our mood, and the one inside the tent that night, was electrifying. This was our maiden performance, and we were determined, after all our practice and planning, to make it memorable.

Whereas before 7 p.m. the tent was filled with an undulating chorus of laughter, squealing, coughing, yelling out names or calling out where someone was sitting, come that moment a self-imposed quiet began to fill the area. It was at that point Frank got up and walked forward to the edge of the stage and spoke.

"Ladies, gentlemen and honored children of all ages, welcome to our show! Please get comfortable. And now let the world of make-believe come alive around you. What you will see and hear this night will amaze, astound and, we hope, inspire you. From this moment on your imaginations are now in our control. Let the rest of you settle back and enjoy the thrill of this night."

At that point he turned, and as he began to walk back to his seat next to Sophie, I came forward and climbed up onto a series of steps that allowed me to speak directly into a microphone. There was no way I could project my voice throughout this large area. On the other hand, maybe I could have barked and filled it, but not by speaking. Reaching the top step, I positioned myself facing the audience and spoke.

"And let me, on behalf of all our performers tonight, thank you for coming to see our show."

Our troop had previously, and repeatedly, discussed the initial effects that my speaking would have on any audience, and we decided to make nothing special of it. Instead, I was just to move on in my monologue, like it was something they'd been experiencing for years with their own dog or other pets. For me to have paused would have likely invited pandemonium. So I had been instructed to proceed like nothing they were witnessing was more than some magical quirk or ventriloquist's trick. There certainly were always people in the audience who looked sideways at each other, but the strategy worked. Panic didn't ensue that night or during any performance thereafter.

"You can follow in your programs," I continued without pausing, "what acts we'll be performing next. And because we don't want to keep you away from home too long tonight, particularly on such short notice, please reserve any applause until we are done with the entire program. By doing so, it will allow us and you to concentrate on each act as one ends and the next one begins.

"So let's begin the tonight's show with a couple of songs, sung by Flo. She will be accompanied by Sophie on the fiddle and Frank on the accordion. She has selected, for your enjoyment, "Stardust" and "Hallelujah". Feel free to sing along, if you like, but please hold any applause until the show has ended. Now I present to you, the one, the only...Flo."

At that point Flo came up to the microphone. She stood on a lower step than I did and held on to the microphone with her front paws. Sophie and Frank were positioned off to her left side. They briefly tuned their instruments, while Flo cleared her throat. The audience giggled nervously, thinking this was going to be some sort of comic act. Then she nodded at them and Sophie began the first few bars of "Stardust", with Flo then easing into the richest entrance to that song I've heard since hearing the classic recording of it by Nat King Cole. Flo's voice was haunting in its beauty. Following immediately after that song was an equally touching version of "Hallelujah".

Without any delay, her performance was quickly followed by Jennifer leaping up onto her trapeze, erected on the far right hand side of the stage. She began her twirls, leaps and balancing as Rita stood by on her perch, whistling a perfect version of "Sweet Georgia Brown", just like you may have heard at one of those traveling sport team's performances. And as Jennifer finished her performance, Rita then began to fly through the tent doing corkscrews, loop-the-loops, barrel rows, flying backwards and stopping to hover in mid-air like a humming bird. And all the while she was doing this, telling one line jokes as she flew. As a finale, she flew back to Jennifer who had released a quick disconnect latch on her trapeze and Rita grabbed its upper support bar. Together, they flew off, circling the tent, as Jennifer swinging back and forth, while Sophie and Frank played a version of "Fly Me to the Moon".

Immediately, after they landed, this act was followed by Walt stepping forward, and lo and behold, he was dressed like a real Wizard was supposed to look this time. He had on some pointy hat and a long bright, shiny, multi-colored robe, holding his magic wand in one hand. He did a few appearances and disappearances of a rabbit, chicken, bowl of flowers and a top hat with a small monkey in it. It was met with assorted "oohh's" and "aahh's", but nothing indicating that they had been thrilled, at least to this point. Walt turned to me and winked, then he motioned to Po, now in his mule state, to

151

come forward from the back of the stage. Using his wand, Walt then transformed Po into the centurion. That generated a collective gasp from the audience.

Quickly, Po, without saying a word, began displaying his feats of skill with his knife, broad axe, sword and crossbow. Finally, he placed an arrow in is long bow and aimed it at a small circle painted on the far tent post and let it fly. It struck the spot dead on.

Then Walt announced, "If anyone here can remove that arrow from the pole, without breaking the arrow, he or she will get a handsome prize. Who will it be? Let's let the family, to the left of the pole, have the first try at removing it."

At that point not one but two families quickly scrambled up to try their luck at removing the arrow. Each family had large men who initially tried; then their wives tried unsuccessfully to remove it, and finally their three teenage kids tried. They all failed. The last one to try was a young girl, about six years old, I'd guess. She did, despite the objection of her parents that it was silly and useless for her to try. But her older brother hoisted her up to the arrow and helped place her hands on the arrow's shaft. Then as she counted aloud to three, she pulled and to the audience's amazement, the arrow dislodged completely. As the arrow came out, she and her brother were caught off balance. They rocked backward, temporarily losing their balance. As they steadied themselves, the arrow she was clutching transformed into a flawless, white dove. It turned its head, looking at the child, then opened its wings and soared around the tent and out the door.

Where it once was, nestled in her hands, now lay five, heavy, gold coins.

"There," Walt announced, spinning on his heels, causing his robe to sweep in a wide arc around him and pointing his other hand, not holding the wand, upward in an emphatic gesture, "never underestimate the power possessed by a child."

His act was followed by Wally and Bernie performing an Irish dance to Sophie and Frank's accompaniment. As they finished their act, the remaining six of us rose to join them. The tempo of the music changed and Rita and Jennifer, Flo, Walt, Po and I began dancing an old fashion square dance. It was festive and lively; getting everyone in the audience involved clapping their hands and tapping their feet.

At the end of this act, all of us came forward to the edge of the stage, and I announced to the audience that we were now going to have a group sing-along, as our finale, just like they or their children may have had in a summer camp outing in years' past. We then sang songs in the round, like "Row, Row Your Boat", "John-Jacob-Jingle-Himer Smith", old songs like "Oh, My Darling Clementine", and finally spiritual and patriotic songs like "Amazing Grace", "God Bless America", and "My Country Tis of Thee".

TWELVE: PENNSYLVANIA - GREG'S PLAN

At the conclusion of our performance, I came forward to the microphone and announced that the troop wanted me to say a few words before our show ended. My monologue became fairly consistent with all our following performances, with the exception that as time went on, and I saw more and more of what was happening to this remarkably beautiful land and its people, my talk became longer, more specific, more urgent, and more demanding. It became a call to arms. And probably this is as good a time as any, in this recounting to you, the reader, to present the final version.

For this first performance, I simply said, "Thank you all for coming tonight. It is our honor and pleasure to be here and to entertain you. As you can see, there are magical forces at play here, allowing unheard of things to occur before your eyes. Things like my speaking to you or Flo singing to you or Walt transforming Po before your eyes. All this is our gift to you, to lift your spirits and to give you a sense of how the impossible can be made possible.

"It takes faith in yourselves, a sense of the righteousness of your cause, and a determination not to let initial failure or obstacles deter you. To change what's not right, to create what gives hope and happiness, to establish or reestablish what once was or now needs to be, you need to have faith, hope, and much charity. And it's our message tonight that you already, as of this moment, possess all of these. You will leave here tonight knowing that you can make a significant difference in what goes on around you and beyond. Remember the impossible you saw and heard here tonight and be emboldened to think, plan and act to accomplish the impossible in your lives."

After that first performance, the tent exploded in applause, whistles and shouting. Kids, particularly, came up and wanted to meet each of us. Their parents were more reluctant to come forward, but Sophie, Frank, Walt and Po took it upon themselves to circulate amongst the crowd, putting the adults at ease. Invitations flew, as townsfolk tried to get us to stay longer. Any sense of threat, hype or the possibility of this being a confidence game was soon dispelled and the audiences that night and the next morning, as ever after, were convinced of our sincerity and of our urgent call for them to take back what had been lost to everyone over these past decades.

So, as I said earlier, probably this is as good a time as any to tell you that as time went on and as we traveled across the continent; I added more and more to this plea for change. By the time our trip was concluded, the following text is what our future audiences heard. The ten of us, who made this journey, have tried to reconstruct the content of that message, as best we all could. It started with this introduction:

"To help guide you on your quest for change, we have assembled the following guidelines for your future discussions. We did this with humility and sadness, but with an urgency born out of the desperation we have witnessed while crossing this land. There is an illness stalking this country of ours. And it wouldn't take much to have it become terminal. You must act, and it must be immediately. Our suggestions for your consideration are grouped under three major headings:

"Part I: The National Level
    1. Disband Congress, the Executive Office and the Supreme Court for four years.
    2. Disband all national political parties for four years.
    3. Instruct the national departments: State, IRS, Treasury, Environment, FBI, Homeland Security, Armed Forces, CIA, Coast Guard, Transportation, Food and Drug, and Commerce to continue operations but only using the existing budget for their present year and for each of the next four. They should be instructed to reorganize themselves for efficiency and productivity, trying to become better and smarter with that funding.
    4. Instruct the Federal Corrections Department to select a site, preferably somewhere within the 50 states, to set up a penal colony. Inside

156

it will be kept all violent, unresponsive criminals, who will provide for their own housing, food and sustenance. Interned there will be those convicted of violent crimes from all federal, state, military and county prisons. All these prisons will be disbanded. The penal colony will be self-sustaining in a remote environment, ringed with security fencing and the necessary security personnel. Once interned there, it will be for the lifetime of the individual. All other prisoners, except those unwilling stop being violent, will be given the opportunity to be freed and become productive citizens. But the same fate awaits them if they cannot make the adjustment to society.

     5.   Declare to the world that the United States of America is now officially a neutral country, but with the will and the power to halt any aggression against us, against our neighbors or against a nation friendly to us. The response would be immediate and have a decisive effect. There will be no half measures, no lengthy, drawn out conflicts.

     In addition, we will remove all our armed forces from any foreign soil, bringing back the troops, materials, supplies, buildings and their contents where feasible. The only bases located any distance from the 50 states would be on U.S. possessions, e.g. Guam, Diego Garcia, U.S. Virgin Islands, and the tip of the Aleutian Islands. All ground troops would be stationed within the U.S. borders. And when returned, they will help maintain our borders' integrity and sovereignty. The Navy, Coast Guard and Air Force will still patrol the air and sea world-wide, but only as it protects our neutrality. Their budgets, likewise, would be frozen at the present level for these four years.

6. All U.S. citizens and those qualified to gain citizenship, other than individuals working fulltime in the delivery of essential human services or in the armed forces, e.g. police, fire, EMT, medical personnel, public health officers and teachers, would have to serve two years in some national service, i.e. The Conservation Corps, Environmental Corps, Agricultural Corps, Infrastructure Rebuilding Corps, Self-Sustaining Industrial Corps.

7. All wages would be adjusted to a minimal sustainable level for all individuals and families to insure that no one was below a designated poverty level for these four years. This level would not allow for frivolous expenditures on housing, personal items, recreational and expensive hobby purchases. Most importantly, no one, anywhere, would be entitled to make more than $100,000.00 a year for these four years.

8. Globalization of corporations would be immediately frozen, with a progressive reversal of those off-shore investments being eliminated during the next four years. Any future investments from the beginning of this four year period would be for rebuilding a self-sustaining country, one able to manufacture its own machinery, technological equipment, clothing, food stuffs and processing its own raw materials. Most importantly, reliance on imported oil would be reduced 70%. We would no longer import oil into this country from any hostile region. If we don't have it, we don't drive it. Public transportation will be the primary mode of

travel, until alternatively powered vehicles are being mass-produced.

9.   Investments, currency exchange, the overall value of the U.S. dollar and the value of stocks and bonds will have to seek their own level. In a sense, we will be returning to a pre World War I isolationist posture. We have to stop our national landslide from the present dysfunctional stalemate into certain self-destruction. With doing so, our country is on a collision course into ruin. In all of past history, great societies and cultures have declined within themselves, due to their own excesses. To reverse this process, a first in human history, will require the nation stop, reassess, reorganize and reclaim the principles of governance. It has never been done before, and it will require a massive commitment, faith and hope in ourselves.

Part II: The State Level

1.   Immediately, any candidate for state office would have to develop a personal policy stance on rebuilding our country at the local, state and federal levels.   There would be no political party to shield or fund his or her bid for office. Everyone is an independent during these next four years.   They will each run for office and be elected on their own merits and ideas.   Everyone 18 years or older will have to vote.   It will be the law, and penalties not to do so will be severe.   Voter apathy and being ill-informed will no longer be acceptable. It will be a crime.

Once elected to state office, the elected officials would have two years to develop plans on how they envision the federal government would be organized and function. Then, those same officials from the 50 states, a number not to exceed 5,000, would travel to Washington, D.C., and for the last two of these four years, they will hold a Constitutional Convention to reestablish a new federal government for this land. It would still require some of the same basic principles of the previous one, including the Bill of Rights, balance of powers, democratic governing, and civilian control of the armed forces. Any and all other options would be open for discussion, vote and change.

2. States that border the countries and Canada, Mexico and the perimeter of the country will be empowered to enlist the National Guard and any other federal agency or forces to secure their respective borders and ports. All individuals, not residing legally within the country, will have to leave. No employers will be allowed to hire illegal immigrants. The two year national service corps will fill any positions left vacant by this exodus of non-legal individuals. Work visas would be issued to foreign workers on an as needed basis, but only for a given timeframe, and they would be strictly enforced.

3. The state legislative bodies would provide the governing authority for the country during these four years. This is a frank admission that the federal government has failed miserably. Lobbyists, political appointments for federal court seats, executive and congressional positions have polarized and eviscerated the governing process. Political parties have become too strong, too self-absorbed, and too agenda-conscious to see and

protect the national welfare. The executive, congressional and judicial systems have become completely interdependent and dysfunctional. Rather than balancing one another, they are intertwined and self-serving. The state governments have to be the governing authority during this four year period.

Part III: The Local Level

1. All citizens have to realize change is now the mandate. We are no longer self-sufficient as a nation, and we are strikingly vulnerable. For almost everything we need or use, we are dependent on a source outside our country's boundaries. And the world is too unstable to think this is an acceptable national policy. This must change. We must start with acquiring the most basic skills and providing for our most basic needs: food, water, sanitation, transportation, personal health. Each individual is now responsible for these and cannot necessarily depend on some governmental body or agency to provide it. We must come together, develop cooperatives, attend local organizational meetings, and interact with other communities to share, develop and innovate.

2. And there are changes required immediately at each individual's and family's doorstep, and they are going to be dramatic and difficult ones. They would involve the Social Contract of our society: for seniors, health care and students.

Seniors will have to have their Social Security and Medicare benefits based on their assets and incomes. A combination of these two amounts will determine the amount, if any, that would be paid them on a sliding monthly scale.

Health care benefits would have to be managed on a state level, at least during these four years. Most likely, a national health care program would have to be developed. No one should be without health care coverage, and the present system of private insurance, state and federal assistance and Medicare has ballooned administrative costs to a staggering level. This cannot be a for-profit business. It is a vital function of a society to care for its own. As all wages and perks would be downsized, the incentive to work in a medical-related occupation would need to shift from monetary reward to dedication to community and nation. Likewise, the patient will need to be made aware that liability lawsuits for medical mistakes, if not from gross negligence, would be ended. The era of indiscriminate liability lawsuits would be over. Incarceration would be the primary penalty.

All students 18 or younger would be required to attend school. They would wear school-designated uniforms and have no electronic devices with them while in school. The schooling would be designed to instruct, inspire and integrate. All reasonable effort would be made to prepare and protect the students throughout this period. Should a student, however, decide to reject this course, he or she would become involved in an alternative, corrective program of intervention, incarceration and isolation.

Inattentiveness, attempting to drop out of school, drug use and poor performance by teachers or students would not be acceptable. Taking or distributing drugs will become a criminal offense, with repeated offenders, if not responsive to treatment intervention, being subject to incarceration and eventually to isolation with few amenities. The penalties would be harsh. And beyond that, if the offenses continue, the individual would face a lifetime imprisonment in the penal colony.

Only by instituting these severe measures, as outlined, would everyone begin to realize the danger drugs and failure to become fully involved in the educational process are to our society. These two widespread developments provide incubation for future terrorism and destruction of our society.

Our society will invest heavily in the students' futures. And the students will have to respect and appreciate that by making full use of their years of learning, they will apply that learning toward a career goal, which could involve skilled vocational, college, university and/or post-graduate training, to conclude with their being in national service for two years.

3. A new attitude and approach would be necessary for our daily lives. We can no longer be indiscriminate consumers. We now have to become conservers, innovators and a resourceful people. This will be the revolution of at least this century, if not for the age.

Environmentally, the world is becoming more hostile to our survival due to our unfettered policy and life styles of consumption. Economically, we have exported our skills, jobs and independence to foreign bodies that have no interest in our survival, other than to be a source to purchase their goods and services, so they can prosper while we decline. Governmentally, our national government has become a disgrace. It must be overhauled from the bottom up. Personally, we've become obsessed with personal agendas, goals and pleasures. Our spiritual lives have gradually eroded and become irrelevant due to a sense of personal manifest destiny. We have begun to feel we are each gods in this universe. A lack of humility and an unwillingness to see ourselves as we are, imperfect and frail, has deluded us. We are preoccupied by 'becoming' something or someone else. We have no patience or self-satisfaction with 'being' who and what we are, simple human beings, needing the love and affection of one another to survive and live a life of hope and love. Recognizing Someone or Something beyond ourselves has become marginalized. We need one another and the everlasting guidance, support and faith in God. Anything else is delusional and self-destructive."

Now, I think I know what you are thinking about now. "Who does this dog think he is? The nerve of it! Discard the major components of our federal system, establish a nation-wide penal colony, SECURE OUR BORDERS!, make everyone age 18-24 serve two years in the national service, GIVE GOVERNMENT BACK TO THE PEOPLE!!!"
"Lynch him!"
I know, I know.
It appears to be the ramblings of a mad dog.

But you should try to see it all from my perspective. And if you did, I think you'd probably agree it is a very sad situation. Maybe you should have a talk with your own cat or dog more, and you'd know what I mean.

And I am particularly sensitive to what you will think are my draconian measures for your school-age children, especially those eight years and older. Bear in mind two things at this point. One is that I did not want these remarks just to be complaints. Cats complain. Dogs try to think of options and solutions. Instead, I tried to offer choices and suggestions. The time for complaining is over. It's time to act. And two, Look around you, if you feel particularly uncomfortable with my suggestions for students. Are you comfortable with what's going on with the public school systems across America? If you are, you fall into one of two categories: you don't care about kids and this country or you have no idea what's going on.

Being a smaller four-legged creature, with an ample amount of body hair, I was able to roam pretty much at will around our old neighborhood in Atlantic City. And then on our journey, I saw over and over in neighborhoods, rich and poor, the same thing. The kids of school age, the majority of them were simply putting in their time. Mostly, I observed school was a social gathering place or somewhere to foster non-academic interests, athletics, marching band, maneuvering to be king or queen on the local social mountain. Sincere dedication to the most urgent reason they should be there was marginalized, by almost everyone connected to the enterprise of teaching and learning. Don't get me wrong. There were exceptions, but they made headlines, wrote books, had movies made about them, and often left prematurely for other pursuits, higher pay, better schools, or entered different careers altogether.

Of all the governmental, political, economic and social issues that I grappled with during the course of our journey, dealing with how to suggest changing the attitudes and approach to education for your youth was my most taxing and frustrating task. You've built magnificently expensive buildings of modern design and utility for them. But, to me, they don't give near the impression and set the tone that the multistoried, gray-stone columned, steep front stair-cased, older schools did. From the outset, the student entering those older schools felt and eventually knew that this was neither a playground nor a place to develop a social network or to hone social and physical skill sets. Of those older schools that remain, many have been left to deteriorate to such a state that they are dingy and forlorn. The atmosphere of challenge, testing and urgency to learn and prepare is lost.

If you would possibly agree that your federal government is becoming dangerously more dysfunctional by the day, then I might also suggest you consider my assessment that the schooling taking place now across this land is non-functional and often non-existent. It's advanced Day Care.

But don't get me wrong. Public schools, like public libraries, are the cornerstones of a sound democracy. Having cadres of private schools is no answer to this problem. And, more tragically, both the public schools and public libraries are being neglected at your peril.

Ok, I know what you're probably thinking. Learn how to use a computer, go online, locate whatever you could find in any library, and probably much more, then get a life. And to all of you my answer, besides a loud bark, is that nothing replaces the aura and mystery of a building full of students, actively engaged in learning and working diligently in a library with thousands of books, periodicals and audiovisual aids, surrounding and encouraging them. A library and a public school are the hot houses, the nurseries, for our children to grow and mature into healthy and productive citizens. The computer and internet are additional tools. They don't replace, nor should they ever do so, the really important tools of learning: a maturing brain, personality and soul; pens; pencils; paper; lab equipment; reflective silence and a deepening curiosity about the world and the universe.

But enough. I realize I jumped ahead of the story to divulge one of my major reasons for making this journey, but like a confession, it's best to get the most difficult and painful issues out in the open first. To back up a bit, I didn't really begin to present the full text of what you've just read until we were about to enter Colorado. It took us traveling through the East Coast and Mid-West states to solidify my thoughts and observations enough to say what I wanted and felt I needed to.

I guess, in short, what I was trying to say throughout our journey was that it's time to do something never done before in history.   This nation needs to put out a large enough sign for all passersby's to see, stating:

"CLOSED FOR REMODELING.   TO
REOPEN IN FOUR YEARS.   SORRY
FOR THE INCONVENIENCE"

And, wouldn't you know, it was about the time I had finally completed what everyone later came to call "Greg's Plan", that our troubles began to multiply.   But that's for later.   Right now, I want to return to our journey after we left Willowdale.

THIRTEEN: PENNSYLVANIA - PART 3

After our morning performance in Willowdale, we headed off immediately. Wally and Bernie were exhausted and slept off and on the rest of that day's travel. The rest of us spent time critiquing our acts, making suggestions how we could improve various aspects of it. I was impressed with how each of us was willing to give and take constructive criticism and praise. I sincerely felt, for the first time that this journey might just work, that we had a chance to complete it and in making a small difference in the lives of some people we met. What could be better?

On April 26th, our eleventh day on the road, we crossed the Susquehanna River, after giving a total of four performances in the last three days. We walked and pedaled across the bridge, so I had no chance to see anything, other than the jetsam tossed out of passing vehicles. I was glad, again, that I was wearing the boots Sophie made for us. What I walked through defied description... That night we slept in Sunnyburn, after giving our fifth performance.

And it was after leaving Sunnyburn that our travels began to take on an additional challenge…hills.   It's true we had some hill climbing during the preceding days, but now they were higher, more frequent and required that Sophie and Frank use the motors on their tricycles to climb them.   Occasionally, I had to ask Wally to get out of the wagon, while Jennifer and I worked our way up to the top of the incline.

And it was during this period that Wally, Jennifer and I started to become life-long friends and companions.   But, even more surprising, was when Po and I became real buddies.   You see, as the hills became steeper, enough so that the folks in these parts called them mountains, even hills that were not much over 2,000 feet high, that's when our progress uphill became pure drudgery.   I guess it was my naughty, dog-like testosterone acting up; but, for me, I agree with those folks who live further out West. For them, and me, if it isn't over 5,000 feet high, it's still a hill.   And if it's located on a plateau over 5,000 feet, then you need to add another 4-5,000 feet on top of that to get a mountain.   Those folks out there know a mountain when they see one.

That said, I also know one when I feel one, and it was when I had to pull that wagon up anything over 800 feet elevation.   It's simply the difference between seeing one and feeling one.   For me, these are two distinctly different definitions that qualify something as being a mountain.   I'd usually call out, as soon as my legs began to feel that grade, "Mountains ho!"   And, believe it or not, the first time I yelled that out, somewhere around Fountain

Dale, where the sign on the outskirts of town said it was located at a 750 foot elevation, or at least that is what Bernie called out to report as we approached the city limits, Po, without a word from Walt, left his position at the rear of our column. Looking all the world like a centurion, which I never got over seeing, he walked up to each of us and attached some extra strapping to our harnesses and to Sophie and Frank's tricycles and then looped it over his shoulders and 'presto' became a mule again at the head of our group. He then began to help pull us up the grade.

We still had to pull and pedal, but it was heavenly to have that extra tugging. He tried to time his stride to match our pedaling and pulling, so that we were in rhythm together. Granted that was more for Sophie and Frank, and possibly Flo's benefit. But for me, with my short, stubby legs, there was no rhythm that could match my stride. I just scampered along as best I could, taking 5-6 extra steps to their one.

Then when we got to the summit, he would return to the back of the column and reattach himself to the chain of harnesses and provide a braking action for our trip downhill. Overall, it made it all so much easier and safer, and I soon developed the greatest admiration for Po.

In between these grades, it got so Po would amble up beside Wally and me, and we'd talk about all sorts of things. But to our repeated questions about where he was originally from or anything of a personal nature, he'd just say, "You'll have to wait until later to learn about that." It didn't bother me that he wanted to shield or protect his past. Even I had things in my past that I wasn't too proud of and couldn't imagine the embarrassment of seeing it splattered all over these pages I am now composing. Maybe you've lived the perfect life and made all the right decisions and walked the middle path all the way until now, but for some of us, myself included, I've walked on the edge of the road, even wandering off it a bit at times. I have no excuses for those times. Being a dog doesn't afford one much justification for any awkward or embarrassing behavior. I just had to find my way back to the straight, and for me, the extremely narrow path, hang my head, whimper for some mercy and make a never-to-be-broken resolution to do better, be better and help others to do the same. You know what I mean?

So whatever Po didn't want to tell Wally and me was ok with us. Wally would often say to me later, "Mr. Greg, Mr. Po doesn't talk very much about himself. Why is that?"

And I'd reply, "Some people are that, Wally. No one's life, even yours or mine, is a completely open book to the world. And that's ok. Often it's the mystery surrounding the life of someone that is their prized possession. Sometimes they might share it with a special someone, sometimes they might save any expression of it until the end of their life, and sometimes they might just take it with them when they leave this life. That's each living beings absolute right: to guard, protect, divulge or to keep secret that essence of themselves."

"Do you think this trip I'm taking will be my mystery?" Wally then asked me.

"Maybe special parts of it," I replied, "but you've got to recognize there are others of us involved in it, so it's not that big a mystery at this point."

"I mean what I'm thinking," he said to that.

"In that case," I answered, "you bet. That will always be part of your mystery."

But I must get back to the trip and stop this reverie. And as I was saying, we had just left Sunnyburn and for some reason Rita, after more than a week hanging back, talking to Frank and Bernie, while she sat on her perch, started coming forward and sitting on the front of Wally's wagon. Sometimes she faced him and sometimes me. From there, she would launch herself off to investigate the road ahead or keep an eye out for a rest stop or a grocery store.

It was on one of those days I ventured to ask how she was enjoying the trip thus far. And turning my head a little further than usual to look backwards, I yelled to Jennifer as well, "What do you think, Jennifer? Has this trip been to your liking up to this point?" Both of them look at each other, as if to decide who would answer first.

"Well," Jennifer started, "I don't like getting wet."

"Not many of us do." I reacted, somewhat defensively. Why I did so, I wasn't sure. It was probably because I hadn't grown accustomed yet to Jennifer's more objective and detached opinions. I was still feeling they were more from arrogance than simply from her a genuinely honest manner. Later, I learned just don't ask her a question, if you don't want a straight forward response. And always be prepared for some comment if her environment was uncomfortable. Whereas, you and I, most likely, will put on some martyr-like airs, feel quietly resentful we were in such circumstances and begin a tedious period of passive aggressive behavior and pouting. Over time, I began to prefer Jennifer's approach: straight at you, with no gloss. I ALWAYS knew exactly where I stood with her.

"It's not the same for you," she went on. "You shed the water more. I just soak it up, and after a while I look like an over-used mop, on the march. And that blasted bird cage I walk in doesn't help either. It sheds water as it rotates, so I get twice the rainfall you do!"

"Never thought of it like that," I replied.

"Maybe I can help," Wally interjected.

"How?" Jennifer asked, somewhat breathlessly, as we had started to make another rather, steep ascent.

"Well, I could get an umbrella and maybe prop it so you got some protection."

"Umm," I said, a little concerned by that idea. "But that might add wind resistance and more work for me and Jennifer."

"No, silly," Jennifer replied. "Wally's got a great idea. You fix it so the wind blows around it, and, anyway, the umbrella doesn't have to be very big to work."

"Yeah," Wally said excitedly. "One like Bernie used to have would be great! It had lots of colors on it and wasn't very big at all."

"Great idea!!" both Jennifer and I exclaimed.

"Wally, you're the Man!" I shouted for all to hear.

"Yeah," Jennifer added, "and one who doesn't bark whenever he gets overly excited."

Wally just beamed at our comments. Little did either Jennifer or I know but he, indeed, was to become The Man. Only Walt was aware of his and Bernice's importance and impact on the future for everyone.

Our trek from Sunnyburn to the Maryland border took six more days. We arrived there on May 2. In between, we had our first full day's rest in Cordorus State Park by Lake Marburg, three miles from Hanover. And while there we made a few decisions on the pace of our journey from that point on. For one thing, we couldn't make any time or distance if we gave performances every day or night. We eventually chose to perform four times a week, which meant those would be shorter travel days. Then three days a week we traveled without performing. Further, we decided that about every two weeks we had to stop and rest 1-2 days, neither traveling nor performing on those days. At that time we could catch up on our rest and do what this most-odd collection of animals, bird, humans, wizard and transformer do. On those days it was like you let caged prisoners out of the hold of a ship, once it was docked. We each either flew off, ran away, skipped endlessly, scratched luxuriously, transformed repeatedly or disappeared completely.

The one notable event during those days, following our layover at the lake campsite, was our crossing the Appalachian Trail. It beats me what the elevation was at that point, but it was the beginning of a long series of steep hill climbs, or "Greg's Mountains", as the other's came to call them. And it foretold the efforts ahead that it would take to cross through Maryland, West Virginia and Western Pennsylvania, much less the Rockies's, the Blue's and the Cascade Mountain Ranges in the Far West. It was probably about then I had my first twinge of regret that we didn't overwhelmingly approve Frank's suggestion to use an R.V. for this trip. But I sensed all eyes and ears were focused on me as we crossed that milestone. So I put on my bravest and stoutest front and said after we finished making that climb, "Boy! Was that exhilarating! That's about as much fun as chasing cars or barking while riding in trucks!"

There wasn't much of a response from anyone to my remarks. But I think I did hear Jennifer mumble, "He must be suffering from altitude sickness."

THE EAST

FOURTEEN: MARYLAND - PART 1

The next phase of our journey took us briefly through two states and then back into Western Pennsylvania. We left Waynesboro on Hwy 16→ Hwy 60 in Maryland→ Hagerstown→ Halfway→ Hwy 11 to Williamsport and across the Potomac River into West Virginia→ Falling Waters→ Hwy 9 West (under I-81)→ Hedgesville→ Berkeley Springs→ Hwy 51 North→ Paw Paw and across the Potomac River back into Maryland→ Old Town→ Spring Gap→ Cumberland→ Alt Hwy 40→ La Vale→ Claysville→ Frostburg→ Keyers Ridge→ Hwy 40 into Western Pennsylvania.

Even though our time, initially, was short in Maryland, it was certainly not uneventful. We arrived in Hagerstown about 1:30 p.m. on May 2. Despite having a population of around 39,000 residents and at the edge of a major metropolitan area, we still hoped to find a rather secluded city park and camp out there overnight. We couldn't avoid this one larger city complex, and Walt wasn't disposed to provide us with his magical truck to maneuver through it. The less traveled roads through the rest of Pennsylvania were too zigzagged for us, unless we traveled on the Pennsylvania Turnpike. And to walk and pedal on less traveled roads, avoiding the Interstate Freeways in Maryland and West Virginia, we had to cut through this one larger city. It was a risk, we realized, both for our immediate safety and for Wally and Bernice's long-term safety.

Sophie had looked at a Hagerstown's city map before our leaving Waynesboro and was confident she could guide us through it without mishap. Her one request was for us to be on the lookout for a safe campsite. And, of course for me by now, I thought if all else failed, Walt could create one if we didn't find one. It's funny how when a little magic enters your life, you're tempted to think you deserve daily doses of it.

We advanced, traveling along designated bike lanes through Hagerstown, to the center of downtown. We were all chattering on our head phones about how pleased we were that the city fathers and mothers had thoughtfully provided them, when we experienced our first significant, but unknown to us at the time, exposure to the world at large.

As we maneuvered our way down North Potomac Street, a busy, one-way street heading south, we came to a stop light at the corner of Franklin/National Pike Street. And after waiting our turn, we began to pedal and walk across the street. By this time moving through the city, we knew that about half of our convoy could maneuver across a crosswalk with the "Walk" light in our favor, indicating it was safe to do so. That first group included Sophie, myself, Wally, Jennifer, Flo and Bernie. Rita, Frank, Po and Walt would then cross when the next green, "Walk" light indicated it was ok. While they did, the first group just waited for them to catch up. Until this intersection.

Flo had started crossing the street, pulling Bernie and her wagon, when one of those huge, all-purpose, car-truck-van combo's decided to make a right turn and hit them. The driver, it was later learned, was distracted. And you could tell that when he got out of his vehicle. There was a dark, very large, freshly spilled pop drink stain on his white, buttoned-down shirt and tie, extending down over his light tan trousers. He was still clutching a partially-wrapped hamburger in his right hand, as he jumped out. And, to our continued surprise and shock, behind his vehicle was a city police car. The cruising patrolman saw the whole event unfold.

What occurred, after we later reconstructed the events, was that Flo had pulled Bernie's wagon half way across the intersection, when the driver accelerated from a dead stop, after hearing he was now late for a 1:30 p.m. appointment with his attorney, handling his messy divorce. In doing so he struck the very back of Bernie's wagon, tipping it over and throwing Flo and Bernie about six feet from the crosswalk.

Red lights and a siren's loud whine were immediately seen and heard. Screeching of brakes, slamming of car doors, shouts of "Oh, No!", "Are you ok?", "Stay Back!", "Is she hurt?", "Look at the size of that dog!!", "Somebody, call for an ambulance", "You mean 911", "Get the police!", "They're already here!", "What is a child doing in a wagon like this?", "Now, I'm really going to be late to that meeting!", "Here, just lay quiet.", "It'll be ok.", and "Make way, I'm the police."

I'm very happy to report that, aside from some pretty large bruises and two rather deep cuts on the right side of Bernie's forehead and elbow, she was ok. Flo had a strained back from the twisting when the wagon tipped over. But she was able to continue pulling the next day after a night's rest. However, I cannot report the same good fortune for the police officer or the driver of the car.

Once it was immediately determined by Sophie that Bernie was not seriously hurt, throughout which there were major objections from the policeman and car driver that she should wait until the EMT's arrive with the ambulance, along with a dispatched fire truck, I began to think we should expect to see the local high school band and their drum and bugle corps show up any minute. And just at this point, Walt walked up to check on Bernie and Flo. Prior to that, Frank had taken it upon himself to clear his tricycle and get Po and Rita settled with us on the other side of the street. He likewise disconnected Flo and I from our harnesses. Mind you, we still had our harnesses attached and were dragging them around throughout this street scene. Frank, bless his heart, had absolutely no control over Flo and me at this point. Flo later confessed to me she, like me, had an almost uncontrollable urge to begin howling and barking. Somehow, deep inside me, I knew both Frank AND WALT, would disapprove. Anyway, it was all beginning to look like something out of the first movie version of <u>The Ten Commandments</u>. But, as I said, then Walt walked up.

Here you had this police officer, with another police car now pulling up as well, the soon-to-be divorced-and-taken-to-the-cleaners-driver, the ambulance and fire truck hurriedly parking in the middle of the intersection, everyone getting evermore excited, and up strolls Walter in his stripped overalls, with one suspender unhooked, as usual, his Big Apple cap cocked to one side and his knee-high rubber boots slapping the pavement. It was the uniform he wore from shining sea to shining sea.

"I need to see how the child is doing." Walt intoned in a most grave and authoritative voice.

"Like hell you do," the police officer snapped. "Just who do you think you are? I'm in charge of this investigation, and we're waiting to see what the ambulance crew says, before anyone touches this child. And lady," speaking now to Sophie, "you need to move away from the child immediately, or I'll place you under arrest."

Again, Walt politely said, "It's important that I see this child immediately."

"Look bud," the officer now shouted, "I don't know who you are or what your business here is about, but from the way you're dressed, I'd say you've started drinking your Jack Juice, from your quart jar, a little early today. BACK OFF! That's an order."

Now, as he said this, the officer made his third mistake for the day. The first was when he didn't follow his wife's advice and call in earlier this morning and ask for a sick day off. The second was that he should have extended his lunch break and not been in the immediate vicinity to investigate this accident. And the third, and most important, was that he had not grabbed a hold of Walt's arm, because what happened next was another of those "Walter Moments".

Understand, up until now I thought Walt's powers were pretty much left to his using that wand of his. I was wrong. It appears he simply oozes magical powers, and if you make uninvited contact with him, particularly, if it has a hostile intent, count your loose change, because you're about to take a side trip into the unknown nether world. You'll need something handy for the return fare. And Rod, our policeman, had none that afternoon.

Quicker that you could blink, where once on that street corner was only a street sign and stop-light standard, there was now an additional ornament, a fire hydrant. I still don't know if it was functional, but it was very authentic looking, and it seemed to mumble.

At the point of Rod's transformation, the errant vehicle driver looked around even more bewildered, but seemed somewhat relieved when he saw the police officer from the backup car walk up. He was hopeful he possibly wouldn't have to explain the migrating stain down his shirt and pants to this second officer. In the meantime, Walt hurried over to Bernie and quickly checked her out. Immediately, he touched her to relieve her pain and bleeding. Actually, he restored her back to normal, the way she looked and felt before the accident. I kind of wanted to go over and ask if he'd do the same with my itchy spot.

So, this episode began to wind down fairly soon after that, except for two somewhat memorable follow-up events. One was that a local citizen had a handy cell phone that took pictures and videos. She made full use of it and recorded all of this follow-up to the accident, until our troop was finally reassembled and moved on. Those pictures made the local TV station's evening news that night. In addition, one of her photos was also picked up by one of the nationally syndicated magazines and hit the newsstands in Atlantic City the next week. The hunt for Wally and Bernie shifted focus after that.

And secondly, as Flo and I were about to be reattached to our wagons, walking by us on the sidewalk, being led by an impeccably dressed woman, were two dogs, one quite large and the other much smaller. Both were dressed up in some bright yellow covers, outlined in white fleece or sheep skin, with Velcro tabs on their underbellies and around their necks. Their entire backs and sides were covered, leaving only their heads, rumps and legs uncovered. Frankly, I was surprised she hadn't put leggings on them, as well. As they walked by me, I couldn't help it, but I called out, "Nice outfit…where could I get something like that?"

And Flo added, "Run faster the next time she approaches you with those."

I never was sure they fully understood what we said, but both of them had the most embarrassed looks as they walked by us. For heaven's sake, EVERYONE OUT THERE, Give a dog a break! If you want to wear ermine and pearls, knock yourselves out. If it's that cold outside, let the dog stay by the fire. Please, don't humiliate him or her with having to wear some silly garment. Maybe it's well meant but what if the situation was reversed and you had to wear a dog hair jacket, say looking like my multi-colored, speckled coat, whenever you went outside. My bet is that you cook up another batch of popcorn and stay by the fire as well.

Anyway, Walt did go over and touch that corner fire hydrant just before we left the area. And in a minute or so a rather bewildered policeman was standing on that corner, with very little memory of that afternoon.

We did eventually find a secluded spot, Doub's Woods Park I believe it was called, at the edge of town, and we quickly ducked in. Walt was aware we had garnered too much attention that afternoon and suggested we break camp early the next day and find a place in Williamsport to rest up before our entering West Virginia and beginning our next set of performances. We all agreed. And Flo needed the rest.

FIFTEEN: WEST VIRGINIA

Our stopover in Williamsport helped us refocus on our trip, after the disturbing and potentially disastrous accident in Hagerstown. Bernie had no aftereffects, especially after Walt did whatever wizards do to accident victims, and Flo was feeling much better. Quite possibly it was Sophie, Rita and I who were the most shaken up by the episode. Sophie was, of course, because she is such a gentle soul. Rita because sitting as she was facing Wally in the wagon, saw the whole incident unfold and could do nothing. And I was, because I'm the nervous type, and I worry. Actually, when I'm not talking to Wally, as we play our Roadside Game, and I'm not thinking about the material I will be presenting at the end of the next performance, I like to worry. It seems like if I worry about something a while, then I can prevent it from happening. Now you may think it's because it was never going to happen anyway, but this is my story, and what do you know, anyway. For me worrying is right up there with clairvoyance, telekinesis, and always having a balanced checkbook. It, for me, is the cornerstone of an organized mind.

So, come 9 a.m. on May 4, we were off to cross the Potomac River. And before we all went to sleep that night, I brought up the subject of how important it was for me, and no doubt others, Flo for instance, to get a chance to see the mighty rivers we were crossing over. Everyone else could. So it was agreed that upon arriving at the middle of the bridge, we would stop, unhook Flo and I and let everyone that wanted to, have a gander at the river.

And true to the agreement, once we were midway, Sophie, bless her heart, stopped and came back to unhook me, while Frank did the same for Flo. Immediately, Flo and I headed for the bridge railing. For her it was easy enough to stand on her hind legs and look over the edge and see everything. When I got up on my back legs, all I could see was concrete. I don't want to discuss the fact that I was the runt of our litter; it's still a painful subject. But it's at times like these that I get a little peeved. But my buddies Wally and Bernie came over and hoisted me up onto the top of the railing, and I could see it all.

And what a marvelous sight it was. I wished for the ability to take pictures, paint or do something that would imprint that scene forever, so others might enjoy it as well. There were blooming flowers, fruit trees and shrubs all up and down both sides of the river. The green grass was manicured and bordered by sidewalks, with well-kept benches and picnic tables scattered everywhere. It was what I would call a dog-friendly vista. The river was brown, which confused me somewhat. The water in my drinking bowl was always clear. I thought about asking about that, but then thought it might not provide the answer that would comfort me. It was only after we got much further out west that streams and rivers were consistently clear. Probably that was one of the major reasons I decided to settle out there. You have to set your own standards for personal hygiene and what you consume. For me, at the top of that list is being able to see the bottom of the bowl that my drinking water is in. And I'd like to think it was always that way. Wouldn't you?

Once we'd had a look at the river, we resumed the trip toward Falling Waters, the first of four communities we were giving consecutive performances in over the next four nights. Falling Waters, with a population of over 7,000, was by far the biggest town we would perform in while in West Virginia. And for the occasion, Walt, to our continued amazement and wonder, provided us with a tent that was twice the size of the one we had been using. We easily had over 1,000 people attend the performance that night. And because of that larger audience, we extended our acts, giving them three hours of entertainment.

From there, we traveled twelve miles the next day to Hedgesville. And I probably should pause here a moment and describe how our Roadside Game was progressing. Wally was leaving me in the dust. As we agreed to, each morning before we began to play, at least on the days he and Bernie didn't devote all their time to schooling. And, believe me, Sophie saw to it that they spent ample time on the three R's: reading, 'riting and riding...just kidding, I want to see if you were paying attention. I meant "'rithmetic". She was a real task-master with their school work, which only made me like her the more. I tell you, she and Frank were heaven sent. But, by now, with all that's been happening, I have to start wondering, if I should say, "both heaven and Walt sent".

What I mean to say is that even though Wally and I couldn't play our game every day, when we did the first few times, and before Rita became a steady rider on his wagon, he won every day. I'd guess a total amount he would find that day, and he'd do the same. Then "bingo", by the end of the day, before Rita, he'd hit it right on the numbers. It was uncanny. That was until Rita became involved. Then he started losing. Finally, I had to say something, particularly when Rita would fly off and then return some time later, and they would have a big conference, out of my earshot.

"Rita and Wally," I called out, when we were walking on a level stretch that allowed me to speak above a raspy whisper.

"Yes, Mr. Greg," Wally answered.

"What's up?" Rita followed.

"What are you guys discussing?" I ask, trying to fend ignorance.

"Umm…," Wally started his reply.

"Why?" Rita quickly interrupted, as if she was going to micromanage this conversation.

"I'm curious," I answered. "You fly off, stay gone a while, come back, talk in hushed tones to Wally, then later you do the same, and repeat this about four or five times a day when were playing our game. Does that seem odd to you?"

"Not a bit," Rita replied, with her yellow crest rising up as she spoke. I know this because I had turned around and looked as she spoke. My reply to that comment was one of my more disarming smiles, tongue hanging out and all.

"Well," I continued, "it seems to me there might be a little hanky/panky going on here. It's ok if anyone helps Wally AFTER we have passed or about to pass an object he might have missed, but it's not right to help him before that."

"I forgot, Mr. Greg," Wally admitted. I thought Rita was just being kind.

"She probably thought she was too, Wally. At least she did when it came to benefiting you. But Miss Rita and I go back a ways, and it wouldn't surprise me that she might not like to rile me a bit. I don't think she has completely gotten over our first truck ride together."

"Ok, Mr. Detective," Rita confessed. "I did try to help Wally, somewhat, to your disadvantage, and you finally figured it out. But, as it turned out, he did much better when I kept my mouth shut. So in fact, I was inadvertently helping you. What do you say to that?"

"Thanks," I replied. And I meant it. "If it's ok with Wally, it's fine with me. I want to win as bad as anybody else. But my hunch is that he'll probably decline your help in the future."

Which he did, and he resumed trouncing me for the next 2, 800 miles. But it was fair and square, and I sure enjoyed playing with that boy. And, again, I figured out, by the time we crossed Kansas, that there was something mysterious going on with the lad, and that it probably had some connection to Walt. The future, I worried, had many surprising twists and turns awaiting all of us.

We traveled further on and performed in the very small communities of Hedgesville, Berkeley Springs and Paw Paw. And as Bernie reminded me later, while I was preparing this account for you, we not only performed in each of these villages, but we also traveled 12, 16 and 18 miles each day along curvy roadways, up and down steep hills and in bad weather. Moreover, Bernie recalled these hamlets only had populations of about 200, 600 and 500 folks. Truthfully, that was one of the reasons we made the extra effort to perform for them. They were so small, out of the way, ignored by the surge of each day's fads and headlines. They were just the people we wanted to entertain, inform, and instill hope and, most of all, to give some promise of change.

Interestingly, it was about this time, as well, that I began to notice that Bernie had an uncanny ability to remember anything and everything: from dates, miles, numbers, names, to events and what we did on any given day. She was my "go to" person for facts, details and comfort. She had a heart, nearly as big as Sophie's. Wally was my best buddy; Bernie was my best friend. I adored her, no bones about it. Whenever we stopped to rest or in the evenings when we camped, you would always find me either lying at Wally's feet or cuddled up to Bernie. Of course, I had some competition from Flo, who also had a crush on Bernie. That meant, oftentimes, Flo would be on one side of her and I would be on the other. Flo and I would defend her and Wally with our last breath, and I somehow think they knew it.

Anyway, our last stop in Paw Paw was the one that had the strongest memory for me. We camped there for two days, due to everyone being exhausted. Knowing we had to keep moving, if for no other reason than for Wally and Bernie's welfare and safety, we mustered up enough strength to leave for Maryland again, crossing the Potomac River once more, on May 24. But it was the night of the 23rd that is most vivid to me.

We had to ask a very elderly couple, who lived in a tumbled down cabin about a quarter mile from the main road we were traveling on, if we could camp on their property, which was west of Paw Paw. They agreed, and we found a spot, adjacent to a spring-fed stream, bordered by trees and on level ground. It offered us a perfect place to rest.

As was our custom on the first or second night at our extended rest stops, we would build a camp fire, invite everyone who was kind enough to let us use their property to join us for supper. Afterwards Sophie and Frank would play, while we all sang and danced. We added songs each time we had these gatherings. That night we added "Down in the Valley", "You Are My Sunshine", "My Bonnie", If Your Happy and You Know It", "Froggie Went a'Courtin'", and "Old MacDonald". Of course, I sang loudest during the songs about animals, especially when they added dogs to the verses of the "Old MacDonald" song.

Sometimes Rita would do one of her stand-up acts, drawing on her endless repertoire of jokes and funny stories, or she and Jennifer would do a joint comedy act, with Jennifer being the "straight man". It was an event we all looked forward to every two weeks. This night we had as our guests three families, including two of Maud and Edgar Smithson's neighbors. It was Maud and Edgar's land that we were camped on.

Unbeknownst to us, however, and even to Walt, was a group of fellows who followed us, but at some distance, from north of Paw Paw to our campout area. They had apparently been terrorizing small communities and isolated families in this region for some time. Their stock and trade were robberies, break-ins, muggings and most lucrative of all, demanding protection money. In discussions later, they reminded Frank and I of the "shake down" hoodlums or "protection" wise-guys the mobs used in New York City. The only difference between them and these local fellows was that the ones we were about to meet used their threats, intimidation and violence over a much wider geographical region. They were thugs, no doubt about it, and they had this region in total fear and control. Even the law enforcement authorities could not seem to find them. But these bad guys found us.

We were all in full voice, having already danced and now settling down to sing awhile before we broke up for the night. The campfire was at a steady-burn stage, with occasional snaps and pops, and the fragrance of pine pitch, mixed with hot, steaming cider in a large pot, filled the air around us.

It was pastoral.

Just at that moment of our singing the last verse of "Old MacDonald", two loud explosions, at least that's what they sounded like to me, erupted around us. Frantically, I focused my gaze and swept the area outside our campfire perimeter; I could barely make out four dark shapes standing in a semi-circle, two of them pointing large objects skyward. Those objects soon turned out to be a shotgun and a large caliber rifle. The other two individuals were each pointing pistols at us.

"Get up!" the fellow with the shotgun ordered. "And get over there in front of those tents, so we can see all of you better!"

We had left all our lanterns on around the tents to make it easier for Maud, Edgar and their neighbors to find their way here and to safely navigate to and from our campfire. That area was nicely illuminated, perfect for the intruders to ply their trade.

"Move over there, NOW!" the spokesman continued his shouting. "If any of you make a sudden move or try to escape, we will not hesitate to shoot you. This gathering is not sanctioned by us, and we don't like strangers squatting on our land. The Smithson's will pay dearly for this infraction of our rules. We're going to make an example of all of you. Line up over here, in a single row," he further ordered, pointing to where Frank had parked his tricycle.

We all stumbled forward, reacting with fear, nervousness and stunned surprise. No one spoke, whimpered, growled, hissed or squawked. Caught completely off guard, we were instantly their prisoners and defenseless. It was a frightening situation, and we sensed something terrible was about to happen to all of us.

After we were lined up in front of the tents, all four of these goons came out of the shadows and faced us, with their weapons pointed straight at us. The spokesman was the tallest. They were dressed in black, looking like some paramilitary marauders that I had seen in a late night movie, while I was still living with Howard and his family. In the dim light I couldn't see any facial features, but there wasn't much to see, as they were also wearing pullover, knit caps that hid most of their face. If their attire was meant to impress you that they meant business, it worked. I was scared, and must confess I did a little wee as I crouched there in that line up.

"First off, to pay for our expenses in having to come all this way," the leader further instructed, "I want each of you to toss in front of you any valuables you have on you. I want to see wallets, purses, watches, rings, broaches, loose change. And do it now!"

I looked at Flo and her at me. We just shrugged, and I wee'd some more.

But then, these fellows' lucrative business venture collapsed. Because coming up behind them, calling out in the most booming voice I ever heard, was Walt, shouting, "I believe that will be about enough of this nonsense!"

Spinning about in total surprise, the four nightriders brought their firearms to bear on Walt and Po. But Walt had already unsheathed his wand

and simply pointed it towards the four of them and made a quick vertical motion with it. And to everyone's continued amazement, but no doubt more so to these uninvited bozo's, they were frozen in place, except for their neck and heads. Walt, it seemed, wanted to have a little chat with them, before making his final decision as to what part of nature's food chain they were to join.

"Having a busy evening, are you boys?" Walt began. "There's nothing like rousting helpless senior citizens and assorted animals and a bird is there. And I must admit it takes a form of courage and daring that leaves me breathless. Speaking of which, are you still able to speak a little?"

In a voice, just above the quietest whisper, the head goon asked, "Who are you?"

"You can, just for next few moments of your more-aware existence, call me Walt. And this is my associate Podesta."

Po was now in his centurion mode, and armed to the teeth. The fierce look on his face said that he could and soon would squash these four dumbbells with one blow. The glaring determination I saw on his face, at that moment, scared me more than they did. After that night, I decided that for any future games, contests, feats of skill, skirmishes, battles or wars that I was involved in, Po would be the first one I'd choose to be on my side. Right after I'd chose Walt.

"Did you fellows plan on robbing and then harming these individuals lined up in front of you?" Walt continued. "Is this what you do for amusement or is this your occupation? Actually, whichever it is has become immaterial, because we're going to update your resume tonight. You've just retired."

"What are you going to do with us?" the hapless leader whimpered.

"Return you to a state in the evolutionary process that best suits your personalities and career goals," Walt answered. "Do you have any final words for these folks who you have terrorized?"

"Please, we didn't mean to harm them. We were just going to scare them a little," the talking head whined.

"Enough," Walt answered. "Your days of threats and violence have ended."

And with that, the wand went into action again and the four frozen figures disappeared. Later, I asked Walt what he did to them. He didn't answer me, which was no great surprise, because by now I realized he was entering into another one of his silent phases. But as we left that site and waved good-by to Maud and Edgar, I looked over to see a flock of Robins busily pecking at the ground where we all stood in petrified fright last night. I could only wonder why.

SIXTEEN: MARYLAND - PART 2

This phase of our journey ushered in our first exposure to rough roads, steeper climbs and even worse weather. While we did have some higher hills to climb up to this point, it was after leaving Cumberland that our trek became much more challenging. However, we still maintained our performance schedule of four a week, giving them in Old Town, Claysville, Grantsville and Keyser Ridge. It was east of Frostburg that we had our first test to see if we were serious about continuing this trip to the finish. We had entered the Allegheny Mountains, and in this particular region they receive over 100 inches of snow a year. And it is not uncommon to have snowfall in May. Moreover, it was 11 a.m. on May 13th, and we were about six miles east of Frostburg, climbing to an altitude of 2100 feet, when we started having snow flurries.

From that point on, I believe we earned every Boy and Girl Scout Merit Badge that they offer. It was a struggle of epic proportions...for everyone.

Sophie alternated using the motor on her tricycle, having Po pull us, having Frank ride tandem with her, having Flo tie up behind Po and having Walt help tug Bernie's wagon.   Whatever we tried was always barely enough to clear the next steep grade, with the next one becoming an even greater challenge.   The further we struggled, the heavier the snow fell.   It blew in swirls and eddies around us, making it almost impossible to tell which direction to go.   Only by Po's innate sense of direction, and detection of the road surface through his hoofs, did we stay on course.   Finally, as we approached the outskirts of Frostburg and the snow pack was now a good 6-8 inches on the roadway, Walt called out.

"Enough, already!"   I turned around to see him reach into his back pack and pull out his wand. Then he began to wave it wildly, like he had some kind of chill.   I was just hoping he wouldn't point that thing at me while he was making all those gyrations.   I dreaded to think what I might be turned into if it did align itself to me.   I'd probably be transformed into a hairy pumpkin or a cucumber with four legs, knowing my luck.

"Hold on!" he quickly added.   "We have to stop here.   There is no sense in going further today. Our visibility is lessening by the minute and it's becoming increasingly colder and darker.   Nightfall will come soon, and we have nowhere to camp.   Po! Turn to the right by that next large tree up ahead. We have to get off this road.   Some car or truck is going to plow into us if we don't."

I wasn't very close to the front of the line by this time, with Po, Frank and Flo each coming forward to lend their efforts to our struggle. As a matter of fact, I was just in front of Walt by then. He became silent after he shouted those last instructions to Po, but it was not like his usual silence. I sensed, with my rarely used canine perception, that he was deeply worried. Something, besides this miserable weather, was affecting his mood. And that worried me more than the blizzard we were presently experiencing.

Po did turn to the right about 100 feet beyond where he was initially instructed to do so. And as he did, we entered a paved, snow-free side road that led about 200 yards to a well-lit structure. There was a roof or halo-like covering over that small stretch of roadway, giving us shelter from the driving storm and the bitter cold. It was dry and warm once we entered it. And by the time I got inside, I looked to see how Wally was.

Unaware what was occurring around me throughout these last four miles, I didn't realize that Walt had taken measures to insure both Wally and Bernie were protected from the storm. Surrounding each of them was a clear bubble capsule, fit over the walls of their wagons. Inside these bubbles, there was a mysterious light and heat source. And yet, they could still communicate with us through their headphones. They had been safe and warm.

The outside of the shelter we were approaching on that side road, as it turned out, was very similar in appearance to Walt's New Jersey cottage. There weren't any come-hither flowers or a white picket fence surrounding it, but it was the most welcome sight I'd ever seen.

"Don't stop at the doorway," Walt cried out. "Keep moving straight on through. The door will open automatically, as you approach. We need to get inside and start getting dry and warm, before one of us catches a chill or worse."

And when my turn came to enter the dwelling, the door swung open and inside was a roaring fire in two native, rock fireplaces, located on each side of a large room. There were lofts overhead, where I presumed the two legged members of our party would probably sleep. Me? I staked out a spot right on one of the large hearths. The large table in the middle of the room was stacked with steaming food and jugs of liquid of some kind. Bowls of food and drink were on the floor for the rest of us who choose not to eat at the table. Walt left that decision, as always when preparing his accommodations, up to each of us. For him, animals had about the same status as the humans. He wasn't very approachable, but he was kind and fair. And that's not a bad epitaph for anyone, even a wizard.

We unhooked ourselves with help from each other, stacked wet clothing by the fireplaces, found a small room off the side to do restroom duties, then all came to the table, or around it, and began to eat, drink and recover somewhat from our ordeal. It was after all this had been done, probably somewhere around two hours after we first entered the cottage, that Walt again spoke to us. And in doing so, he rose and stood at the far end of the table.

"I think it best if we let Wally and Bernie head off to bed now. They are completely exhausted, I know.   Sophie, would you mind tucking them in upstairs?"

She nodded she would, and without any objection from the children, they scampered up the ladder to the loft bedroom.   Within five minutes Sophie was back at the table, drinking some steaming, hot chocolate.

"Everyone, I need to fill you in on some details about Po and I.   In addition, you need to know what is happening around you and how you came to be in this place and with us. It was not by accident, as I'm sure you've guessed by now.   I had planned on delaying this discussion with you for a few more days or weeks, but our accident eleven days ago in Hagerstown changed that.   There is a looming threat now facing all of us, and I know Greg has sensed that I have become quite concerned about something.   Haven't you?"   He asked, looking at me.

I nodded my head, wondering what else he knew about me or about what I was thinking or feeling.   But, then I reassured myself that he had much loftier things to think about than to focus on my thoughts or feelings.

Walt then followed up with, "Later, I will talk more about Greg, Flo, Rita and Jennifer's abilities, but for now, I need to start at the beginning.

"Po and I come from an entirely different 'Verse' than yours.   It was called the 'Anteverse'. It was a cosmic realm similar to your present Universe, but predated it.   Your Universe began forming about 18 billion years ago.   Our Anteverse arose before that time.   In fact, it predates even the

'Multiverses' that your cosmologists are now theorizing about. Ours was the first 'Verse'.

"Hints of its existence have crept into many of your early myths and legends. No doubt spawned by the emissaries, about whom I'll discuss in more detail later. That early connection and awareness of your world of mine came through your ancients' recording sightings of winged creatures and spirits, such as angels, winged horses, and fairies. These creatures did exist in our Verse, and they represented the goodness and beauty of our world. Physically, it was a world similar to yours, but ours was the only one of its kind throughout all the Anteverse. Our world was full of humor and goodwill. All living things were able to communicate freely with one another. It possessed life's perfect harmony.

"In addition, there was an assortment of wizards, like myself, who moved freely throughout that world. We provided comfort, assistance and protection where it was needed. We were commissioned to be that world's guardians. But we were overwhelmed and defeated. And that was because enough pure evil can triumph over the best and strongest wizard.

The decline all started, innocently enough, with the appearance of the 'horned' creatures. They were simply the emissaries' messengers, and they were the first to arrive. What they brought was simply the temptation for mischief, which in our realm at the time, seemed innocent enough. But over time, that same temptation became twisted and evolved into more sinister pursuits. With that transition, an evil force came into being, fostered by the 'emissaries'. Now those mischief pranks were replaced with suspicion, envy, greed, lust, distrust, intolerance, self-importance and a laziness of spirit and purpose. Eventually, our ability to see goodness in all around us, to speak with all living creatures and the protective powers of the wizards were lost. Our world was slowly destroyed, leaving the Anteverse devoid of life. And this was all due to the subtle forces of evil and corruption, first established by the 'horned ones'.

"So successful was that occupation and destruction that the emissaries were eventually sent to your Universe. There were only four worlds like yours scattered over the expanse of your cosmic realm. But nowhere did the beauty and majesty of creation flourish as it did on this world. Knowing the emissaries were venturing into your cosmos, it heightened the urgency for our Order of Wizards to send 'vanguards' to your four inhabited worlds to aid and protect you. I am the 'vanguard' wizard who was sent to your world. Our Order felt that because of our devastating loss that we had a responsibility to protect and defend the beauty of this world and its precious life forms. I came to New Jersey over 300 years ago. Prior to that, I lived for hundreds of years in various lands that are now called Europe. Eons ago, I learned that the other three inhabited planets, so very similar to yours, had all suffered the same fate as my home world did. Only yours is left. It, alone, holds the last promise of lasting goodness, beauty and the hope of being able to speak with all major life forms.

"That brings me as to why you are sitting here tonight, listening to me at this moment. You each have a role to play in this universal battle, and you must be made aware of it immediately for your own safety and, most importantly, for the safety of Wallace and Bernice.

"Specifically, the emissaries sent to this world are responsible for the death of Wally and Bernie's mother and family. They are desperate to find them and to begin finalizing their complete conquest of this world. Their mother was what we called, in our world, the 'vessel'. That means only she could give birth to either a 'vanguard', 'herald' or a 'protector'. Only under the most extraordinary circumstances could a vanguard create a vessel, and it is only possible to do so once. Each of us on these four planets had the power to do so, but those wizards on the three other planets never got the opportunity to do so. Events began to move too fast and their chance to do so was lost in the pell-mell chaos that preceded the final destruction of those worlds. I was able to do so, but only after I realized the rapidly deteriorating and desperate state that this world was in.

"Wallace and Bernice's mother was my vessel. I know my time is running out. Po, on the other hand, is still youthful in Anteverse terms. He will be their 'protector' during their time of maturing and fulfilling their mission in this world. I am an ancient one.

"So, Wally and Bernie have within themselves the capacity to become a 'herald' and a 'vanguard'. But I have no idea who will be which.

You already have some idea what a wizard can do. A herald, on the other hand, is unknown to you. They have the capacity, through their knowledge, insight and goodness, to guide the leaders and governments to realize and achieve a harmony and peace only known briefly on our world ages ago. The herald can assist, in countless ways, how to address needed changes and reforms. And, most urgently for this world, she or he can speak to the spirit of humanity, indeed to all creation, how to have and to keep this kingdom for all time.

"Your roles in all of this have already begun. None of it was by accident. I didn't manipulate you; that's impossible, even for me. But it wasn't by chance that you came together like you did in Atlantic City. The ability that Greg, Rita, Flo and Jennifer have to speak is the beginning of that communication between all creatures. Plus, each one of them has special talents that will become evident as this journey progresses. They, as a collective group, would be called 'harkeners' in the anteverse. They are the ones who listen and watch, then warn and help save what's good and change what isn't. Sophie and Frank, as you already know, are the 'nurturers'. Without them, the children of the 'vessel' would perish.

"You must understand that within your midst are the most precious beings on this world. Wallace and Bernice will help guide the change that is needed to make this world capable of communicating between all living creatures or beings. They will help direct this world toward everlasting peace. But most important, even beyond their roles in all this change and evolving mystery, is Who reigns above all these 'Verses', be it the Anteverse, Universe or Multiverses. It is God. Know it, believe it, honor it, worship and take strength, knowledge, grace and hope from accepting it. "Finally, even wizards pray, and my fervent prayer for you and for your world, is that peace everlasting can be yours.

"But, of course, my telling you all this seems too fantastic to accept and too frightening to imagine. And yet from what you have witnessed, by my hand up to this point, will serve as my proof that I speak the truth. I will not let harm come to any of you, and I already see you will do the same for each other and for Po and I.

"So, where do we go from here?"

Well, by now, for me, the answer was simple. We stay right here. It's warm, dry and there's lots of food and something to drink. All my friends are here. What's to discuss? And yet, there was my more adventurous side, possibly even my altruistic self, that said, "Push on, mates. There are still millions of hearts and minds to touch and to change. We can help alter what is now into what can be." As I thought further about it, I supposed that was my noble self speaking, sometimes far removed from my barking self, dancing around in the back of some pickup truck. So I made myself settle down and listen further to what Walt was saying.

"For now, we continue to travel as we are. Be prepared, however, to have three significant, but I hope after tonight's revelations less startling, changes occur as the need arises. One is that each of you will exhibit and pass on a special ability to a particular individual; another is that there will be a change sometime in our mode of travel; and the other will be that you may need to be transformed, like Po has been from time to time, for your safety. Quite likely, despite all your feelings and commitments to the contrary, there may be times when it becomes so dangerous or so difficult for us that you cannot travel as we do now."

Right away, I was in favor of voting for the alternative mode of travel to start immediately. I'd even volunteer to help drive it. That was music to my pointy, little ears. BUT, I couldn't say the same for the first and third scenario. I had sincere reservations about his use of the terms 'special ability' and 'transformed'. And having now seen the transformations Walt had been performing lately, it was not something I wanted to stand in line to experience. Becoming a fireplug or ground feed for a local flocks of birds wasn't what I bargained for when this trip was first being planned. Right now, I was thinking those were the really good ole days. Even Howard and his mob, and my bed on their front porch, seemed more inviting about now. So, without thinking, I blurted out to Walt, "Special Abilities? Transformations? You must be kidding! Does it hurt during and after these things occur? I think I want to change my job description. Can I?"

"Good questions, Greg," he answered. "And probably it's time that I do address some concerns and questions from all of you. I realize what your initial goals and plans were for this journey, and it is not my intention to hijack them. In fact, I will do all I can, given the circumstances I just described for you, to help your trip be completed as you originally planned.   But to do so will require my intervention at times, just like our being inside this retreat here tonight.   So let me first answer Greg's questions, then I want to address any others you may have.

"Your special ability and any transformations will be painless.   Ask Po.   And as to what the transformations would be, my thoughts are that they should blend into the surroundings as much as possible.   The emissaries have no ability to divine my thoughts or actions.   Their psychological power and thought control is strictly limited to other life forms, not generated or created by me.   However, their capacity to do physical harm is almost limitless, again except to Po and me.   Using their powers in that way, all of you are frighteningly vulnerable.

"Because of these circumstances, I assure you that the transformation will appear almost fanciful to you at the time.   However, I don't want to tell you in advance what these changes will be. The element of surprise will add to your spontaneous acceptance and the natural mannerisms that will follow.   It all has to appear completely natural.   For now, you'll have to trust me.   As I have said, I will protect you.   And as to the special ability, that too will be a surprise, but it will be most pleasant and exciting for you.   Trust me on that as well."

"What can we expect to accomplish during this trip, given the ominous circumstances you've described," Sophie asked, semi-rising from her chair as she asked.

"Probably, much of whatever you originally

planned," Walt answered. "You still should complete the trip to the West Coast, and we will continue to take the back country roads along the way. At least the emissaries don't know what our destination is or the routes we'll follow. Here on the East Coast the vast network of roadways is to our advantage. There are so many more side roads now, compared to later in the journey. As we progress further across the country, the roads become fewer, which will make us more vulnerable. It is at that point we may have to change our mode of travel."

Then Flo asked, "How are we to treat Wally and Bernie now that you have told us all this?"

"Do not change anything you are doing," Walt replied. "One of the most satisfying events of my entire, eons-long life, is seeing how you have come together, without any prompting or influencing by me, and adopted and loved these two children. Their respective future roles will evolve as they mature. And certainly their innate capabilities will become enhanced day by day, but none of this is something you have to be concerned about. Much of that development will be my responsibility. However, a great deal of it, as well, will be a part of their own natural development.

"Most of all: don't change how you approach them. Love them. Care for them. Treat them as you would any child. Over time, during the course of this trip, you may occasionally notice some changes, but even those should not alter your relationship with them. Remember: they are not here to harm or threaten; they are here to help you individually and collectively."

"When will they approach the peak of their powers and influence?" Frank followed up.

"I cannot say," Walt responded, to everyone's surprise. "I've never been involved in this process before. As I mentioned earlier, each Vanguard had only one opportunity to create a Vessel. And there is no instruction booklet accompanying her creation and that of her offspring. I will be filled with as much wonder as you. But if I had to make an educated guess, I'd say between ten and twelve years of age there will be some noticeable changes. But I could be wrong. This is a process that will be a surprise and adventure for all of us."

"What changes should we be looking for?" Rita snapped, now sitting on the large table immediately in front of Walt, looking up at him with her yellow crest almost perfectly erect. This probably indicated some impatience and, more likely, general disbelief with the whole matter under discussion. Rita did not suffer fools, nor apparently heralds and vessels, readily. It was evident to me that this conversation was becoming too much for her to accept quietly. She was becoming deeply troubled by all this wizard talk. She had gone from having a nice, steady gig on The Steel Pier and living in a snug den under the Boardwalk to now facing global annihilation. Boy! She was going to give me the business once Walt's briefing was finished.

"That's a more difficult question for me to answer," Walt stammered uncharacteristically. "Obviously, I recognize wizard powers, but I was too young when I arrived on this world to know how I came to possess the wand. I was aware of some powers before that, but they were nothing compared to what happened once I had the wand. In addition, it depends on whether it is Wallace or Bernice who is the wizard, and the unique personality he or she will bring to the powers of this office. My earliest memory was my ability to make myself disappear and reappear. It didn't involve anyone or anything else to make that happen."

That answer caught my attention. If I'm supposed to be calm and serene if and when I was playing the Roadside Game or having an innocent conversation with Wally and he suddenly decided to disappear before my eyes, I knew at that moment there was no way I could take that event casually. Let me take this moment to remind you, again, that I am still just a dog, no matter what other magical objects Walt waves in front of me or potions he has me ingest to make me otherwise. And if human beings are going to be disappearing before my eyes, that will cause me to reassess this entire venture.

Walt continued, interrupting my mounting anxiety, with "But I have had no experience with heralds and how their powers develop or manifest themselves. My presumption would be that you'd notice Wally or Bernie having significantly more insight and a stronger desire to become more involved in public discourse and implementing needed changes. This individual will be the orator, the organizer, the 'public wonk', as they say these days. Who knows if we will be around when any of these signs begin to appear? My guess is that if any of us are, we'll soon be sharing that experience with the others."

"Then should I still be doing my talking bit at the end of our performances?" I asked nervously.

"Most definitely. Your perspective and insight are seminal to the formation of Wallace and Bernice's eventual roles in this world's affairs. You are the most appropriate one to perform this task of us all. You also have all the right qualifications for the job. It is one of your unique contributions to this journey and to our troop. You did initiate some recruiting for our group's present composition, but the comments you make about avenues for change are your particular charge and challenge. Keep it up. As for your other contributions, you'll have to wait until later to find those out"

"What about the rest of our so-called, unique contributions to this enterprise?" Flo asked, sounding, uncharacteristically, rather miffed.

"Never you mind your feeling ignored or minimized, Flo," Walt countered. "You've got remarkable gifts that will amaze even yourself, as it will be with each of you. But neither Greg, nor any of you, will prompt me to reveal them at this time. The spontaneity of their revelation is as important as the gifts themselves. Mark my word, by the end of this journey, all of you will have shared your gifts and made your contributions. To have that happen is one of my major responsibilities as a vanguard and wizard. Please Flo, be patient."

"Getting back to the emissaries," Jennifer interjected, "how many of them are there? Did they multiply once they came to these four worlds? And how are you going to combat and eliminate their threat and influence?"

Walt sighed and looked down at the table for a minute before answering. "That is the hardest question yet to answer. And wouldn't you know that it would come from Jennifer, our no-nonsense, tell-it, say-it, ask-it, get to the point cat. No one can cut through the fog and chatter like you.

"The emissaries supposedly came in teams of ten to each of your Universe's other three inhabited worlds. And I'd have to assume the same would be the case here on your world. Bear in mind, though, that they are much older than I am. They've been here for many eons, taking on different forms, influencing and corrupting rulers, conquerors, despots and any unsuspecting individual. At first, they simply caused mischief, and then slowly, throughout the thousands of years they've existed here, they have advanced their cause with fouler deeds and manipulations.

"There is a time limit for their life span, just as there is for mine. And just as I came here as a young wizard, so did they. Their advanced age and the fast-approaching end of their existence make them all the more desperate. All I can do is estimate that there are anywhere from two to four of them still actively sowing their hate and destruction. And, for added impact, I might add, it is customary for them to always travel together. It makes for an almost indestructible force to counter when they act in unison. Make no mistake about it, they've been very successful over the span of these millennia. Chaos, anarchy and the final, total destruction of this world is certainly not out of the question, given the rapidly deteriorating state I see all around.

213

"And if that happens, they will have succeeded and the light of this world will also die. Even this magnificent country of yours, one that I have taken so much pride and pleasure watching mature over these last 300 years, is rapidly losing its will and soul. Greg, as you know, is speaking to that issue at the conclusion of our performances. This land and its people have been serving as the lighthouse and lifeboat for the nations of this world, but it has a rot forming at its core, and it's sapping away its goodness.

"And to try to answer Jennifer's last question, I am only able to say that I will combat them with all my powers and all my wits. I have not come face-to-face with them before. I've always tried to work in the background. I was outnumbered and could easily have been overwhelmed. That's what happened on the other three of your sister worlds. Their wizards acted prematurely.

"My hope has always been that your fellow beings would somehow triumph, provided I gave needed insight, direction, and minor intervention here and there. However, now I've had to enlist your help to insure that Wallace and Bernice can survive and be able to add their protection and powerful forces to this struggle. This is my last, desperate attempt. And when I ultimately face these evil doers, my hope is that you are safe and secure. Further, I hope that I can triumph over them and you over the damage they've created and spawned around this world. It will be my last act, of that I am certain. Unfortunately, I cannot provide any of you the actual details of this final battle. Surprise is my most potent weapon.

"So, are there any more questions, folks?" Walt asked, concluding a rather lengthy explanation to Jennifer's questions.

"Yes, I have one more," Sophie spoke up. "Just how did this deterioration in our world occur to such an extent? Was it from the influence of these emissaries alone? Are you saying that it's due to the old line, 'the devil made me do it?"

"No, I'm not," Walt quickly answered. "And that's an excellent question to end this evening's conversation. The darkness the emissaries bring to this world is external. There is another, less tangible darkness that dwells within each human being. Where that originated from I cannot say. For the lack of a better explanation, scholars, sages, theologians and skeptics have credited sin, the id, personality disorders, internal chemical and hormonal imbalances and evil influences from some satanic presence. Suffice it to say, for all its beauty and wonder, the human being is not a perfectly finished product. And these imperfections can be manipulated and magnified both internally and externally. From what I've witnessed in my time amongst all of you on this world, I'd say each of you need to constantly apply checks and balances within your own lives and insure that the same is maintained throughout your society and government.

"You need to do this through self-awareness, self-control, sacrifice and prayer. For all your many accomplishments, I have continuously observed that you are a frail lot. You can be easily tempted by power, ambition and desire. The emissaries know all this, and they've manipulated you magnificently to their will. But they needed a receptive host before they could begin that transformation. And that's why 'Greg's Plan', as we now jokingly call it, needs to be presented wherever we give a performance across this land.

"Saying all this, I think now it's time to have a last cup of something hot to drink and call it a day. You've heard a story of enormous impact tonight, I realize. As our trip progresses, what I have told you will unfold and any doubts you may have now will pass. Try to get some rest now."

THE MID-WEST

SEVENTEEN: OHIO

Needless to say, I had a sleepless night after Walt shocked us with his revelations.   Come on. Before this trip, my world consisted of lounging on Howard's front porch, occasionally parading down a few blocks to the Boardwalk and then happily strolling along it when the weather was nice.   Now, after his story, most of which I sincerely doubted, I was confronted with having to accept his accounts of life-ending Armageddon, intra-universal battles, disappearing worlds and children who become wizards and heralds.   All this made my talk at our performances seem like backwoods drivel.

Within minutes, I got very depressed, almost even despondent.   And it was my buddy Wally who came to my rescue that next morning, as we were preparing to leave the shelter of the cottage for the highway.

"Mr. Greg," Wally called out to me as I was carrying my wagon-pulling harness in my teeth out the front door.

"What Wally!" I snapped, feeling my old dog temper beginning to resurface after the last night's disappointments.

"Could you come over here for a minute? I need to talk to you," he said in a most sincere, yet insistent manner.

"Alright, alright," I said, sighing and dragging the harness back inside.

He led me over to a corner next to the left hand fireplace, away from where everyone else was still eating breakfast and planning the next leg of our journey. Their conversation was, at times, loud and rather intense. It seemed all of us were on edge after last night.

"I already knew what Mr. Walt told you last night. He and Bernie are not aware that I know, and you are not to tell them. I trust you. You're my buddy, as I am yours. And I know that you are unsure what to think or do. But you must go on EXACTLY as you were with what you've been doing and saying. Keep observing and telling our audiences what you see and hear. You're not just a Harkener. You have also been given the gifts of a Sage. But you are not to discuss this with anyone but me, not even Bernie for now."

"Why are you telling me this?" I asked, now completely bewildered.

"Because I sensed your despondency and doubts, which are a natural reaction to Mr. Walt's talk last night. But you mustn't continue that way. I need you to stay the way you were. It's very important that you do so. But don't ask me why."

I stood there a few moments just staring at

him, and then it just came over me, 'what did I have to lose'. This trip was supposed to be an adventure, as well as a possible opportunity to perform and speak. So what if there is to be intergalactic or cosmic turmoil, I've got my friends here and a six year old buddy, who now talks and thinks like a tenured, university professor. So despite it all, I decided to just bark. And I mean really bark: at Wally, at the fireplace, the table full of food, the cottage, and then I ran outside lugging my harness and barked at the wagon, snow, trees...everything! "Bring it on!" I barked and shouted.

In retrospect, maybe I began to feel that what Wally told me put more 'zip' into what I was saying at those performances. Maybe I'd even been too timid, too reserved with its content. And so it was that after this series of revelations from Walt and Wally that I introduced the 'Disband" portion of 'Greg's Plan'. I decided it was time to grab the audiences' attention immediately. Maybe it was now time to stop listing all the ills of our society. Instead, this was the moment to be vocal and forthright with a plan, any plan, just something to get people talking, thinking and working at making desperately needed changes.

I certainly didn't care what became of my particular plan. How could I? My qualifications were a little scant and my degrees and pedigrees were non-existent. My only claim to any authority or insight was the word of a wizard from another 'verse'. He wasn't even from this universe...and that makes it unusually difficult to verify your resume. But, anyway, the tone, intent, ideas and wording of my performance talk took on a more concrete format after this detour to the snow cottage. And the audiences from Keyser Ridge to the Puget Sound were told, in no mincing of terms, to go forth and plant the seeds of change. I began to think of myself as the Johnny Appleseed of the Second Constitutional Convention that was to be held in Washington, D.C. five years from then.

Following that final climactic revelation by Wally and once he helped connect my harness to his wagon, I was ready to head off, well before anyone else. I was energized and wanted to run around and yell at everyone else to hurry up and get ready to go.

By the time we were all assembled and on our way the snow on the highway had turned to slush. The dangers of last night had passed. We traveled on through Grantsville, after giving a performance in Frostburg late that same morning. It was in Frostburg that Frank purchased goggles for all of us to use in case we ran into severe weather again. I was so proud of my pair that I wore them all the time. With my old flight helmet and goggles on, I fancied that I looked rather striking, like a true ace.

Our last performance in Maryland was in Keyser Ridge on May 15th, and after that we reentered Pennsylvania on May 16th, 30 days after beginning our journey.

We crossed into Western Pennsylvania on Hwy 40→ Addison→ Farmington→ Uniontown→ Hwy21→ McClellandtown→ Paisley→ Khedive→ Morrisville→ Waynesburg→ Rogersville→ Wind Ridge→ Ryerson Station→ back into West Virginia→ Rocklick→ Hwy 250→ Pleasant

Valley→ Limestone→ Moundsville→ crossing the Ohio River into Ohio.

It was May 26th when we entered Ohio, having traveled through mountain ranges and valleys. They were not overpowering by out-West standards, but they were enough of a challenge for me at that point. Along the way to Ohio, we gave performances in Uniontown, McClellandtown, then in Morrisville, Rogersville, Wind Ridge and Ryerson Station. We camped one extra day in the State Park outside Ryerson Station. We were exhausted and needed the rest before venturing further into Ohio.

Once in Ohio, our route was from Steinerville→ Alledonia→ Malaga→ Lewisville→ Summerfield→ East Union→ Sharon→ Meigs→ Malta→ Sayre→ New Lexington→ Junction City→ Lancaster→ Circleville→ Williamsport→New Holland→ Washington Court House→ Sabrina→ Wilmington→ Oakland→ Waynesville→ Springboro→ Franklin→ Germantown→ Gratis→ Camden→ into Indiana. You will notice that I have purposefully left out highway numbers at this point. I did this because once we got out of the congestion of the East Coast states, the route could easily be followed by following the towns we passed through. I hope you will agree.

It was between Williamsport and New Holland, almost exactly in the middle of Ohio, that another, and more ominous, 'Walter Moment' occurred. We had been traveling through altering stretches of forested areas, mixed with orchards, fields planted with corn, soy beans, alfalfa, timothy grass and pastureland stretching to the horizon, when we came to a more open area of rolling hillsides. Scattered across them were herds of grazing livestock, wood-framed farm houses, many needing a rescue coat of paint, barns that had passed their prime, some even sagging or bulging, but all proudly announcing their birthright.

Barns, to me, even more than the homes, signified the resolve and will of the earliest settlers to make a lasting success of their family's settlement on the frontier. It housed their animals and rations for the harsh winter ahead. Their homes kept them dry, fed and warm. The barns provided the means to do that. You may be a house person or a horse, cat, vintage car, pickup truck, or even a dog person. But me, I'm a barn dog. And I never tired seeing them along the way. They comforted me, in an odd sort of way. But Walt interrupted this idyllic reverie when he called out with the following, urgent instructions. As he yelled them out, he seemed to me to be almost in a panic.

"EVERYONE! At this instant, move off the roadway and make your way up that dirt path on the right. Quickly, move forward past the fence line. DO IT NOW!"

Without any hesitation, we each turned ourselves in that direction, Sophie leading the way onto the dirt path. The path was surrounded by a two-to-three foot high stand of Johnson grass, Cat Tails and Sweet Pea vines. Beyond the fence line that bordered the road we had just left, there was some farmer's pastureland. Scattered about it was a large herd of Hereford cattle, some grazing and some lying about. None of them took any notice of our frantic retreat off the paved road.

When we all got well beyond the fence line, Walt then commanded us to get back away from our gear a good ten to fifteen feet. But he said to do it quickly!! It probably would have helped if we'd had a couple of practice drills before doing this in a crisis-like atmosphere. To me, it looked like a mob scene of people trying to flee war-torn Atlanta, as depicted in an old movie I once saw. And, to tell you the truth, right about then I was beginning to miss watching those late night, movie reruns at Howard's place. If I'd known how, I would have started screaming about then.

"Is everyone out of the way?!!" Walt then shouted.

We all looked around at each other and nodded, Jennifer being the last one to detach herself from her squirrel cage and ambled over. Hurrying a cat, no matter what the occasion, is not a good way to try and prove your magical powers.

"Then stay back!" Walt again loudly announced, as he pulled his wand out of his backpack and sheath. Then pointing it at our wagons, tricycles, carts and assorted harnesses, tack and supplies, he made a clockwise motion with the wand, and they all disappeared.

And did that ever make me feel more secure. Now we get to walk the next 2,500 miles, with no provisions or protection. "You've really done it now, Walt" I thought to myself.

What followed next is still vague to me, but I do remember him pointing the wand at me and raising it vertically. It was only later that everyone else told me they had the same experience. The next thing that I remember is looking down from a height of about 50-75 feet onto that pasture of Hereford cattle and seeing a mule and a large draft-size horse underneath me. In addition, I noticed a small flock of birds on a couple of higher limbs, with two larger birds above them. Underneath me, looking up at me was a large grey squirrel. And then it struck me, I WAS THE TREE!

Almost immediately, after this transformation had occurred, there was a sound of something coming, and then passing over and around us. It was like a strong gust of wind, but it had an angry, menacing quality about it. And the area darkened as it passed. There were no clouds at the time, but the shadow it cast was distinct. I remember that much. And associated with it was a terrible sense of doom and helplessness, of finality. It was terrifying.

Following the ominous shadow's passing overhead, the largest bird that was above me, which I surmised was most likely a Red-Tail Hawk, took off and swept out over the entire, visible valley. And probably within five to ten minutes it returned and appeared to coax the other large bird and the smaller birds gathered immediately above me, to fly down to the ground beneath me. At the same time the squirrel flipped its large, bushy gray tail repeatedly and chattered nervously at me for a minute, then it, too, scampered down the tree trunk to the ground. Then, within a matter of seconds after that, I found myself standing on the ground next to Walt and Po.

Walt spoke first. "I am sorry to have

scared you and then to have given each of you such a dramatic transformation, with no warning or foreknowledge. Our window of escaping detection was very narrow, and I had to act fast. From all indications that I observed in my scouting the area around us, we did succeed in hiding from the emissaries. It was they who swept over us. They, too, can transform themselves to adapt to a particular circumstance. In this case, they need to travel quickly and over a large area. To do so they have adapted to being a swirling maelstrom. It had no definition, but, believe me, if they had found what they were looking for, you can be assured they would have regained their grotesque features of the horned ones. It was something that we soon learned to dread seeing when I was still in the anteverse.

"Each of you took on a transformation that was unique to your particular role that will become known to you, and to others, as our trip progresses. You were each aware that you had assumed a different form, but you couldn't communicate with each other or with anything else at the time. In due course there will be some additional changes associated with that transformation, but now is not the time for that aspect of your developing talents to be revealed. I know you must have many questions, but remain reassured that no harm or damage to you has or will occur. For now, we must quickly move on.

"The emissaries will not be returning to our location again. And I doubt we will be bothered by them for some time to come. They are scanning the entire region for us, and by now they will be many miles away. Given the distance they have to cover in their search for us, I would doubt we will have to hide from them again for another 3-4 weeks. Eventually, without question, it will be necessary to stand up to them, but that time is not going to be of their choosing. For now, we must be on our way."

Little did we know that what happened to each of us was like an imprint that would create a linkage between us and all living beings. That wasn't truly recognized until much later, when we all gradually began to experience remarkable capabilities and to further discover that they were transferable. In the meantime, while we witnessed Walt reappear all our gear, I was so relieved to be back into my more natural appearance that I did something that, so far, had been lost in the rush of preparation and traveling. I chased my tail. You should try it sometime. It's pure exhilaration.

Mounting up, sometime after my tail-chasing, we were off again to New Holland. We had given performances in Sharon, Meigs, Sayre and Junction City. We were due to start again in Sabrina, Oakland, Springboro and Gratis before getting to Indiana. The crowds were growing, but we had begun asking, before and after each performance, that the audiences not give our presence wide publicity. We were trying desperately to avoid the exposure we had in Hagerstown. And we didn't want an uncontrollable crowd stampede our venue. It was a balancing act to advertise, somewhat modestly, our presence in each community, but to avoid over-exposure at the same time. And through it all, Walt would estimate the size of the next audience and provide the magic tent to match it. By now, I was convinced he had to be a wizard or an amazing tent maker.

Our performances seemed to have stabilized at three hours in length. We had a twenty minute intermission half way through it. And over the course of the four performances each week, everyone managed to substitute something new into their act. Except for me. My talk, by the time we exited Ohio had reached its time limit. From there, it just took on different flavors, depending on what I witnessed during the preceding days. And our entire troop agreed that I should limit it to 15 minutes in length; it was to be no longer than that under any circumstances. Otherwise, they would strike up some music and start singing and dancing. The first time they did that I spun around and snapped a quick bark. To that, they just played louder and laughed at me. I got the hint.

I need to comment on one final item before we leave my recollection of Ohio, with its magnificent dairy farms, brilliant roadside wild flowers, dense stretches of forests and hillsides of apple orchards and grazing cattle. We all were badly shaken by the sudden appearance of the emissaries, so much so that we never spoke of it. The event had lodged deep in the furthest reaches of our fears. Everyone, by a certain age, knows life is a gift with finite limits. But to have it stalked by something so dark and so terrorizing requires an extra measure of faith to proceed. For each of us, it became our new mission, expressed with unspoken determination, that we would outmaneuver the emissaries, that somehow goodness would prevail and the needed changes would be made within ourselves, our governments and our world. Nothing was ever so clear to me, without it being voiced by anyone. And with that resolve, we headed into Indiana.

EIGHTEEN: INDIANA

Our journey through Indiana started on June 2nd, after we rested two nights in Camden, Ohio. Our route took us through Liberty→ Connersville→ Rushville→ Shelbyville→ Franklin→ Martinsville→ Gosport→ Spencer→ Patricksburg→ Clay City→ Lewis→ Fairbanks→ Graysville and then into Illinois.

From my perspective, walking along roadway shoulders, and having Wally call out the debris along the road or the sights around us, it seemed that nothing changed too much when we crossed the border into Indiana from Ohio. It was lush country, as well. And I welcomed the forested areas. They offered us some protection that open stretches of meadows and farmland didn't. And at this point I should note that, whether or not Wally was having pity on me or not, I had begun to win a few of the Roadside Game wagers. Sophie and Frank were taskmasters for Bernie and Wally keeping up with their studies. Somehow, I had the feeling Wally, and probably Bernie as well, were kind of playing along with them. These children knew a whole lot more than they were letting on. Occasionally, Wally would wink at me when he answered a question that Sophie had called out to him. But he was always so kind and generous with both Sophie and Frank. I was convinced he and Bernie both loved them as much as they did them.

But it was Indiana that provided the opportunity for Rita to demonstrate her newly-acquired, Walt-induced, world-altering gift. It was somewhere west of Martinsville that Rita experienced her first gift to us and to our world.

We had pulled over to have a picnic lunch, something we weren't always able to do. We were only traveling a total of 17 miles that day, and the road was fairly level, allowing us to make good time. And, we had no performance that night to worry about. After we had lunch, we each settled back to take a nap in the lovely, afternoon sunshine. It was luxurious. I had Wally unhook all my harnesses, and I just rolled over on my back and slept like a puppy.

In the meantime, Rita decided to explore a little, while everyone else rested. About 30 feet from our picnic area was a small grove of maple trees. She decided to head over there to check out some fellow-bird activity. All the chirping and squawking indicated that there was a serious argument or dispute going on. Rita wanted to enjoy the show and decided to fly over.

Landing on a branch just above the loudest, most boisterous bird, she looked down to see that it was a sparkling, red bird. It stunned Rita; she'd never seen or heard of one before.

"Whoa!" she let out a whoop. "Get a load of you! Did you fall in a bucket of red paint or get tagged by a gang of crows from the hood? But, I forgot, your kind can't speak, can you? I guess I've got the corner on that market. Too bad. It would be nice to have at least a little conversation with my fellow species. I guess they're all just a little too dull to develop that skill." And with that, Rita began to launch herself to another limb.

"Rather proud of yourself, aren't you," the cardinal answered, catching Rita completely by surprise.

Spinning around, Rita stared at the little red bird and exclaimed, "What did you say? Or did I imagine you said something?"

"No, you conceited airhead, I just addressed you," the smaller bird answered. "While it's true, this is a first for me, and I know of no one else in my group that has spoken before, it's a real privilege for me to do so and to put the hammer down on your prissy ways. I can tell you're not from around these parts. And maybe you should just head back to wherever you came from, if this is your attitude towards us natives."

"Believe me, I didn't know," Rita answered. "And I sincerely apologize for being so arrogant. I had gotten used to the idea that I was the only one in bird land who could talk in complete sentences and then even make some sense while doing it. This is GREAT! Please accept my apology."

"Ok, that seems fair enough," the crested red bird replied, "but how did this all come about? Am I to be like you, wandering around talking, and no one answering or knowing what is wrong with me? My breed chirps mostly, with some monosyllabic melody occasionally associated with our twittering. You haven't jinxed me into being some kind of carnival showpiece, have you?"

"Honestly," Rita replied, "I don't know what is happening. And if I told you what I think is behind all this, you wouldn't believe me anyway. Suffice it to say, there have been some really strange events taking place in my life over the last few months. I'm beginning to wonder, at this moment, if I am undergoing an emotional breakdown. You see, I'm originally from Atlantic City."

"Where or what is that?" Red asked.

"Hmm, this is going to be even harder than I thought," Rita replied, sighing and looking over nervously to where Walt and her fellow travelers were napping. "It's a city on the Atlantic Ocean, in New Jersey."

"What's a New Jersey?" came the quick reply.

"Gad. Your speaking doesn't come with an index of place names, geography highlights and packaged in some kind of historical context, does it?"

"I don't think so," the redbird answered. "All I know is that I can now speak. Beyond that, I only know vaguely where I've been and why I've even been there. Actually, why I've been doing what I'm doing is even more of a mystery. It's not a stretch to say, I don't know jack. Being chosen as the Indiana State Bird doesn't leave me much time to travel widely. I stay pretty close to these parts, which doesn't appear to be the case with you.

"No, quite honestly, I'm beginning to think that I am traveling way too much. And I guess all I can say is that you have a gift, unlike any that other birds, except me, have possessed. I have no idea if it is a transferable gift, like it was from me to you. If it is, then share it wisely, if you can."

"Can you give me any tips on how to do that?" the new talker asked.

"First off, and most importantly, stay away from stray, grayish white and blue dogs, particularly those with the name of 'Greg'. And be really suspicious of anyone, who has a mule for a companion, and who is dressed in stripped overalls."

"Right..." Red answered. "That's really nice advice. I'm glad I asked."

"Well, I don't mean to transform your entire existence and run, but I need to be off. I have a duty to survey the area around our rest area to insure there is nothing strange going on."

"And you don't think this encounter was strange?" the little bird asked.

"Not as strange as it can get. Take care and don't talk to strangers." And with those sage remarks, Rita flew off.

What she didn't know until sometime later in our journey was that Little Red set in motion a tidal surge of events amongst the birdlife of this world. It was like a global pyramid scheme. He talked to a buddy, who then talked to his or her buddy, and so on and so on, until, within a month, every bird in the state of Indiana was talking to each other and to their keeper, if that was the case.

A good example of how that evolved happened just up the road from where Rita and Little Red first met. It was somewhere near Brown Country State Park, on a chicken farm. Early one morning the mistress of the farm entered their chicken house, as was her custom every morning to gather the eggs laid over the last 24 hours. She had a small stand near the highway, in front of their farmhouse, where she sold these eggs and any extra produce from their garden.

On this one memorable day, Ms. Caine went into her chicken house, as was her custom. She then reached into the first nest, with a hen still lying on her brood of freshly laid eggs, to grab a hand full. It was something she had done at least 329,439 times before this, without incident. Except today.

"Hold on, Missy," the hen replied, as she reached underneath her. "I believe those are my eggs you're trying to remove."

Recoiling, like she had touched a live wire, carrying a thousand volts, Ms. Caine rocked back across the chicken house and landed on one of the feeders, tripping and falling onto the one water tray in the house.

"You're going to have to get us more water, now that you've emptied that one," the chicken then observed.

The only recorded sound from Ms. Caine that morning was a piercing shriek, as she ran toward the farmhouse. It wasn't long after that the sign, advertising "eggs for sale" was removed from her front yard.

Thus began a process where the birdlife of

this planet was beginning to voice their concerns and demands for equal and fair treatment. It was a major revolution within numerous industries and pursuits. For example, the effect was immediate for turkey growers, chicken farmers, duck and geese hunters, penguin fanciers, bird feeder enthusiasts, bird watchers and feral cat predators. If there was a listening device hooked up to the planet for other other-world beings to eavesdrop on these conversations, after that first month, the volume of speaking rose dramatically. Not only was there bird songs in the verdant forests, but there were now arguments, discussions, bidding, bargaining, and protests. Birds, of all kinds, had been empowered. And Rita set it in motion. That was her first gift.

And, of course, Rita didn't fly off to scout out the area. Instead, she made a dash for our napping area, yelling as she landed, "Everybody, listen up! I've got amazing news! I'm contagious...I made a bird speak just like me...simply by insulting it... Well, maybe that wasn't the actual cause, but it did talk back to me, just like you do to me, except she thought I was an arrogant twit."

Briefly the thought passed by me, that I, too, had entertained such notions, but after all, I'm only a ...So, swallowing my urge to press that line of thought a little further with Rita, I said, "You mean this other bird actually spoke back to you?"

"You bet," Rita answered. "It was a small red bird, with a darkish crest. It hasn't been out of the area much, from the sounds of it, but there was no question, he could speak as well as you or me."

"Did this bird say it had been speaking like

that for a long time?" Frank asked. "And is it planning on joining us?" which you could tell by the tone of his voice would not have been a good plan.

"No, Red, as I called him or her, said this was the first time ever. And I'm sure it had no intention of traveling with us. He or she had local obligations."

"Given that Red, as you call it, is bright red," Sophie added, "by your description, Red is a male cardinal."

"Well, he was dashing," Rita added. "And I wonder what happens to him, now that he can talk?"

"Who knows," I commented, "maybe start his own traveling circus..." However, just at that moment Walt had caught my attention and shook his head at me. He didn't comment about this development, but at that moment I knew it was somehow all part of his Grand Plan. By the time we crossed Illinois and were about to enter Missouri, we discovered how significant Rita's experience really was.

Our trip through Indiana included performances in Rushville, Shelbyville, Franklin, followed by a three day break from performing, then resuming them again in Lewis and Fairbanks. And true to Walt's word, there were no further flyovers by the emissaries during our crossing Indiana. Slowly, we were regaining our calm and perspective, ones we had before Walt's revelations. Indiana had been a needed balm to our battered spirits. It was a lovely state. I felt like I might have had relatives still living there, it felt so comfortable being there.

NINETEEN: ILLINOIS

Come June 11th, we crossed into Illinois and still had two more performances to give before we had completed our schedule of four a week. We gave the last two of this set in Eaton and Gila. Our route through Illinois took us through Eaton→ Gila→ Effingham→ Beecher City→ Ramsey→ Hillsboro→ Gillespie→ Piasa→ Fieldon→ and on to Winfield in Missouri.

It was after the performance in Gila that my concerns mounted about school children, more specifically those 8 years or older, that I had been seeing since we left Atlantic City. I hadn't yet incorporated anything about education of kids in my performance talk, and I knew I had to say something. So I turned to Sophie and Frank that evening, once we settled into our campsite and everyone else had quieted down for the night. Sophie and Frank always had a last cup of coffee together before they went to sleep. I was so proud of them, at how they had handled this trip and all the wizardry that was swirling around us.

"Sophie, Frank, can I talk to you for a

moment?" I asked, walking up slowly to them, so as not to startle them.

"Sure, Greg," Frank answered. "What's on your mind tonight?"

"Well, it's like this. I need to add something to my presentation about school age kids and education. To me, even though I've never had a chance to have any of either, getting a good education seems the most important job of their lives, almost more important than the jobs they are to have afterward. And, from what I'm seeing, both during the time school was in session and now that the summer break is here, there is not the dedication to learning and applying themselves that I hoped to see. It worries me."

Sophie then set down her coffee cup and reached over to give me a scratch. I had sat down between the two of them; obviously hoping one of them would do just that. She never let me down.

"You're right, Greg," she began. "There is a major breach developing between what needs to be learned, how to teach it and the motivation and diligence it will take our children to learn, absorb and apply it. That disconnect is getting wider by the year. There are too many diversions for the students. Self-discipline and an eagerness to learn have to be reinstated during their school years. What do you propose to say to call attention to that need and to change the course of what's happening?"

Taking a deep breath, I then outlined my thoughts on education, the material you saw at the beginning of this story. I admitted to both of them I was well aware of the harshness, even draconian nature, of the plan. My reasons for it being that way was that there appears to have been a major shift in priorities and a kind of fatalism about even trying to learn for many students. I noted that our society's emphasis has been on material matters, acquiring wealth and finding the easiest path to accomplish ones goals. I finished my description of the plan by asking what they thought of it.

Frank was the first to reply. "You'll sure get everyone's attention. And I think you should expect some major pushback from parents, politicians and the students themselves. But, deep down, I don't think there is anyone who is sincerely analyzing our educational system who wouldn't agree that something dramatic and stunning needs to be done to save our children from finding themselves in the nightmare of living in a third world country. I say go for it. Say what's on your mind. It will at least get people thinking."

"I agree," Sophie said. "If our own children had not applied themselves in school, I would have almost threatened them with what you are suggesting. Frank and I had worked too hard to see them just throw away their educational opportunities. It's ok, Greg. There will be some outcry, but say it anyway. Frank and I are proud of you."

That did it. A good scratch, a complement from these folks and I slept sounder than I had in weeks after that night's conversation. And by our next performance in Hillsboro, I had added the part on education you previously read. And there were always gasps from the audience when I got to that part, if there had been none before that. But, having the support of Frank and Sophie, I persisted saying it all the way to the Puget Sound in Washington.

As far as the next bit of magical wonder that Walt had imbedded in each of us, it was when we were having our two day rest in Ramsey that Flo came center stage. During our second evening there, Flo decided to take a walk into the woods. But these weren't your ordinary woods. They were congested with thickets of thorny bushes and vines, made impassable by boggy areas covered with wetland plants and half-submerged logs, and densely covered over with older oak and maple trees. In addition, everything was in full foliage, so line-of-sight visibility was nil. No matter. Flo had a nose on her that could track a polar bear at twenty miles. There was no way she could get lost…in the arctic, that is.

She had been lunging through the woods and underbrush for about 30 minutes when she decided maybe it was time to circle back to our campsite. And circle she did, over and over again. She became hopelessly lost, and her barking, even her yelling, was swallowed up by this jungle. Eventually, she began to run pell-mell through the woods, in an obvious panic. And it was at this point she had her first lucky break. She ran right into a very large, white-tail, male deer.

Now, it was never completely explained to me how this business of speaking was transferred to other beings, but there was some mention of it being through direct contact, either by one's voice being directed at someone or by speaking while making physical contact with someone. It was the latter method that Flo used that particular evening.

"Ummpfff," she cried out as she hit the deer broadside. Then reacting out of her natural tendency to be polite, Flo apologized. Very soon thereafter, she realized that it was actually a really stupid thing to do. How would the deer know or care what she was saying? And her next thought was that, with the deer now looking at her and sporting a large rack of many-pronged antlers, he could very easily impale her out of self-defense.

"Please, excuse me," Flo said out of habit. You see, I am lost and I was just bounding through the trees out of sheer panic." Then, recovering somewhat, she added, "Oh, this is so silly of me saying this to you."

To which the deer reared its stately head and looked Flo squarely in the eyes and replied, "I beg your pardon. What's so silly about it? You struck me, and then you apologized. It's common courtesy to do so. Where are you headed?"

Shaking her head from the collision and then realizing what she had just heard, and from whom, Flo looked up at the large face gazing down at her and nervously replied, "Back to our campsite, but never mind that, you're talking to me!! I must have suffered a concussion and am now delirious."

"You may well be both of those, for all I know," the deer answered, "but in actual fact I am speaking to you. I grant you it's a first for me, but I've had a lot on my mind for years, and it's nice to finally be able to start getting it off my chest.

"Speaking of which, that was a real thump

you gave me. You're not originally from around here are you? I've never seen your like before."

"No," Flo answered, feeling just a slight bit less nervous and threatened. "I'm originally from Siberia."

"Oh," the dear replied, "is that anywhere near here?"

"Uh-uh, it's a long way off. It's where it's cold and icy most of the time." Pulling herself up straight, she added, "I'm a Siberian Husky."

"Do you have a name?" the deer then asked.

"It's Flo."

"Well, Flo, I'd really like to get to know you better, but this is a busy time of the year for me. I'm in the rutting season, and I've got to keep moving about."

Confused by this, Flo replied, hoping to be helpful, "You don't look stuck to me."

This comment caused the deer to roll his eyes and sigh. "I haven't time to explain right now. For now, let's just work on getting you back to your friends. Are you the ones camped out east of here?"

"That's us," Flo replied excitedly,

"Then follow me. I'll get you back on the path to your camp."

"Would you like to meet them?" Flo then asked. "I think you would enjoy their company."

"Not tonight," White Tail said. "I've got a potential date later on tonight. Maybe another time."

And within ten minutes Flo was bounding out of the woods, excitedly telling everyone as she ran up, about her encounter with the deer. Because we had not had any contact with Rita's talking birds, it was still not known to us about the transference of this speaking ability. And by early the next morning White Tail had made contact with three or four deer, ran into a couple of cows and one horse. Each of them left those encounters, speaking the King's English. And again, within a month's time most of Illinois' larger animals were catching up on a lot of local gossip.

I never knew if English was the only language spoken by the birds and animals. I guess I figured if they wanted to learn another language they would just have to apply themselves and find a tutor. That seemed the only logical course to me.

But I have to tell you the most amazing thing about being in Illinois was in leaving Illinois. It involved crossing two rivers, The Illinois River at Hardin and then taking a ferry across THE MISSISSIPPI RIVER!! We crossed from Batchtown into Winfield, Missouri. Love of my life! It was almost too much for me. This wasn't just crossing two wonderfully large rivers in one day, but that the Mississippi river was SO BIG. It was like the Atlantic Ocean had been channeled. It was too much. They had to drag me off the ferry. I would have stayed on it until my last breath.

TWENTY: MISSOURI

We walked and pedaled off the ferry heading into Winfield on June 21st.   From there, we traveled on to Hawk Point→ Olney→ Middletown→ Santa Fe→ Middle Grove→ Clifton Hill→ Indian Grove→ Tina→ Braymer→ Lathrop→ Wallace→ and finally into Atchison, Kansas.

My mood was euphoric practically all the way to the middle of Missouri. Having seen the Mississippi River was a highlight of my trip so far. I realized there were cosmic events taking place all around us, and possibly the survival of human and animal kind hung in the balance, but after I have had my say at the end of each performance, I regress to being what I was always meant to be: a happy go-lucky, shaggy-ass, herd dog, who really, really loves big rivers. I figured once I got wherever we were going to eventually settle, I was going to find a bridge over a big river and spend every waking hour just watching the water go by. Truth is, with all the talk about how the climate is going to get much dryer, I envisioned I might have a lot of company on that bridge.

It was during our layover at Clifton Hill, the last day of rest before we started our next series of four performances, that Jennifer had her own, personal "Walter Moment". Or at least that is what we surmised much later. It had to be his doing that was creating all this upheaval in the animal and bird world.

Jennifer, as it was her natural-born habit, would often go out at night on the prowl. She wasn't looking for mischief or some companionship. It was just her way of reducing that day's pent-up tension and stress. I actually encouraged it. It kept her from whining at me during the day, particularly when we were pulling a succession of hills. I never knew exactly what she did during these outings, but she was always refreshed and ready to "Do the Cage", as she called it, the next day.

Well, on this particular night, things didn't go as was her routine. It appears, from what she told me later, that she wandered into the exclusive territory of some particularly, uptight raccoons. The way she tells it, she was just ambling along, when four large animals confronted her. They were all growling and snapping at her, making moves like she might be their midnight snack. Out of self-defense, and not knowing anything else to do, she looked the biggest one in the eyes, and shouted, "Don't you dare touch me you big, overgrown rodent!"

It seemed to have its desired effect, because that same raccoon halted his forward advance and blurted out, "You called me a rodent! Why did you do that? That really hurts my feelings. I'm a proud member of the Procyon lotor species or raccoon family. I am descended from a long line of distinguished mammals."

But their brief exchange didn't stop the advance of the other three hunters. Jennifer's life was in peril, and she knew it instinctively. But to her amazement, the fellow she had just insulted, turned to the next one of his companions in line to have the second bite of Jennifer and said, "Did you hear that! This cat doesn't know the difference between us being rangers of the night and common rodents."

And apparently the leader was close enough to his nearest partner, that to Jennifer's amazement, he or she was able to reply, "The nerve of it." And then these two came to a complete standstill. By now the other two, less articulate members of this party, stopped as well, because they were concerned what had happened to the first two. They weren't doing the usual growling and snarling, like were proper in these circumstances. They were babbling instead. And that's when the first two spoke directly to them as well, and the first recorded four-way conversation between raccoons in any forest of this planet occurred.

Mind you, Jennifer was not lost in the moment. A recorder of world-shaking events, she wasn't. Drawing on her much-repeated, athletic performances over these past months, she crouched quickly, then did two high leaps, one incorporating a complete summersault and a back flip, and was clear of the hunter's circle of death. They all, in turn, watched as she corkscrewed and back flipped down the path out of sight.

It was too much for one night, for each of them. First off, their speaking amongst themselves and then watching their night's meal perform agile acrobatics to escape out of their clutches left them limp and disheartened. Finally, their leader asked, in a reverential manner for fear something else incomprehensible was going to happen to them, "Who was that lone cat?"

And as if Jennifer knew what they were experiencing, she turned briefly and yelled back at them, "Hi Ho, Silver, Away..."

And like Rita and Flo before her, once Jennifer returned to camp and related this encounter to us, with the added twist that these four were able to transfer the ability to speak to each other, we knew something mighty big was afoot. But Walt still remained noncommittal and mum about the whole process. I could only surmise this process had not fully played itself out.

And it was on this same night that I had another conversation with Sophie and Frank. During the course of our trip we had passed a number of jails and penitentiaries. They set me to thinking that something different, possibly more drastic, had to be done to discourage a wasted life of violent crime. Granted, every society has to take care of its own, giving each person as much help, guidance, education and hope as possible for a descent life. That's a given. But sadly, that promise is often eclipsed by those in power or seeking power. What I proposed to Sophie and Frank was a return to the times when there were penal colonies. No frills, nothing supportive or the offer of rehabilitation.

Everyone incarcerated now, except those deemed the most hopelessly violent, would be given the opportunity to become integrated back into a new environment. And it would include them also serving two years in a national service corps, like the rest of the population, ages 18-24.

Frank's response to my suggestions was, "Again, Greg, it sounds harsh, like your educational incentives. And I'm sure there are going to be those in the audience who will shout you down."

But Sophie, interrupted with, "But, dear, what are we going to do now with the millions of imprisoned individuals. We just can't keep shuttling prisoners to their present fate; probably losing forever the potential most of them might have developed. Greg's right, with the present system, too many are beginning to view their punishment almost like it's a reward for harming society. Victims stagger off to try to recover from their loss. Perpetrators are confined in a lock down situation, but other than the danger from other prisoners, they are fed, clothed, kept entertained, with minimal effort on their part. Something has got to change. I say let Greg have his say. You bet, it will stir up the crowd, but at least it will start them thinking about some alternatives to the present situation.

And so it was, after that brief conversation, that I added that part into "Greg's Plan" for the remaining performances. And Frank was right. By now, with what I was offering as alternatives was getting the audiences really steamed up. Sometimes Po would have to walk with me as I left the podium. But being a dog, it wasn't like I was that big a threat.

It made me think that it is words that are the ultimate force that moves a society, not whose saying them. So I just kept on talking.

Probably I should let you know that we experienced countless rain and wind storms since that one on our first day on the road. And we took all the necessary precautions when it appeared one was going to be more than just a light shower. However, it was on July 2nd, that we saw first-hand nature's full fury. It was as we approached the overpass that would cross over Interstate 35. As expected, everyone was alert to any gathering of dark clouds, and this was particularly so in the Mid West's tornado alley. About 3 p.m. Frank called out to the rest of us, "We better find some shelter. Just pulling off the road doesn't look like it will be safe enough for us. There is an accumulation of threatening clouds ahead, and the swirling nature of them aloft looks ominous."

Sophie then called out, "There's an overpass ahead. Let's get on the access road and try to find a spot underneath it. Between it and the freeway, we should have some protection."

Hurriedly, we shifted off the road we were on and made our way along a dirt road to the overpass. Once there, we dismounted and unhooked our harnesses and huddled under the bridge. Already, cars were beginning to stop on the freeway under the overpass, because hail stones were starting to fall and the wind was picking up. Within minutes, the sounds of hair-raising wind, hail, lightning and thunder filled the area around us. Never having been in such a situation, I wasn't at all sure we were going to survive. And looking around at the others, it appeared I wasn't alone. Even Walt and Po looked as if they were cast adrift in this storm.

In what seemed like a hour, but probably was only a few minutes, the storm passed and the sun eventually came out 30 minutes later. But as we were climbing back on the roadway and crossed over the freeway, we could see ahead of us tremendous destruction. We later learned there had been a strong tornado, one of a string of them that hit the area.

We were the first on the scene of a large, mobile home park that looked like a combination mammoth wrecking ball and counter-top blender had twisted its way through the 108 homes. I couldn't tell what was what. But immediately Walt yelled out, "Frank, Sophie, Po unhook Greg and Flo and let them begin to sniff out survivors. Rita, fly over and see where the worst damage is located. Po you come with me and we will start clearing and moving debris off the survivors. Sophie, until the authorities arrive, you and Frank find blankets, mattresses, anything that will cover and comfort the people we find."

After I was unhooked I ran up to Flo and asked what I should do. She told me to bark whenever I sensed someone or something was alive under the rubble. She then said she'd take the buildings to our left and I should go to the ones on our right. We'd work one street at a time, with Po, Walt, Sophie and Frank following us. Rita would soar down periodically and tell us which street needed to be cleared next.

Walt had gotten out his wand and worked it swiftly, once we identified someone trapped underneath the wreckage. Po would alternate between being a mule and a centurion, lifting and pulling as he went along. There was so much confusion in the region; no one noticed what we were doing. And the survivors were so relieved and stunned by what had just happened to them with the storm, they didn't notice what the makeup of our rescue party was.

We started at the front of the park and worked toward its far back side. That way, as rescuers arrived, they could tend to the victims behind us and let us do our search and rescue unimpeded and undetected.

The one thing I did notice during all this rescue work was that as time went on, my acute sense of smell got less sensitive. Whereas, ole Flo just kept on locating injured people at a stunning speed. She probably located twice what I did. It was a marvel to watch. And I was so proud of her by the time we had reached the end of the park's destruction. We never counted how many people and children we located, but it was enough that we had a renewed sense of purpose. We were no longer just a traveling troop of entertainers, and it felt good to have helped some folks in a desperate time.

As we worked our way into Lathrop, where we stayed three nights for our two week respite, we were able to rescue many more folks along the way. We finally found a secluded park that sheltered us from all the commotion. Sirens wailed into the night, as did the sounds of heavy trucks and equipment being brought into the area. By midnight we finally settled down and slept all the next day. It was later that I learned I had experienced my first tornado.

By the time we had crossed Missouri we had given performances in Winfield, Hawk Point, Middletown, Indian Grove, Tina Braymer and Lathrop. Two days later we crossed into Atchison, Kansas.

THE WEST

TWENTY-ONE: KANSAS

We arrived in Atchison, Kansas, on July 6th. From there we traveled to Horton→ Fairview→ Baileyville→ Marysville→ Washington→ and a very long day's march to Rydal. It was on that day we crossed Hwy 81, which for me divided the country into East and West. From this point on we were in the Western United States. It was an arbitrary decision, I admit, but from that point on the distances seemed vast between settlements, the land was flat and expansive. It just seemed to fit. Then from Rydal we went on to Montrose→ Bellaire, which was almost in the exact geological center on the contiguous United States. For us it marked the half way point of our journey, whether it really was or not didn't matter that much. Again, it just seemed to fit the occasion. And from Bellaire we marched on to Agra→ Prairie View→ Reager→ Overlin→ Atwood→ Bird City to Hwy 27, heading to Wray Colorado. We camped that last night in Kansas at the Arikaree Breaks.

There were no further shocking "Walter Moments" from within our troop. It appeared, at least for now, that we had stopped sowing global disruption amongst the status quo. But I still had issues to discuss with Sophie and Frank, before my presentation was completed to my satisfaction.

The last two issues I had to discuss with them were the proposed isolationist posture of this country during the massive restructuring process and the drastic economic measures I suggested to equalize the disparity of income.

As far as leveling the wages, all I was trying to do is level the playing field, by trying to put everyone at the starting gates together. The national, economic game plan now is tilted too much in favor of certain special interests, industries and top executives. Obviously, I realize everyone has different talents, abilities and intelligence. Why wouldn't I. Just take another look at me? But it's all about starting over!

And the isolation was simply a way of saying to ourselves, and to the world, that we had to pull back, reassess, rebuild, and restore our nation and reset our moral compass. Our greatness is in our people, in the beauty of our magnificent land and in the genius of the Declaration of Independence and Constitution. I needed Sophie and Frank to hear me out, to see if saying we needed to hang out a sign, which could say: "Closed for Repairs. Be Patient. We'll be Back in Business Soon.", was ok for the audiences to hear..

And after I presented my ideas to Sophie and Frank, as we were camping in Horton, it was Sophie who summed it up best. "Greg, your efforts to suggest concrete avenues of change, rather than just complain and moan about the way things have become, are admirable. You are not suggesting revolution or anarchy. And you're not being defeatist. You are suggesting that we, as a country, get back to the basics of living, educating, governing and protecting ourselves. Go for it. Frank and I will support you, as I know the others in our caravan will."

And from then on, once we crossed the Colorado border, "Greg's Plan" was pretty much as you have read at the beginning of this story. I never had any clue why it was me that was doing this, other than it appeared to be one of Walt's "gifts", as he called them, that Flo, Rita, Jennifer and I had. Believe me; I was never particularly observant or full of ideas before this trip. I just seemed to sense when something was not right and wanted to suggest some changes, to someone, to anyone. I have no idea what effect it had or will have. That wasn't necessarily my goal. All I wanted to do is insure this wonderful land stayed wonderful.

But, about three miles from Atwood, we confronted the Terror, face-to-face, that would do harm to everyone and to everything. Rita had been on one of her scouting missions, looking for a good location for us to camp that night. What she found instead was a major roadblock and an inspection station blocking the road we were traveling on. To her, it appeared that maybe the emissaries had returned. She swooped in over our column calling out, "Stop, something is happening ahead of us about five miles that you should know about."

Walt, upon hearing what Rita had seen, once more called out from the rear of our column, "Everyone, off the road quickly! Sophie, turn into that stand of Willows over there by that pond."

Our previous exposure to this same kind of urgent command from Walt heightened our anxiety level, to one that demanded we should now be in a stampede. Sensing this, Walt tried to calm us as quickly as possible, and explained what he had to do

"We will have to go through that roadblock; there is no way around it. It appears the emissaries have set up inspection sites up and down the country, in hopes of locating us. And by a process of elimination and tips, they may have discovered a pattern to our stopovers. In doing so, they have determined we should be about this far along by now. They probably are still unsure exactly which route we are taking, but they are in the process of narrowing it down. I'm afraid we're going to have to switch our mode of travel for a while, particularly to get through this roadblock.

"If you will, one more time, stand back from your gear and then stand apart from one another. I will be transforming some of you again, but this time you will be able to communicate with each other. We will all meet again two days from now at the Arikaree Breaks, some 70 miles northwest of here. You will have to remain in your transformed states until then. Rita will be with you for protection, should any raptors be in that area. I am sorry to have to do this, but everyone's safety is at stake as we now are."

So, before anyone could voice any reservation or objection, Walt had whipped out his wand, circled it at our gear and then vertically raised it, while pointing it at Sophie, Frank, Wally, Bernie, and Flo. Po was already in his mule phase, as I came to call it. Only Flo was not transformed into a small flock of cedar waxwings. Flo was now the Belgium gray draft horse I had seen earlier from atop myself, when I was a tall tree. This is all getting a bit bewildering for me to relate, so don't think you're the only one confused. Only Jennifer and I were left untouched.

Quickly, then, Walt pointed his wand at the ground where our travel equipment was and moved it horizontally to the left. Immediately, in that same spot, there was now a large PICK UP TRUCK!!! And hooked behind it was an equally large covered trailer. I nearly swooned.

All this transformation was followed with a variety of comments, coming from the birds, Po and Flo. Mostly, they were concerned who was riding where. The conversations became quite excited, and I noticed that Jennifer had to fight back some primitive urge to snag one of the juicy, little birds. I reminded her who they really were. Instinct trumps reason every time, I decided then, because her back was still arched and her stare was still unwavering. She remained poised to have a small bird snack. I had to walk in front of her and sit down to block her view and quickly calm her down.

To bring order back into this melee, Walt then instructed us where and when we were to go. For the transformed birds and Rita, he asked them to take off right away, making a heading due north about five miles, then head west to the Republican River and the Arikaree Breaks. They were instructed to obey everything Rita told them, which when you tell a collection of humans who recently became birds that they should obey a rather temperamental cockatoo, it is a bitter pill to swallow. With sighs and a lot of "oh, ok's, whatever you say Walt." they launched themselves up over above us; and with Rita at the head of their "V" formation, they headed northward. I think it was probably Frank that I heard say as they flew off, "This is definitely not what I had in mind when Greg suggested a cross-country trip."

For the remainder of us, Walt opened the rear doors of the trailer and told Po to get in one side of the horse trailer, and Flo, now a 1200 pound draft horse, in the other. Jennifer was also told to get in with Flo, and to make herself comfortable in the straw bed at the front of the trailer. She was there, ostensibly, to calm Flo, and that is exactly what he was going to be telling the inspectors. And she should be prepared to act accordingly, not set off on one her snits or acrobatic performances.

As for me, Walt opened the passenger side of the pickup truck and lifted me up into the front seat. This pickup was so big that it had another set of seats behind the front ones. It was luxurious. And between the time he closed my door and walked around the back of the trailer to secure those doors, I became so excited I began barking, scratching and trying to catch my tail...all at once. I just hoped Walt didn't have any somber plans for me, during this inspection, because I had lost all perspective on saving humanity. I was, at that point, a purified and rarified dog, and I was possessed with no other ambition than to be that. And most amazing of all, that's exactly what Walt wanted me to be. It was as close to heaven as I'll ever come to, of that I am sure.

What I didn't know was that Walt had outfitted the back of the trailer with a wide variety of show tack, as well as countless ribbons, supposedly won at various competition events in county and state fairs. In addition, I had no idea what he was dressed like until he opened his door to get in the truck. He had transformed even his own appearance! He was newly cleaned-shaven, his hair pure black and he was wearing the most outrageous cowboy outfit I ever saw. Naturally, I hadn't seen very many of those when I lived in Atlantic City. He had rhinestones stuck everywhere all over him, in his belt, in his cowboy hat, on his boots, on his bolo tie, shirt and pants. Here was the perfect rhinestone cowboy.

All I could say, when he sat down and closed the truck door, was, "Do you glow in the dark?" He just looked at me, said nothing, and started the truck engine.

And within 20 minutes of pulling off the highway we were back on it, heading in the direction of Atwood and the emissaries inspection stop.

As we got up speed on the highway, then Walt spoke. "There are a couple of things I want you to do when we have to stop for the inspection. First, don't talk! Second, create as much noise and be as excited as you want. Bounce back and forth from the front to the back seats, lick the inspector's faces, bark, whine, scratch and chase my tail. Just don't talk. And don't stop doing what I have asked. Even if I tell you to stop, ignore me. I want you to create a scene of total chaos for these inspectors. And through it all, I will be introducing you as my Grand Champion Sheep Herding Dog, accompanying my two Grand Champions in the trailer: Po, as my prize mule, and Flo, as my prize draft horse. And if they make me get out of the truck to inspect the trailer, I want you to try to get out as well. When you do, run around the truck barking and howling, making out like you want to get back on the road again. Pull at my pants leg; jump up and down in front of me. Be absolutely obnoxious."

Now, it was my turn to look at him. And I smiled. At that point, he knew he had created a monster.

We pulled up to stalled traffic about a half mile from the inspection station. We were silent up until there was only one car ahead of us at the roadblock, where the inspectors were stopping everyone. At that point Walt reminded me again, "Be yourself. Be completely natural. Don't let their appearance or manner stop you from doing what we discussed earlier. They are acutely aware of any variation from normal behavior, either from humans or any other living species. Here we go."

As we pulled up to the two individuals standing on either side of the truck, the one on Walt's side leaned over and motioned for him to lower the window on his side. As he did so, that seemed to me the best time to trigger my routine. I began barking, jumping back and forth from the front to the back seat, running up to Walt and coming between him and the steering wheel, trying to poke my head out his window. I was a complete jerk.

In the midst of all my commotion, the two inspectors were trying to ask and get audible answers out of Walt. From all that I was doing, it was difficult to hear any of it, but it seemed to go something like this.

"Good afternoon, sir. May I please see your identification and vehicle registration?"

"Certainly," Walt replied. Then he asked, "Is there something wrong, officer? I don't remember there being an inspection station here before when we came through this way."

"Two prisoners have escaped from our State Penitentiary about thirty miles from here. We have to set up roadblocks throughout this area to stop them. They are armed and extremely dangerous."

"Well," Walt added, "We haven't seen anything along the way that looks particularly suspicious, and we've been traveling all day along this same highway."

"Where are you coming from and where is your destination?" the man dressed in black asked. In fact, he was entirely covered in black. Even his face was covered in one of those knit caps that cover everything but your eyes, mouth and nose; it was exactly like the ones those zero's wore, who tried to rob us, that night in West Virginia. It must be a fashion statement for so-called, tough guys. Their helmets were huge, appearing larger in the backside than seemed normal. I assumed maybe it was due to some kind of communication gear inside the helmet. And they wore those high-top boots, that were shaped to their lower legs, like officers used to wear in the long-ago, horse-drawn caisson regiments. Their black surface was polished, to such an extent, that they were like a mirror, which reflected everything around them. And they each had side arms and large, complex-looking rifles that were slung over one shoulder. But none of that deterred me from continuing my barking, jumping from window to window, stopping just at the window and just staring, wagging my tail and twitching my ears, like I wanted a good scratch from these bozo's.

"From our farm outside Braymer, Missouri," Walt answered with a mid-western twang. "And we're headed to the Weld County Fairgrounds in Greeley, Colorado," he added. As he said this, he reached into the glove compartment and got out some papers, pushing me aside to do so, and then reached into his back pocket and got out a wallet and handed the inspector his driver's license.

"You'll see my registration and driver's license both indicate my home is Braymer, or on our farm just outside it. And I apologize for my dog, Rufus; he gets overly excited around strangers. He wouldn't hurt anyone. Or possibly, he could lick you to death, if you let him." That little exchange gave me a moment's pause. He could at least have used a better name than "Rufus". It sounded too much like "Dufus", the connotations of which, were disturbing. And I hardly lick anything, except what's in my water bowl. I felt Walt was being a little too whimsical about me, so that spurred me on;

I raised the ante on my behavior. I started to howl.

"I see your papers are in order," the black figure said, somewhat hesitantly. "Would you mind now getting out of your truck and opening your trailer, so we can see what's inside? And what would be the purpose in your traveling to Greeley?"

Opening his door, which allowed me to jump through as well, Walt replied, "I own prize show animals. Believe it or not, Rufus, here, is a champion sheep-herding dog. And in the trailer I have a champion mule and draft horse." And once I hit the ground I was all over this guy, jumping up on his pants' legs, running in circles around him and his buddy, and even occasionally chasing my tail. I bet if Jennifer had seen me, she would have had to say something. And that would have been our doom.

"That's interesting," the all-black attired inspector said. "Your dog doesn't appear to me to be very well disciplined."

"Oh, that's customary for their breed. They are very high strung and protective of their trainer. Put him in a paddock with a flock of sheep, and he becomes all business. It's a transformation that is hard to believe right now, I know."

Walking around to the back of the trailer, with me jumping up and down all the way, Walt unlocked the doors and opened them wide to expose Po and Flo in their altered states of mule and draft horse. Surrounding them were all the ribbons and tack. And on the floor in front of Flo was Jennifer.

"What's the cat for?" the inspector asked sharply, as if he was confirming some previously reported information.

"You mean Samantha. She is always brought along to calm Babe. There is no way I could even load, much less keep this large horse in here, if she didn't see Samantha lying in there. It's an unspoken relationship that escapes me, but it keeps Babe quiet and manageable as long as she's in front of him."

Throughout all this conversation and inspection I continued my unruly behavior. Both inspectors seemed haggard by the time the lead one turned to Walt and said, "I don't see anything here to be worried about. You're free to be on your way. Just be on the lookout for anyone or anything suspicious."

Like talking animals and fanciful wizards, I thought to myself.

"Well, I hope you catch who you're looking for before anyone gets hurt," Walt called out as he closed the truck door, pushing me over into the passenger seat.

"You can be sure that we will. No one escapes from us," the now sinister looking figure said, as he stared long and hard at both Walt and I.

And with that, Walt started the truck engine and eased away from their checkpoint. "Nice work, Greg. You nearly had me pulling my hair out. I do believe we threw them off track for a little while longer. Their seeing Jennifer almost gave us away. But all of you maintained your calm, or as in your particular case, your infectious romping. Thank you."

Maybe it was the effort or the stress of what we experienced, but I was exhausted after this encounter, and lay down on the front seat and was sound asleep almost before Walt ended his words of appreciation.

Walt pulled off the road in Atwood, where we spent the night. He didn't want the emissaries to somehow think we were dashing away in fear. And traveling a short distance the next day, we camped in Bird City the next night. It was the following day we finally rejoined Rita and the others in Arikaree Breaks. It was a joyful reunion. They weren't sure we had made it safely through the roadblock, until they saw us roll down the dirt road into the one of the picnic areas. It was one of the few areas that had a few fair-sized trees. Most of what we saw in this region was high prairie grass, mixed with high desert vegetation. Trees were at a premium, unless you were next to a riverbed. In a matter of minutes after we had stopped, Walt had transformed those of us needing it back to our original selves. The rest of that night was spent with everyone recounting their out of body experiences and just enjoying being alive with each other.

All told, we did eight performances in Kansas and our next one would be in Wray, Colorado, on July 22nd. We didn't need to have extra days' rest along the way due to our staggered driving and flying to the Arikaree Breaks. And, besides, we were eager to be on the road into Colorado. Being in Kansas had scared us.

TWENTY-TWO: COLORADO

Walt had Rita do a lengthy fly over to see what had happened to the emissaries since he left them. Her report to him was that prior to our leaving for Wray that day, she saw a road block being set up by Trenton, Nebraska. Apparently, the emissaries were extending their search northward, rather than further west at this time. Knowing this, Walt said we could continue our trip on foot and tricycle, at least until we reached Brush. Our route through Colorado went from Wray→ Yuma→ Akron→ Brush→ Greeley→ Windsor→ Fort Collins→ Hwy 14 to Steamboat Springs→ Yampa River State Park (near Craig)→ Maybell→ Elk Springs→ Blue Mountain and into Jensen, Utah.

We did performances in Wray, Yuma, Akron, Brush, Elk Springs and Blue Mountain. By the time we reached Colorado, our entire performance had become fixed in place; there were minimal to no variations thereafter. And I began to observe carefully the audiences' reactions during and after each performance. During the actual show, there was invariably, the animated appreciation, with clapping, sometimes members of the audience joining in singing, and the children always laughing at the antics of Rita and Jennifer. But, as a rule, the tent was hushed by the time I finished. There were no cheers nor was there stone throwing. The entire show was simply received with silence. It was not our intent; certainly not mine anyway, to plumb what folks were thinking afterward. We were planting seeds, saplings and sometimes fully matured trees in their midst. How they husbanded them was their decision.

But it was in Brush that our mode of travel changed again, and even more dramatically than before. Furthermore, this wouldn't be the last time we had to use it. As had been the case throughout our entire journey, we almost always tried to camp on some farm or ranch property outside of a town, usually close to a creek or pond, and always surrounded by trees or high shrubs. Our privacy by this time was even more important, now that the emissaries were casting their nets so wide.

The next morning after our performance in Brush, we awoke early for some strange reason and Walt called us together once we all had finished breakfast and were about to start breaking camp.

"Folks, we have a very full day ahead of us. We will need to put many miles between us and this campsite before nightfall. The reasons are twofold. One is because our route will take us through the heart of the Rocky Mountains. We'll be crossing Cameron Pass, whose elevation is 10,276 feet and Rabbit Ears Pass is at 9,426 feet, neither of which we could pull without totally exhausting ourselves and taking weeks to cross. And the other issue is how close the emissaries are to us. We must put some distance between us and them as soon as possible. I'm not sure how much longer we'll be able to avoid detection, and we are not fully prepared yet to take them on. And finally, I wanted to give each of us a well-deserved day's rest and allow you to watch some stunning scenery, without struggling so hard for a change.

"So, if once again, you will please stand back away from our gear, let me rearrange a few things."

I was about ready to put my paws over my eyes, because by now, when Walt said things like this, I knew, full well, that I was going to probably become transformed a dog, taking on an unimaginable form or be placed in a terrifying position. But not this time.

In a matter of seconds he had spirited away all our gear and replaced it with a gleaming thirty foot recreation vehicle. It was fully stocked with food and drink, sofas, beds, fluffy chairs, floor pillows and a perch.

"Climb aboard," he said. "And Frank you'll take the helm again. I'll let Sophie ride beside you, and the rest of us will find our own spots. Wally and Bernie immediately sat at the kitchen table, while Po prepared them some hot chocolate. Rita headed for the perch for a good preen. Jennifer took her time jumping up and down off all the sofas, chairs and pillows. After a light snack, she settled on a window sill, basking in the sunlight. Walt laid down on one of the sofas, stretching out his tall frame and was soon deep asleep. His overalls were still only hooked on the one side. Flo found a deep piled armchair to settle into and swiveled it around so she could look outside. And I ran back and forth up and down the hallway. I had been given strict orders by everyone not to bark, even once. After a while, I settled down and dragged some pillows up between Frank and Sophie and was able to sit high enough to see the road ahead.

We traveled over 300 miles during the next twelve hours. Frank did amazingly well going over the mountains. His talents and contributions to this trip were unheralded, I thought. And I repeatedly told him throughout this drive how amazed I was how he managed to handle this big rig so well.

We arrived at Yampa River State Park at 7:30 p.m. that evening. It had been an exhausting drive for Frank, but the rest of us were fully rested. Frank collapsed on one of the beds in the back of the bus and slept till sunrise the next morning.

And while he was still sleeping, I crept outside the vehicle and into the surrounding trees. They were large, majestic Ponderosa Pines, and they were breathtaking. I had been noticing them as we drove along yesterday. As dawn was breaking, I walked into an area that was shaped like an oblong circle, which was formed by these tall trees. I just sat and gazed up at them for the longest time, wishing that I could somehow communicate with them. The stories these old and majestic giants could tell me. And then, I remembered that Walt had transformed me once into a tree. It seemed a really odd thing for him to do. I certainly don't resemble a tree in any way. I wondered why he did that, just as I was overpowered by a need to scratch. Without thinking, I backed up to one of these immense trees, with their thick, jigsaw-patterned, reddish-orange bark and started scratching. It was the perfect scratching post. I was beginning a nice daydream, as I swayed gently back and forth, when out of nowhere came a voice.

"Enjoying yourself?" the voice boomed.

I immediately stopped, thinking that Walt, Po or Flo had followed me out here. And then I scanned the area. There was no one there but me and these trees. "Who said that?" I nervously stammered, in reply.

"I did," the voice said, echoing through the trees.

"Where are you?" I persisted, getting ready to run away.

"Right behind you," came the reply.

Running around the backside of this four foot diameter tree, I saw no one or nothing. "What do you mean, behind me? There is no one here but trees!"

"You are an observant one, aren't you," the voice continued. "That's right. You're looking at the voice."

Staring straight ahead at the huge tree, my mouth fell open, and I gasped. "You're talking to me? A tree is actually talking to me!!"

"That's right. And now that we've taken so much time to establish that fact, can we move on to more important details?" the tree continued.

"Like what?" I summed up the courage to ask.

"Like your ability to get me talking. Where did that come from?"

"Hey, I'm just a dog, as you can see. I have no powers or abilities. I was simply having a scratch at your expense."

"All I know," continued the pine tree, "is that for all these hundreds of years I've wanted to speak to someone and never could. Then along comes a rag-tailed dog, scratches his backside on me, and I'm now talking."

Just then a breeze came up and blew the upper limbs of the trees, causing needles to intermingle with one another. And before I could answer him, other trees were starting to ask questions and make unflattering comments about me. The whole forest was starting to talk!!! And so it was, whether by leaves, limbs, needles touching other trees, this ability spread up and down the Rocky Mountains, across valleys and into other ranges and forests near and far. No longer did trees stand silently as the world passed by or abused them. They could speak, and they had something to say.

I spent the next 30 minutes talking to these trees, trying to calm them down somewhat, and relating what little I knew about Walt's particular predicament with the emissaries, and how the outcome of that final encounter may affect them as well. We parted with them reassuring me that in return for me giving them a voice, they would work to keep us posted on any dangers that might lie ahead and try to help us in other ways if they could.

When I arrived back in camp, Walt had already transformed our gear back to the wagons and tricycles and carts. He looked at me as I ran up and said, "I know, Greg. The speaking trees were your second gift to Wally and Bernie." And that was all that I needed to hear.

We walked, biked and performed for the next three days and on the fourth day; we finally arrived in Jensen, Utah on July 30th. And by this time, even I could sense that something approaching a cosmic event was building up to a climactic finale. The verses, and all the good and evil that had been spawned by them, were about to collide.

TWENTY-THREE: UTAH - WYOMING

Jensen, Utah, was our next layover and performance.   From there we went on to Vernal → Fort Duchesne→ Myton→ Duchesne→ Fruitland→ Heber City→ Kamas→ Hwy 150→ Evanston, Wyoming→ Hwy 89/16 →Hwy 30→ Garden City, Utah, and then finally on to Fish Haven, Idaho. Other than in Jensen, we gave performances in Vernal, Fort Duchesne, Fruitland and Garden City.

We were now walking and pedaling in high, plateau country, and our energy reserves were not that great.   We tired quickly and needed to rest often.   Finally, at Fruitland Walt had witnessed enough.   None of us had said anything, but he could see that we were nearing complete exhaustion.   That next morning, after our performance the previous night, he set us apart and reconstituted, or whatever he does, that same motor home we used in Colorado. Relieved and worn out, we all climbed aboard. Walt later admitted he was also relieved, due to the constant worry he had about the emissaries showing up to challenge us prematurely.   Right after he loaded us all into the motor home, he advised us that we would stay in it for a considerable distance this time. And no one argued with him.

It was on Highway 150, between Kamas and Evanston that the next major revelation took place. And as was the case, but unknown to us at the time, all the first revelations that Flo, Rita, Jennifer and I had before today were also for the benefit of Wally and Bernice. Today's revelations began innocently enough, with those two reviewing with me what I had been saying at the performances. They asked me many questions about the content of my message and how I arrived at the various conclusions and suggestions.

And at the end of this conversation, they both reached forward to hug me, and then they each thanked me. Oddly, they specifically thanked me for my wisdom, deep spirituality and speaking with the trees, the first two of which I had no idea what they were talking about. Anyway, I was tickled that they did, and I certainly enjoyed the show of affection. It was like they were dipping into a wellspring of some kind.

And stranger still was that after they had spoken and hugged me, they called Flo, Rita and Jennifer over and went through the same ritual with them. Both Wally and Bernie would tightly hold each of my three compatriots at the end of their conversations. It seemed odd, but by now I was glad they were being affectionate with all of us. It only seemed proper and fair that they show no favoritism. And it signaled to me that we were becoming more than just buddies.

Odder still was that Walt and Po were not in

the room when all of this was happening. Earlier, they both had retreated to the back bedroom. I later found out they were going over strategies for the upcoming battle with the emissaries. Likewise, Sophie and Frank were totally engrossed in driving and seeing the remarkable scenery around us. They were oblivious to what was going on behind them.

Being the curious critter I am, I couldn't help but eavesdrop on what Wally and Bernie said at the end of each conversation with Flo, Rita and Jennifer. They were brief, but poignant comments. And I will never forget what they said to each one. For Flo, they thanked her for her strength, courage and speaking with the large animals. For Rita, they thanked her for her intelligence, discipline and speaking with the birds. And for Jennifer, they thanked her for her objectivity, honesty and speaking with the small animals.

It was Bernie who did all the talking, with Wally simply nodding his head at her comments and expressions of gratitude. But he did participate in holding each of us, and he did so with great emotion and sincerity. It was as tight and comforting a hug as I've ever had. And as I was about to leave his embrace, he finished it by whispering into my ear, unlike with the other three, "You and I are not done yet." To which I thought, "Of course we aren't, silly boy! We've still got another 1,000 miles to go before we reach the Puget Sound." But I just scampered down off the cushioned seat, wagged my tail and wiggled my body and ears in gratitude. This trip was all I could ever have hoped it might be. I was, at that moment, the happiest I had ever been.

We pulled into Garden City, Utah by 5 p.m. and promptly began our preparations for the night's performance. It was a lively audience, even after I finished talking at the end. There were lots of questions and comments from people of all ages. That was one of the nice things about having us animals and the bird along. The children weren't at all hesitant about coming up and touching us and asking us lots of questions. And given the magical nature of the performances, no one was particularly alarmed by our speaking. It seemed to them like it was all part of the show. Just more magic.

The next morning Walt informed us we were going to continue our trip in the motor home, at least to Swan Valley, Idaho. After that, we would resume walking and pedaling, at least into parts of Oregon, if not all the way through into Washington. Just hearing those states named was exciting to me. Our journey was nearing completion. A dream, my dream, was coming true for once. I knew this was going to be a good day.

TWENTY-FOUR: IDAHO-WYOMING

On August 6th, we entered Idaho, still riding aboard our luxurious motor home. Walt seemed somewhat more relaxed after our having traveled all this distance in it. The route we took from Swan Valley, Idaho was to Ririe→ Idaho Falls→ Hwy 20 and camped 10 miles west of Idaho Falls→ Highways 20 and 26 crossroads and camped one night there→ Arco→ 30 miles further west and camped west of Crater of the Moon National Monument→ Picabo→ Magic River Reservoir and camped one night there→ Corral→ Andrews Ranch Dam and camped one night there→ Mountain Home→ Grand View→ Murphy→ Marsing and then on to Adriana, Oregon. Performances were given in Swan Valley, Ririe, Arco, Corral, Mountain Home, Grand View and Murphy. We spent three nights in Marsing before crossing into Oregon. It was our last rest stop before the horror of what awaited us in central Oregon.

Our travel through Idaho, once we left the motor home, was all-in-all very taxing. We rarely stayed overnight in any town, often we just camped along the highway, miles from any settlement. And then when we approached Corral the smoke from Bureau of Land Management and National Forest lands began to alter our visibility and made breathing more difficult as we walked and pedaled.

The intensity of the smoke and fires only increased as we came to the Anderson Ranch Dam area. Finally, we had to pull off the highway onto a side road. But as soon as we got off the highway, we were stunned to see an immense gathering of animals of all sizes and varieties and many species of birds, all standing in the road, blocking our passage. Surrounding these hundreds of creatures were the large ponderosa pines that I had first seen in Colorado. Unsure what to do, Sophie stopped pedaling immediately upon seeing this disturbing sight. And the rest of us pulled up alongside her and formed a line facing our roadblock.

It was Walt who spoke first. "Why are you gathered here in this manner? What has happened to bring you together like this? Is there anyone amongst you who speaks for all of you? Do we need to help in some way? Are you in trouble?"

"Probably," was the first response. The voice came from an elk, which had a headdress of horns like I'd never imagined. He then took a few steps toward us and continued. "But it is your party that apparently needs the most help at this moment. It appears that you are in grave danger."

"Why?" Sophie interrupted, not letting Walt continue with his interrogation. "How could this be? We've done nothing and not been exposed to any outside media for hundreds of miles."

"Apparently, that is not exactly the case," the elk continued. "It seems that someone in Idaho Falls saw you pass through town and took some pictures of your entourage. They ended up being posted on the internet and got national attention. And someone else, who is very powerful and very angry with you, saw them and apparently knows now where you are. It seems this party is creating the fire and smoke you are seeing. They are driving you to a particular area for some reason."

"Oh…, me," Walt sighed. "Time is running out, folks. Right now, we need to see what gives with this collection of animals and birds." Then turning to the ever-growing audience before us, Walt asked, "Does anyone else with you speak?"

"Are you kidding?" the elk answered. "EVERYONE DOES! However, you're the first humans we have talked to. No one else knows of our ability."

"How did you know to look specifically for us?" Rita asked nervously.

"It was the trees that told us. Apparently, some dog got them talking and concerned about your welfare. As you crossed the states of Colorado, Utah and up to this point in Idaho, the trees have kept track of you along the way. And flocks of birds have kept us posted on who is responsible for these fires and where they are being started. The rest of us are here for your protection, if you ask for it.

Then, the most amazing thing happened, if it was possible to top all of this. Wally and Bernie got out of their wagons and walked over to the still, ever-growing assembly. Standing directly in front

279

of the elk, it was Bernie who spoke.

"We are so grateful that you have risked your lives and come together like this to warn us. It is, after all, because of us being here that all this is happening. We've known for some time what was occurring, but we were waiting until the right time to let others know, including those we have been traveling with. Your warning us gives us that last bit of foreknowledge to be able to make preparations for the final battle to determine the sovereignty of this world. The fires you have been seeing are set by forces committed to the extinction of all life on this world and, with that, throughout this universe. The outcome of this battle will decide whether good or evil finally triumphs.

"We need you to keep alerting your fellow beings what is happening; and tell anyone who can, to make their way after us, over land, along waterways, and in the air, to the place where our final stand will be made. Do not needlessly endanger your lives by coming, but all who can, will be needed. We must show this evil that all life, that is able to come, is there to speak with one voice. God bless you and us in the days to come, and God bless this world."

After Bernie said this, she and Wally each hugged the elk and mingled amongst the other animals and birds that were in their immediate vicinity. All that could be heard was a low murmur, as they all spoke to one another. In the meantime, the rest of us in our troop, including Walt and Po, just stood there transfixed and dumbfounded. Eventually, the group parted and the two children walked back to where we were standing. As Bernie was climbing back into her wagon, she turned to Walt and said, "Ok, Mr. Walt, now you can go ahead with your plans."

And I swear I heard Walt reply, "Yes, ma'am. Thank you."

Then he walked over to the now-huge gathering of four legged, two legged, hairy, woolen and feathered beings and said, "We must spend the night here with you. Then in the morning we will continue our journey, just as if we know nothing of what you have told us. My guess is that from here on the emissaries will only be burning the brush and grassland from here to central Oregon, where our clash will occur. But I would advise you to have all, who can, graze and trample down the thick underbrush that is growing on the forests' floor along the fire line. In that way, we can prevent these fires from reaching the crowns of the trees and killing them. We need whatever trees there are to be alive in the area where the final battle takes place. That is extremely important. They must have a voice in this conflict.

"We should be in Marsing in three more days, and we will rest there for three nights. That will give you some extra time to rally any additional forces you can, to cross over into Oregon. Alert everyone! We will need you. We cannot defeat them alone. And any of you who want, can spend the night with us here tonight. But we will need to travel alone tomorrow. To have a large entourage on the roadway tomorrow would attract too much attention. And as Bernice did, I speak for the rest of us when I say, thank you so very much for being here, for risking your lives, for speaking to us about these things. We WILL stand and speak with one voice when the time comes."

And sure enough, after we left the next morning, the smoke and grassland fires followed us, stopping only at the Snake River, but beginning again on the other side. Throughout it all, we tried to maintain our same schedule of performances and pace of travel. It was difficult at times. Why? Well, for me, because I was afraid. I don't know where courage comes from, but at that point I didn't think it was something that you wore, like a collar, all the time. Courage, I thought, just happens. And I prayed it might come to all of us, especially to me who, no doubt, was the most frightened of all.

THE PACIFIC COAST

TWENTY-FIVE: OREGON

We crossed the Oregon border on August 22nd. And nowhere around us did we see any sign of our animal or bird companions. It was like we were all alone for this upcoming battle. And realizing that put me in a state of deepest dread. Unfortunately, we had no choice but to push on, as if we knew nothing of the emissaries plans. Our route took us from Adrian→ Vale→ Brogan→ Ironside→ Bates→ John Day→ Mount Vernon→ Hwy 395→ Beech Creek Summit region→ Long Creek→ Monument→ Spray→ Hwy 19 camping at Butte Creek Pass→ Mayville→ camped at North Condon→ Wasco→ Biggs and into Goldendale, Washington. Prior to our coming to Beech Creek Summit, we gave performances in Adrian, Vale, Brogan, and Ironside.

It was at Mount Vernon that Walt made his surprise move, having us detour from the prearranged route the emissaries had forced us on. Their scheme to corner and surround us was now

283

being altered by Walt's own plan. We were unaware at the time, but while we were passing through Unity, on Highway 26, approaching the edge of the Malheur National Forest, Walt had instructed Rita to fly into the nearby woods and tell the trees that we were deviating from this highway onto Highway 395 at Mount Vernon. Apparently, he was never sure the message got through to who or whatever might be following us or traveling from that area, because Rita could not report that she had any feedback when she flew into the forested area and repeatedly called out what Walt had told her to say. All she heard in return was the rustling of pine needles. That worried Walt, but he knew they had no choice but to face this evil body on his terms, as much as was possible.

The actual area he chose to make our final stand was at the northern end of the Beech Creek Summit. The actual area where we took up our battle positions was an immense, sweeping valley. It was heavily wooded, to the south of us, almost down to the valley floor. The valley itself had at least three miles of clear visibility along its east-west orientation. The valley floor and its northern hillside, where we stood, had endless acres of low grassland, having been kept that way through regular grazing by both large herds of cattle and sheep. I'd estimate the valley was over a mile wide at the point Walt had us stop and pull off the highway.

He asked us whether we'd like to be transformed into more unrecognizable forms for what was about to happen, but all of us declined. By now we were a team, maybe not one that could offer much help at this point, but we were united in our will to protect Wally and Bernie.

Walt figured we had about three hours before the emissaries figured out that we were not traveling on their predetermined route, and they would begin swooping over the area to find us. I dreaded the thought of how they would arrive. That thought, alone, terrified me, much less what might eventually happen to us.

As in any preparation for battle, Walt sat us down and went over his plans, which basically consisted of Po and him fighting them alone. There was no indication that the hoards of communicating animals, bird life and the trees had extended this far into Oregon. So that was not something he could incorporate into his plan. He had originally hoped that he could. He became grim, as the time passed.

And the rest of us decided to line up facing the northern flank of the Beech Creek Mountain, whose summit we had recently crossed. We were positioned about a third of the way up the opposite side of the valley. It gave us a wide-angle view of most of the valley and the direction from which the emissaries would most like make their advance. The afternoon was warm, even at this altitude. It was sunny, and because we had departed from the smoke-filled route dictated to us by the emissaries, we were relieved to have a clear view around us. And the forests were lush and intact as far as the eye could see. There was a scent of pine tar in the air, mixed with sage and mesquite. No breeze stirred the grasses or forests. It was absolutely calm.

That was until we heard the scream of four,

incoming fireballs. They rushed in from the direction of Mount Vernon, low over the mountain tops, but not low enough to set more fires, as they had over the grasslands. Clearly their arrival was meant to demonstrate a determination of will to kill. And we were the targets. And as quickly as they zoomed into the valley, they had landed about 100 feet from Walt and Po, who were standing another 100 yards ahead of us.

As the fire and smoke from their initial appearance faded, what was left standing before us were four figures, transformed into two-legged, cloven hoofed, scaled   beings with slanted eyes, and small horns, curved backward over the top of their head to their neckline.   Immediately, I thought of the extra large helmets these figures were wearing at the inspection station in Kansas. And the only objects they carried were like pitchforks or tridents. These figures were uglier than anything, I had ever seen or imagined. Sophie and Frank said, after the battle had ended, that these four reminded them of the gargoyle-like figures seen on buildings and in paintings produced during the Middle Ages. Later, I thought about how being consumed with evil must, in itself, cause someone to change in appearance. The longer the evil reigned, the more horrid the appearance. And then they spoke.

"At last, the mighty, earth-Wizard is finally cornered. Your journey of escape is ended. And now we can finish our work, started so many eons ago on this world and nearly completed in Atlantic City. Actually, having all of you here in one place is better. We can wipe out the obstacles to our destroying all hope of this planet surviving, having your fellow-travelers assembled here. Your little evening performances were pathetic and served no lasting purpose. There is no one or thing around here to help you, you miserably, pathetic creatures. You are isolated and alone in this valley. No one will ever know or mourn your passing. Do you have anything to say before we complete our work here, wizard?"

In my preoccupation with looking over the valley and its surroundings, I had not noticed that Walt and Po had changed their appearances. But I did begin to notice, as I scanned the area, not passed over by the emissaries, that there was movement at the forests' lower edges, where the grassland began. To my amazement it was due to animals, hundreds of thousands of them, beginning to pour down the mountain slopes. And with them were people, coming by the thousands as well. They were pouring down off the highway, like a multi-colored river, merging into the flood of life coming forward out of the trees. Even the sky was darkening over them, as birds, their numbers beyond counting, began appearing overhead.

At the same time this mass movement could be seen, a gentle breeze began blowing, which gradually grew in force and volume. To me, it seemed as if it had begun to cover their appearance and advance. But at the distance we were from them, it was hard to tell if they were making any sound. From what I could hear, they were not. It was a mute invasion of life forms.

What struck me about Walt and Po's

appearance, after I turned my attention back to them, was that they'd changed their traditional attire or at least any I had ever seen. Walt was dressed in a stunning uniform with blue trousers having a burgundy stripe down the pants leg, a white jacket and dress blue hat, both with burgundy trim and gold braid. Po was dressed the same, but with what appeared to be less braid. Neither of them bore any arms, and most stunning of all, Walt did not appear to be holding onto his wand. They both looked defenseless.

At that moment Walt answered the black form's question: "Only that your reign of terror will come to an end soon. And it won't be by my hand. You won't succeed with this world like your comrades did on the other three in this Universe and like you did throughout the Anteverse. This world will be different. These people are different. These animals and all life forms are different. My time here on this world has proven that to me. You are finished."

"Enough," yelled their apparent leader, and the one who sounded like who inspected our pickup truck and trailer in Kansas. "We are going to force you two back to your worthless band of misfits and child pretenders and eliminate your presence in this world once and for all time. There is no power, influence or magic left in you. You are a spent old man, as is your so-called protector."

After saying that, they began advancing step-by-step toward Walt and Po. And with each stride they took toward them, our two protectors each stepped backwards. The emissaries had lowered their tridents as they advanced. But what impressed me the most, despite my impending urge to flee, was the calm that surrounded everyone else in our party. I, despite my misgivings, was sort of proud of myself as well. I knew, all the same, that I wouldn't have stood still, if they weren't here with me. Our band was standing firm.

It was after the black creatures had taken about 15-20 steps forward that Wally, standing beside me, leaned slightly toward me and whispered,

"Mr. Greg, it's time for you and I to go into action. You must now take on your role as a harkener. Listen to me carefully, and do exactly as I say. You are to close your eyes and clear all thoughts and emotions immediately. Then I want you to swing your tail around behind me, moving a little closer to me as you do so. I need to be able to reach behind me and make contact with it."

Bewildered, I set about trying to do what he asked. This wasn't the best time to demand that I become a disciplined monk. I thought I'd been doing pretty well not taking a nervous wee. But I closed my eyes and tried to be really calm, fearless and thoughtless.

"Steady," Wally whispered. "That's it, clear all your thoughts now! You must be perfectly still and quiet!"

Then, as I reached a moment that I don't have any memory of, I was startled awake by someone yanking, what I thought was hair from the tip of my tail. It was all I could do not to bark and start chasing it. I couldn't imagine what was happening.

Wally then whispered, "You did perfect, Mr.

Greg.   All this time, even before you started learning to speak, Mr. Walt had already implanted in the tip of your tail the magic silk fibers that would become my own wand.   And in my hands they are now transformed and wait my moving it.   Now you won't have the constant urge to chase your tail.   The foreign body has just been removed."

Well, now, what could I say to that?   Here I had the keys to saving the universe with me all along. It certainly shows what can happen when you have the right tool in the right hand, at the right time. Deep down, I was probably a little miffed at being used, but because it was for Wally, I soon forgot that thought.   What are buddies for anyway, if you can't pack a magic wand around in your tail end?

Then a series of events unfolded that probably will echo down through the rest of recorded time.   First, Wally held the small wand out in front of him and swept it horizontally to the right.   I'd never seen Walt move it in that direction before. Later, Wally told me he would only use it once in that manner, and could only do so because he was so young and had the unused power to do so.   And this was the moment.   It brought something from the anteverse forward to our world.   It was the only thing that could contain the emissaries.   It was a hovering, transparent, protective shield that surrounded them and protected all of us standing there, as well as those approaching the dark forms from the forest side of the valley.   They still were not powerless, but they were unable to escape the shield, at least for a short time.   Soon they would be far from harmless.   Their evil was still capable of influencing others without them lifting a forked finger or leaving the shielded area. Wally had to work fast.

Next, Wally turned to me and yelled, "Speak! Mr. Greg. Speak with all in your power! Yell out, 'NO MORE!' And keep yelling it, so that everyone begins to yell it!"

Startled, but wanting to do something, I did as he commanded and the first one to join me was Flo. It was like you had let her loose on the arctic tundra, and she was shouting for all her life to be home at last. Raising her head, taking a deep breath, she howled in her most, booming voice, "NO MORE! NO MORE! NO MORE!" over and over again.

The rippling of our cries was like a chill down every living being's spine. By the sixth time we called out, our entire troop was yelling it, including Walt and Po. And with Po's voice, it probably was carried back to the Utah border. In seconds, it was being chanted by the people pouring into the valley. Then the animals and birds joined in. And finally the loudest, collective voice of all was heard, above all of us. It was when the trees began to chant it. It was a roar! It echoed up and down that valley. It spread across the mountain range, through other valleys and into the surrounding prairies for hundreds, if not thousands of miles. It seemed all living beings were shouting "NO MORE!"

It seems, there were only two possible ways to defeat the evil ones. One was individual and personal, involving goodness, love, forcefulness, yearnings to be free from tyranny and terror, and rejection of the endless lies and deceptions. But it had not been in sufficient numbers to be totally effective. The other way was collective. And it involved directing the all-encompassing voice of the world's living and speaking beings crying out to the emissaries, something that no other world had been able to achieve. Only by combing the individual and collective wills and voices could victory occur.

As our chanting increased in volume and as the mass of life descended down into the valley, the dark forms began to shrink. It was like a jack hammer pounding them into the earth. They had thrived on the silence born of their intimidation, fear, resignation, hopelessness and loss of faith. The voices, of our countless number, went on and on until we could shout no longer. And when that moment came the emissaries, who had occupied this world so long, were gone, never to return.

What followed was a celebration of thanksgiving and joy beyond anything you could imagine, unless you were there. Everyone knew much more lay ahead to rebuild a world, torn by the effects of their evil and our acceptance and involvement in it. But we had been freed at last of their kind. Everyone and everything was speaking to one another. Discussions were taking place with huge trees, birds with cats, rabbits with wolves, Sophie and Frank with some bears, Po with mules and horses, Flo and I with children and Wally and Bernie with Walt.

We stayed there in that spot for three nights. People, animals and birds continued to flow into the valley for days afterward.   Some say a monument is to be built there one day.   Apparently, the word had spread by trees, birds and animals to those who had seen our performances.   And from them, the word spread to other people, who then talked to their pets, and their pets to other animals, and so on and so on it went.   There was a cascading effect of speaking to one another, and everyone who could, came to this place.

We concluded our time in Oregon by still giving performances in Monument, Spray, Mayville and Wasco.   We arrived in Goldendale, Washington, on September 7th.   Of course, by now there was no avoiding the crowds.   What happened near Beech Creek Summit, Oregon, finished our unobserved and unaccompanied portion of the journey.   But because we were still in back country, we were able to travel with some ease.   That all changed by the time we got to the Columbia River. By then, our walking and pedaling days were essentially over.

TWENTY-SIX: WASHINGTON

The decision was unanimously made that we still needed to maintain giving our performances in Washington. Despite overcoming the threat of the emissaries, we still felt strongly that our show and my talk should continue until the end of the trip. Our route took us from Goldendale→ Gleed→ Packwood→ Randle→ Morton→ Winlock→ Pe Ell→ Menlo→ Humptulips→ and finally to the farmhouse along the Hoh River.

It was also quite obvious, at least to me that something quite disturbing was happening to Walt. After the confrontation and battle at Beech Creek, he'd lost much of his energy and forceful drive. It was as if he'd expended all his energy and now had little left for anything but barely existing. He rode on Po through the rest of Oregon to Biggs, which was located on the Columbia River. He only did the most routine magical tricks during our remaining performances; and when we got to Biggs, he convinced us to finish our journey using the motor home again. He said returning to it was due to the crowds that we now attracted with our walking and using the tricycles. But I knew it was even more so due to his exhaustion. Once we started using it, he began sleeping in the back of the R.V. whenever possible.

And when we started using the motor home, Po was no longer transformed into the centurion or a mule. Now he wore the same style of clothes that Frank did. I was shocked the first time I saw him dressed in a pair of blue jeans, flannel shirt and hiking boots, wearing a baseball-style cap that had an insignia of some sports club on it. His dress also indicated to me that something was changing with Walt. Po was no longer his protector.

And for your information, Flo and I continued to wear our same uniform: the flight helmets with our goggles resting on the top of our heads, unless there was a bright sunshine or high wind. Then we pull them down over our eyes. They were our signature uniforms that we wore with pride; those, along with our boots, of course. We were now down to our last pair of boots that Sophie had made for us. We put them on when we left the Beech Creek Summit campsite. Even now, whenever we go for a hike or a long trip somewhere Flo and I will don our travel gear. It's a habit now.

But back to Biggs. It was there I first saw the mighty Columbia River. And I confess she is my favorite of all the many rivers we saw, crossing America. The starkness of the canyon walls surrounding her, the dark blackish-blue color of the water, bordered by the many shades of tan along the hillsides and the browns and reds of the cliffs were a breath-taking setting for this mighty river. And

295

given her history of the many floods from collapsing ice dams , which resulted in 1,000 foot high walls of water scouring the hills, carving the gorges, and laying down silt for the orchards and crops that surround her, it's no wonder I fell in love.   She doesn't spread out and meander like normal rivers do in the flatlands.   Here she had to carve and slice her way through snow-capped mountains, volcanic rock and great forests of the Pacific coast.   What's not to swoon over?   I stood on the bluff overlooking her and felt my heart beat with a flutter.   I felt deeply in love at that moment.   It just happened to be with a river. My foolish heart.

From Biggs, we performed in Goldendale and Gleed before crossing the Cascade Mountains on Highway 12 over White Pass.   The view of Mount Rainer, as we rounded one particular curve, convinced me that we were certainly headed in the right direction.   I never heard Sophie and Frank talk so excitedly.   You could tell they were approaching what they thought was a pathway to heaven on earth.

It was after our performances in Packwood, Randle, Morton, Winlock, and finally in Pe Ell, that Walt mustered up enough energy to give us the remaining background and details on how and why he and Po came into our lives.

We had finished eating supper and were scattered around the motor home, joking and chatting, in an atmosphere that clearly reflected our relief that Wally and Bernice's were no longer being chased by the emissaries and that our journey was just days away from completion.   We thought we were going to wind our way up some side road to

Tacoma and begin our search for their grandmother tomorrow. It was when Bernie casually mentioned how eager she and Wally were to meet her that prompted Walt's final revelation.

"Dear friends," he began. "I have one final explanation to discuss with you. It entails where and why we are going to finish our cross-country odyssey. First, I'll discuss the why.

"I know the grandmother of Wally and Bernice. In fact, I know her very well. In the anteverse she would have been called the Hostess, which means she is the one who provides safety and shelter for the Vessel, before someone like Wally and Bernice are born. She is, in fact, their mother's mother. Only she could give birth to a Vessel. And only one individual like her was sent to each of the four inhabited planets in your Universe. To my knowledge none of the other three were able to carry out this most precious act, as those worlds perished before they could. She and I have been on this world for an equal amount to time. We are, as you say, contemporaries. We were both involved in helping insure that their mother came into existence.

"And that leads me to where we are going. It is, indeed, to their grandmother's residence, but it is not in Tacoma, as was suggested months ago. It is a place where Wally and Bernice can restart their new lives, and you can bring your journey to an end."

"Where is she exactly?" Rita asked.

"Off onto a side road about ten miles up the Hoh River on the western side of the Puget Sound Peninsula," Walt answered. "She lives on a rather large farm there. It has an adjoining general store and market fronting the roadway."

"Is it near the ocean?" I asked. After all, my plan all along was to travel until we got to it.

"Yes," Walt replied. "The Hoh River empties into it at the Hoh Indian Reservation."

"Can we go to the ocean there?" Wally then asked.

"I don't know," Walt answered. "But, anyway, we will go right by it before we reach the Hoh River turnoff. My guess is that the tribe may let us see it from their land, but I'm just not sure. To be safe, we'll stop before the turn off, so you can get your feet wet."

"Does she have any pets?" Jennifer then asked, somewhat anxiously.

"No, I'm sure not." Walt said rather emphatically. "And that was at my insistence. You see, our plan for some time has included all of you assembled here. And if you like what you see, you are most welcome to stay on and live there as well. She and I will no longer have the stamina to manage the farm and store. I say this even though I, myself, have never lived there. My time spent there was always brief. It was her home, like my cottage in the woods was mine. But we've tried to prepare it with all of you in mind. And it is yours to have and to become your own home, if you like what you find there."

"Is she nice?" Bernie asked quietly.

"You will love her dearly, as I know she will you." Walt, equally as quiet, answered. "And that goes for all of you. You are not coming as unexpected intruders. Your arrival has been planned for centuries. We just weren't sure who exactly would be coming."

"How soon will we get there?" Flo asked anxiously.

"How about tomorrow?" Walt replied.

To that, all of us looked at each other, grinned widely, and nodded our heads eagerly 'yes'.

"That's it, then. Tomorrow our trip concludes, but only after Greg, here, has a chance to dip his paws into the ocean."

And that I did, at a place called Kalaloch. And I must tell you the Pacific Ocean there was nothing like the Atlantic Ocean by Atlantic City. The beach was covered with huge driftwood logs, and there were cliffs and small islands offshore in the distance. I was told there often were seals on the rocks of those islands. It was paradise, for sure. And the Trees. They were magnificent! They'd been forewarned that we were coming and greeted us in the deepest base and baritone voices. I knew then I could live the rest of my days here, walking among these ancient rainforests, talking and listening to the tales these trees could tell.

We arrived at our final destination by 5 p.m. on September 11th. As we pulled up to a very large farmhouse, which overlooked a well groomed, open meadow, subdivided by wooden fencing and scattered with assorted horses, sheep and cattle, we saw a woman about Walt's age exit the front door. It was Willa, the children's grandmother. She was wearing a colorful, calico dress, with a three-quarter length, cream-colored apron tied around it. She had as wide a smile as I had ever seen. Our arrival, though expected someday, was a complete surprise to her today.

Introductions, hugs, kisses, hikes around the property, investigations of the farm house, barns, store along the roadway, meeting and talking to her livestock filled the rest of that afternoon, evening and the next day. Wally and Bernice, most of all, were enveloped in a loving atmosphere and were at peace. Their grandmother spoke often about their mother, not ever wanting her memory to fade.

And for the record, there was no actual father. Apparently, that's not the way it happens with Vessels. It all seemed a little too mystical for me at this point. If it were up to me, if there ever was a need to go through this vessel business again, I'd vote for a Vessel and a Vesselier. I even thought Po would have been perfect in that role. But, then, what do I know? And by this time, you are well aware of that.

In fact, Po did become a father figure to Wally and Bernie. He was, after all, still their Protector. But his gentle nature blended perfectly into the role of fatherhood.

Sophie and Frank loved the area and the general store so much that they convinced their children to sell their market in Atlantic City and all of them move out here as well. Sophie and Frank never returned. They, too, were home now.

Interestingly, as we drove up that Hoh River road the first time, Flo spied the snow-capped Olympic Mountains at the end of it. It wasn't long before all of us were hiking up to the snow fields for Flo to roll in. She eventually would pull Wally and

Bernie in a modified sled that Frank and Po made. It was enough of the arctic life for Flo. She later also told me this was home.

Jennifer settled in quickly. A large stone fireplace became her base of operations. From there she resumed scolding me and Flo for tracking mud indoors, shedding hair, scratching fleas, and for just being dogs. It was right out of a chapter from Hearth and Home.

Rita had a couple of indoor perches, one by Jennifer's fireplace and one in the kitchen where she could gossip with Willa, Sophie and Walt. Walt quickly became confined to an armchair that was kept mainly by an old Cannon, wood stove in the kitchen. He and Rita became fast and dear friends in the days he remained with us.

Wally's abilities and powers increased rapidly, but he kept them to himself, sharing them only with Bernie and myself. The two of them spent a great deal of time together. I was sure it was working out how to best help us and, more urgently, how to help the world at large. Soon enough they would be thrust into that arena. For now, I wanted them to taste the joys of the love and friendship of those around them.

Bernie continued to blossom as the Herald she was destined to become. Her oratorical skills and her ability to understand and organize were to become legendary. She was a repository of the Anteverse's goodness and what promises lay ahead for this world. Wally was the wizard to help make it possible.

And me, what can I say? I could talk to and

herd the farm animals, or any wildlife that stopped by, and sometimes even the birds that migrated through. And most rewardingly, I could sit and converse with the ancient trees for hours. In between, I lay on the farmhouse porch and celebrated the passing seasons and the joy of being with family.

Finally, I need to mention what happened to "Greg's Plan". It was one day; about two months after we settled in with Willa and Walt, that Frank brought in a local newspaper and called out to me.

"Hey, Greg! Get a load of this! Washington State's governor, and those in all the other 49 states, has unanimously voted to set up elections for new state representatives. And in two years, after their election, they are all going to Washington D.C. to form the Second Constitutional Convention. What do you think of that?!!"

I just looked up and smiled at him. I only wished Walt could have been there then to hear the news as well.

www.ingramcontent.com/pod-product-compliance
Lightning Source LLC
Chambersburg PA
CBHW031250170626
46807CB00001B/65